Under Fire!

I braced myself at the controls and tried to watch all the monitors at once. The wait felt like forever, but it was probably less than ten seconds till I caught sight again of that shuttle-shaped shadow against the stars. She fired before I did, but only just.

Her shot hit. Mine didn't.

I felt the whole rock shudder under the impact of her laser blast. The computer screamed—a brief electronic howl of overload that sounded like a startled woman. I wrestled with the big guns while the computer sorted itself out and slammed home the big plasteel doors down the corridor between us and the airlock where the shot had hit.

It worked a lot faster than I did; the shadow got in another shot at the viewport while I was still manhandling the weapons. . . .

MELISA C. MICHAELS

FLOATER FACTOR

A TOM DOHERTY ASSOCIATES BOOK
NEW YORK

FLOATER FACTOR

Copyright © 1988 by Melisa C. Michaels

A TOR Book
Published by Tom Doherty Associates, Inc.
49 West 24 Street
New York, NY 10010

Cover art by Maelo Cintron

ISBN: 0-812-54578-8   Can. ISBN: 0-812-54579-6

Library of Congress Catalog Card Number: 88-50628

First edition: November 1988

Printed in the United States of America

0 9 8 7 6 5 4 3 2 1

To the three bears
Chuck, Judy, and Erich Dinges
cherished hostages to fortune
aloha nui loa

Chapter One

WHEN THE AIRLOCK SIGNALED READINESS TO OPEN, IAN and I were positioned strategically with our handguns ready, one on either side of the lock, ready for anything. Anything, that is, except what we actually found. Our intruder was approximately two months old and, if the noise it made was any indication, was just as displeased with being there as we were to find it there. We both stared at it, dumbfounded, for seconds before I recovered enough to punch up the scanners, to try to get a glimpse of the departing shuttle that had left it; and by then it was too late.

While I was activating the scanners, Ian examined the physical evidence: the infant itself and the accoutrements that came with it. By the time I'd given up on the scanners, he had the baby in his arms and was patting it affectionately on its heavily padded rear. A very touching scene, that. Except that the brat was still howling: a thin, irritating little wail, fretful and impatient, that was probably designed to make the average nice, gullible adult human go all weak-kneed with parental concern.

"Can't you get it to shut up?" Parental concern just isn't one of my better tricks.

Ian went on patting and bouncing it while I stepped into the airlock to get a better look at it. I was not much impressed. It had a wrinkled, red little face like a cross old man, with its eyes scrinched shut and its mouth wide open and wizened little fists flailing spastically at Ian's shoulder. He was making peculiar little gurgly noises at it.

"What's the matter with it? Why's it making so much noise?"

He glanced at me, but most of his attention was still on the infant. "I think it needs to be changed."

"Changed?" I scowled at it, wondering what the hell had prompted somebody to dump it in my airlock. "Changed into what?"

"A dry diaper," said Ian. "You going to shoot it, or what?"

"Oh." I holstered my handgun. "Well, *do* something, don't just stand there *bouncing* it. It sounds like it's in pain. Fix it."

He gave me an odd look. "*Fix* it?"

I glared at him. "Make it stop that godawful noise." We were both raising our voices to make ourselves heard over the creature's increasingly robust expressions of discontent. "If it's supposed to have dry diapers, *give* it some."

He grinned suddenly. "That's my Skyrider: all woman."

"What, you think a couple of X chromosomes make

2

a person intrinsically maternal? You're damned right I'm all woman, as you've just had occasion to determine for yourself." We had been in bed together when the intruder alert sounded. "But I am *not* that thing's mother, and I don't want to be."

"Of course you have a reputation to maintain: risk taker, law breaker, outlaw queen—"

"Just get the brat to shut up, before I space you both." I must have sounded like I meant it, because he stopped goading me and took the little monster, along with a bundle of its accoutrements, out of the airlock and off toward the bedchamber.

Of course he was partly right. But only partly. It's true I set more store than I ought to by my reputation as a hotshot shuttle pilot with no emotional ties to the human race. It's also true, however, that not all women have any inclination at all to nurture small, helpless—and noisy—creatures. I'd never had the smallest desire to reproduce, and I don't go all moist-eyed at the sight of infants, housepets, or stuffed animals. (Those of you who think otherwise because you've seen that tape of me in the toy store can just go stuff yourselves. I wasn't *cuddling* the damn bear. I was holding it, prior to purchase for my cousin's kid. That's all.)

Once Ian had taken the small noisemaker away so there was peace and quiet in which to think, I looked around the airlock and through the brat's remaining accoutrements to see if I could learn anything useful about it or about the people who brought it. There was no note or anything. Just a big crate of baby supplies, the basket the brat came in, and a few loose diapers Ian had dropped on his way out.

I couldn't guess how anybody got past all my alarms

and safeguards to deposit a baby in my airlock. My rock was as secure as the Company Store. Or I thought it was. The number of guard buoys, trip stones, fence beams, and sensor nets I had out bordered on the ridiculous; even I tripped at least one alarm on the way in most times, and I knew where I'd put them, not to mention having all the keys. I'd have sworn nobody in the Solar System could get past all that without error. Except maybe Ian Spencer, boy wonder. Since he was a computer wizard, an electronics genius, a very slick con man, and the designer of about half the redundant alarm systems I used, I'd have suspected him if he hadn't had such an unimpeachable alibi . . . and no apparent motive.

Well, who did I know who *did* have a motive for dumping a kid on me? Nobody. Nobody who liked the kid in question, anyway. Unless it really had been Ian, who knew he'd be there to take care of it if I didn't. But why would he want to? And where would he get a kid anyway? I was pretty sure it wasn't his; but not, of course, *quite* sure. There wasn't much about Ian that anybody could feel *quite* sure of, except that he was the best con man in the asteroid belt.

I hadn't heard a peep out of Ian or the infant since they left the airlock. There was nothing to learn from the scanners there, and I had little desire to look upon the infant again just yet, so I headed for my rock's main control/computer chamber to see if I could pick up anything on the long-distance scanners. I was halfway there when the periphery alarms started sounding.

Without a scanner picture there was no way of telling whether it was the baby depositors getting clumsy in their departure, or a different intruder less skilled than the self-styled stork. I sprinted the rest of the way to the control chamber, checked the location of the alarms that had been tripped, and punched up the scanners for those coordinates.

It took a moment to spot the intruder: she was a sleek little fighter painted flat black all over, visible only as a shadow against the stars. I could see no identity markings or registration numbers of any kind, but the computer could see plenty of weapons and it said they were all armed, all aimed at us. The information was redundant: she had begun to fire by then. For a small fighter, she was exceedingly well equipped. It looked as though she intended to vaporize my whole rock in one swift pass. The notion did not please me.

That was why I had set so many periphery alarms; any competent smuggler is bound to make a few enemies in the course of his or her work, and I wasn't just a competent smuggler. I'd made my share of enemies on both sides of the law, and I saw no reason to make things easy for them.

This one was fleeter than most, and a little too quick on the trigger. The alarms gave me time to get ready, but if she had waited to fire till she was in range, she might have got in a lucky shot before I was sure she was hostile. As it was, I knew almost as soon as I saw her; and knew, too, that I had the range on her. I could hit her before she hit me.

Still I hesitated. For some people, that kind of firefight is easy. They don't have the quality of imagination required to understand in any but an intellectual way that when you kill a ship you're killing its pilot just as surely as if the two of you were face-to-face. They target on metal and plastic, and that's all it really is to them. In a face-to-face battle they'd be a little slower on the draw . . . and maybe they'd die for it.

When somebody's shooting at you, you have three clear options: die, run like hell, or shoot back. If you're going to shoot back, there's no merit in hesitating. But I have a very vivid imagination: and the hard-ass attitude I had toward killing, before the Brief War, had got itself as frayed at the edges as the rest of my mind by too damn much killing during the war. I didn't even know who the hell I was fighting here. Despite my queries, the Comm Link stayed obstinately blank and silent.

I've gotten more reluctant to kill, but I'm not suicidal. When that blazing black shadow got close enough to singe my rock, I fired. Exit one well-armed black shuttle, stage right, in fragments. The afterimage of the explosion, even screened through a shielded port, left a blue-green blind spot in the middle of my field of vision. I reset all the alarms very carefully before I left the control chamber to see how Ian was doing with our pint-sized intruder. At least that one was probably still alive.

The bottom half of the bedchamber door was closed and the warning light was blinking over it, indicating that Ian had turned off the gravity inside. We'd been keeping it on low anyway, so there was less clutter in the air than there would have been in a chamber in which we'd been accustomed to constant full-Earth gravity. Ian and the brat were floating near the bed, and I had a chance to watch them for a moment before he noticed I was there.

The brat was feeding. Ian had sort of wrapped himself around it and was holding its bottle, watching its wizened little face with a look of besotted adoration. His own smooth boyish face looked as youthful and defenseless as ever. Maybe even more so, in the throes of infant worship.

I couldn't see his eyes, which were both his most enigmatic and his most beautiful facial feature, but I could see the curve of his cheek, the line of his jaw, the way his hair fell across his forehead in a disarming veil across one eye even in freefall, as though it were so well trained to its job of masking his cunning with childlike innocence that it defied the laws of physics in order to maintain it.

I could also see most of his sleek, hard-muscled, devastatingly graceful body, since neither of us had taken time to dress when the airlock signaled the brat's arrival. Golden skin rippled smoothly over stringy muscles and elegant bones, with the jagged scars of a hard childhood and reckless adulthood marring the gold, but not the beauty, where they cut across his back, angled down one leg, and traced a long, thin, puckered line from shoulder to elbow on his left arm. The baby and its trailing blankets covered the long curve of an old knife scar across his chest and ribs, and decorously concealed his groin. The laser scars were on his right side, away from me, but I knew well enough they were there. All in all, he was nearly as battered a specimen as I was.

I leaned on the top of the half-door, staying in the gravity field for no particular reason except to keep a safe distance between me and the erstwhile noisemaker. "How did you get it to shut up?"

He glanced at me: one quick, startled glance of wide blue eyes before they went oddly silver and guarded, their usual expression, wholly unreadable. I had never

7

been able to decide what color they really were: gray or blue or mirror-colored, with startlingly vivid flecks of amber around the pupil. The amber was the only color that never changed. "I turned off the gravity," he said. "She's a freefall mutant: look at the bottle that came with her."

It was the collapsible freefall model. "That doesn't prove anything. She probably just shut up out of greed. That kind of bottle works just as well in gravity."

"I didn't realize you'd made a study of baby bottles."

"I haven't. I've just seen them in use." I pushed open the door and launched myself into the chamber. "Did you change its diaper?"

"That's how I know she's a girl." He grinned at me laciviously. "Speaking of such things, I certainly admire your costume."

Like him, I was wearing only my holstered handgun. "You're a fine one to talk."

He reached down to arrange a fold of the baby's blankets. "I'm more cleverly concealed than you are."

"And you look very well indeed, draped in baby blankets, my love."

"Thank you. I assume you took care of whatever tripped your infernal alarms? Was it the kid's departing parents, or just a wild rock?" He was convinced my precautions were excessive.

"Neither." I found a short pullover robe in the closet that was slit high enough up one side to leave my holstered handgun free when I pulled it on. "I don't know who it was, but it wasn't the brat's parents unless they don't much like their offspring. They

8

weren't leaving. They did their best to wreck my rock, so I had to kill them."

"Usually a pretty effective form of discouragement."

"They wouldn't answer the Comm, so I didn't have a lot of options." I don't know what my voice sounded like, but it made Ian give me a very odd look.

"Sorry, kid. I didn't mean to criticize."

"Don't call me that."

"Sure, kid."

The alarms sounded again before I figured out how to hit a man who's hiding behind a defenseless infant. I forgot about hitting: if this intruder was as quick as the last one, I didn't have time for hitting.

It's a lot easier going into a freefall chamber than it is going out of one. I can do it gracefully when it matters, but when I'm in a hurry I don't worry much about appearances. People have different ways of doing it. For me, the quickest is a curled-up dive, elbows, knees, and head tucked in, so that when I enter the gravity field I have plenty of forward momentum to roll onto my feet and come up running. I did it that way, and got to the control chamber in time to see another flat black shuttle hurtle like a broad-winged shadow across the glittering starfield, swooping in for the kill. The first lasers hit us before I could reach the weapons panel.

Chapter Two

MY ROCK WASN'T SHIELDED. ON SOMETHING THAT BIG AND that sturdy, shielding is a plain waste of energy. But that meant there were some vulnerable areas. My reason for deciding against spot shielding for them had been that it would take a very lucky shot for somebody to hit a soft spot before I hit back. That didn't mean it couldn't happen. The second black shuttle that attacked us clearly meant to make it happen. Her first shot was aimed at the control-chamber viewport, and it rattled the chamber enough to knock me off balance. The viewport was polarized, and it held, but I was slow to get to the weapons console.

She was as sleek and swift as the first one had been, and her pilot knew more about my rock than I liked; she knew my blind spots and found one before I could fire. I didn't even see which way she went, so as far as she was concerned it didn't matter that she couldn't hang in a blind spot for long. I couldn't be ready for all the possibilities. The odds were in her favor that she'd get another clear shot or two before I found her. That could be all she needed.

I braced myself at the controls and tried to watch all the monitors at once. Ian came in, saw I was poised for battle, and didn't say anything. I was only peripherally aware of him; my whole concentration was on those monitors.

The wait felt like forever, but it was probably less than ten seconds till I caught sight of that shuttle-shaped shadow against the stars. She fired before I did, but only just. Her shot hit. Mine didn't.

I felt the whole rock shudder under the impact of her laser blast. She'd gone for the empty landing dock: the airlock where we'd found the baby. It was another soft spot. The computer screamed, a brief electronic howl of overload that sounded like a startled woman. I wrestled with the big guns while the computer sorted itself out and slammed home the big plasteel doors down the corridor between us and the damaged airlock. It worked a lot faster than I did; the shadow got in another shot at the viewport while I was still manhandling the weapons.

It wasn't my kind of fight, and I hadn't had much practice with those big movable guns. I was used to firefights in my shuttle, where the guns were less mobile but I was more so. I knew how to play very efficiently with a ship's mobility, but my rock wasn't moving, at least not in that sense. It was moving through space, in a rather eccentric orbit around the sun, and it would continue to do so in exactly the way it always had, unless something a lot more powerful than I decided to move it. I couldn't flip and run and dodge and chase. All I could move was the guns.

Luckily the shadow's pilot wasn't worthy of that swift little shuttle. The shot at the viewport was way off the mark, and then I had the big guns tracking. This time I didn't hesitate. When the shadow was lined up perfectly on the laser screen, I fired. The shadow's shields sheeted brilliant green and went dead. A fraction of a second later the shuttle-shaped shadow was transformed into a rolling ball of yellow-white flame like a miniature sun. Then it was gone, and the screens showed only scattering shards of shrapnel: minute new asteroids of charred metal and plastic and maybe a fragment or two of bone. I closed my eyes.

"Did somebody start another war while I wasn't looking?" Ian's voice was oddly plaintive, like a child's.

I looked at him, into those jeweled mirror eyes that never smiled, and I wondered, not for the first time, what went on behind them. "What did you do with the brat?" He had pulled on a pair of pants but no shirt or shoes, and he wasn't carrying anything.

"She fell asleep. I anchored her to a retaining panel and came to see if you needed any help. Any idea who was in that thing?"

I shook my head. "None. At a guess I'd say they were both Earthers, but it's just a guess."

"Both?" His eyes were unreadable, his face expressionless.

"This one was the same style as the one a few

minutes ago. Matte-black shuttle, no markings; probably modified Starbirds from the configuration, but that's a guess too. I never got a really good look at either one of them."

"We can run the tapes back and see if the computer can pick up anything you missed." His eyes were pure silver now, even the amber oddly reflective, and there was the hint of a smile pulling at his lips. "Why Earthers?" It was not a good sign when Ian Spencer smiled. With his beautiful, boyish face, the usual expressions of irritation, anger, and even rage tended to look merely petulant; he'd long since trained himself to substitute smiles, and they were deadly. His grin could chill a person's bones.

I shrugged. "The way they flew. They were used to working in a deep gravity well. Like Earth."

His eyes were blue again, as pale as Earth. The smile was gone. "I thought maybe you just called them Earthers for the hell of it." At my lifted brow he added, "As an insult."

"You're paranoid, Earther. You know me better than that, or you should." I had reset the alarms. Now I called up the computer's automatic tapes of the two brief battles and again watched the shadow shapes swoop in for the kill. Still no visible markings, but this time, knowing where to look, I saw what had not been obvious before: they were both going for the airlock. The first one never got close, but that was where she was headed; and the second one didn't choose a blind spot at random. She chose the one that would give her the best shot at that airlock. "That's weird: the viewport's a more vulnerable target, but they both went for it only as a second choice."

"Maybe they were after *Defiance*."

I shook my head. If they'd wanted to hit my shuttle, either one of them could have, but neither had even tried. "No, they wanted the empty dock. Why, d'you suppose?"

He glanced toward the bedchamber. "Maybe they were after the baby."

"For space sake, why?" I frowned at the monitor and turned off the tape. "Even if they wanted to kill the brat, which why would they, they'd have had a better chance while it was still on the shuttle that brought it here."

"Her."

"What?"

"Her. She's a girl, not an it. Maybe they tried that, and couldn't catch it."

"Her."

"What?"

"Her. A shuttle's a she, not an it."

"Sexist."

"Nonsense. What are you going to do with it?" The screens and the viewport showed a blank starfield outside. I picked up a tool box and headed for the corridor.

"With what?" He followed me. I couldn't see his face. His voice was as mild as always: almost as unreadable as his eyes, and in some ways as boyish as his face.

"With the brat." The corridor was efficiently blocked by the emergency plasteel barrier the computer had slammed home to protect the atmosphere in the rest of my rock when the airlock was hit, and the monitor on the little lock centered in the

14

plasteel reported near-vacuum on the other side. I would need a space suit to effect repairs.

Ian caught my shoulder and turned me to face him. His eyes were pale and beautiful. "What am *I* going to do with her? What do you mean, what am I going to do with her? She's your problem, not mine!"

I shook my head. "Oh, no."

"Oh, yes. It was your rock somebody brought her to, not mine."

"You don't own a rock." I put down the tool case beside the nearest suit locker.

"Don't evade the issue."

I opened the locker and reached for a suit. "Ian, I wouldn't know what to do with an infant. Don't be silly. Of course you'll have to deal with it."

He caught my arm before I could pull out a suit. "Melacha." He almost never called me Skyrider except when he was grinning with anger . . . which wasn't, as a matter of fact, an uncommon situation; but this time we hadn't yet reached that stage. "The repairs can wait a few minutes. You can't wear a suit over that dress or whatever it is, anyway. And you're not going to solve that little girl's problems by pretending she doesn't exist, or by shoving her off on me."

He was right about my robe: it would fit in a suit, but not comfortably. "So what, you think I should go tend the brat and you should make repairs to my rock? You think that arrangement would make more sense because I'm a woman and you're a man?"

He stared at me, clearly perplexed; which was not unreasonable. That wasn't the sort of accusation I had expected to hear myself making. I wasn't really quite sure why I'd said it. He tilted his head as if to view me from a new angle and said in a voice not quite as mild as usual, "What is it with you? The presence of a baby sure seems to turn you hell of touchy all of a sudden."

"It's not the brat that does that, Earther." I hadn't meant to say that either; but having said it, I was too damn proud to retract it, so I braced myself for a fight, instead.

If he'd been a Belter, we would have fought. But Earthers are more civilized than we. They avoid fistfights. Armed warfare is more to their taste. Vast armies engaged in wholesale slaughter is acceptable to them, but one-on-one unarmed combat is not, except as a sporting event. Ian had been living in the Belt long enough to pick up some of our ways, but not long enough to lose the more ingrained Earther concepts. He smiled, and it was not a friendly expression, but he made no move to follow through with action. In fact, he lifted his hands in a placating gesture and called me Skyrider. "I don't know what I've done, but I'm sorry, for crissake."

After a long moment I relaxed, and sighed. I'd rather have had a rousing good fistfight; my adrenaline was still up from the firefights with those black shuttles, and there were afterimages of death in my mind. But I wouldn't force it with him. "You haven't done anything. Space and damnation." I couldn't quite bring myself to apologize, either, so I changed the subject. "What *will* we do about the brat? Nobody's ever dumped an infant in my airlock before. I've no idea what might be the proper response."

"I suppose there's someplace to put them. An agency or department of the Company. The govern-

ment's supposed to be prepared for anything, right?"
There was an odd note in his voice as he said that. I
couldn't identify it.

"Maybe." We were headed for the bedchamber so I
could change clothes. "But you said the kid's a Faller.
Would the Company treat it right?" The Company
was the Belt branch of the World, Incorporated, the
Earth-based government to which he referred. Being
based on Earth, where the population consisted almost entirely of Grounders, it was not overly sympathetic to freefall mutants, probably even in the infant
state, though I had no firsthand knowledge of that. I
knew well enough how they treated adult Fallers. My
best friend, Jamin, was a Faller. An Earther med-tech
once, in my hearing, referred to him as a monster. She
was not speaking figuratively.

Words, even from a med-tech, usually aren't very
hazardous; but it did show how deep the prejudice
went. With her medical training, she *had* to be aware
that the physical differences between herself and a
Faller were no more monstrous than those between
people of differing races and skin colors, but the
awareness was intellectual at best, not emotional.
What would a person like that do with a defenseless
Faller infant?

"The only alternative," said Ian, "is to find out who
gave you the baby, and give her back. And I don't see
how we can do that."

"There must be a way." We had reached the bedchamber, which was still set for freefall, with the brat
sleeping peacefully pinned to a retaining panel. I
launched myself toward the closet. "I didn't think to
ask the computer whether it had a tape of the baby's
delivery."

"It won't have. The alarms weren't triggered, and they're what triggers the tape system."

"I could still ask."

He made an expansive gesture, forgetting he was in freefall. It sent him tumbling but didn't seem to affect his mouth. "The optimism of the ignorant. So okay: ask." He caught at a handhold and turned himself the same side up as I was.

"I intend to. After I mend the damaged airlock . . . if I can. It maybe hasn't occurred to you that access to the *Defiance* is not going to be easy till we can get that emergency bulkhead out of the corridor."

He shrugged. "If we need to get to her, you've got plenty of space suits."

I nodded toward the infant. "None that size."

He had the grace to look moderately embarrassed. "Oh." He frowned. It made him look childishly cross, though I don't suppose that was quite what he intended. "And no rescue bags?"

I'd found a work suit and was pulling it on. "Nope. Meant to get some, in case Collis comes visiting, but I haven't got around to it yet." Jamin's son, Collis, was older than the brat by seven years, but still not big enough for an adult-sized space suit; and there's no sense stocking kid-sized ones just for emergencies, since kids grow faster than seems reasonable.

"Then I guess you'd better go do some repair work," said Ian. "And I'll dutifully baby-sit while you do it." His lips twitched with the effort not to smile: he wasn't much more comfortable with this situation than I was, apparently. "After that, we'll talk, right?"

"What about?"

"About the fact that knowing how to tend a baby is not the same as wanting to."

"Oh, that." I launched myself for the door and caught a handhold by the frame to let myself out into gravity carefully. "Sure. We'll talk."

Chapter Three

THE DAMAGE TO MY ROCK WASN'T AS EXTENSIVE AS I'D feared, and the repairs were tedious and time-consuming but not really difficult. The most arduous part of the whole job was getting through the cramped little airlock in the emergency bulkhead, and I comforted myself with the thought that I wouldn't have to do that twice: the area that had lost atmosphere was small enough, and my reserve supplies large enough, that once the repairs were complete I would have only to wait a few minutes for the atmosphere to cycle back in, then tell the computer to withdraw the emergency bulkheads so I could walk out.

When I'm stuck with a job that occupies my hands but not my mind, I have a regrettable tendency toward introspection. I fight it, especially when I'm in a foul mood and not very proud of recent behavior, but I don't often win the fight. I didn't, that day. I knew damn well that if I took a good hard look at myself I wasn't going to like what I saw, and I looked anyway. I could hardly avoid it. I'd been playing surface games with Ian ever since that brat arrived, and that just wasn't my style. Before this morning, it had been a long time since I'd called Ian an Earther except in fun, and I had never before hassled him about his attitude toward women. What was it to me what he thought of women in general? He probably did have some of the typical male Earther prejudices, but he'd never displayed them in his interactions with me. He had always judged me on my own merit. This morning I had not been judging him on his. Why?

The easy answer, of course, was that the way this day had started was not my favorite: the drowsy, lazy lovemaking had been hell of good, but ought not to have been followed by babies and firefights and death; that sort of thing could take the edge off the best memories of warm morning playtime. Too sudden a dose of harsh reality can take the edge off damn near anything, and I'd call babies and death two very harsh forms of reality. Alpha/omega. In the beginning is the seed of the end. I hadn't even had my morning coffee yet!

And I knew damn well that was an excuse, not a reason. I had started too many of the mornings of my life with death to start getting fussy about it now. I hadn't often experienced such a graphic progression of sex, then baby, then death; but it was still an excuse, not a reason, for the way I had behaved. Why had I struck out at Ian? It hadn't been just the usual need to expend excess adrenaline. If it had been that, I would have picked a fight with anyone else who was handy, but with Ian I would ordinarily have picked sex over fighting any day; it, too, is an excellent way to expend excess adrenaline.

Okay, so maybe the relationship was wearing thin and I just hadn't noticed. I have a remarkable talent for self-deception: it may not be a requirement for the role of self-conscious hero cleverly disguised as a mercenary who scuffs her feet in blushing astonishment when she's caught rescuing the populace from yet another fire-breathing dragon, but it's a useful adjunct. Had I been fooling myself about Ian?

Unbidden images of him popped into my mind: Ian, serious and tender, silly and gentle, in bed with the space-tanned, self-styled outlaw queen and smiling, with mist-colored eyes; Ian, poised and grinning with his handgun leveled and his eyes polished silver; Ian, angry, his smile growing broader and his voice getting softer as his anger increased; Ian, in an unguarded moment of sheer joy, laughing out loud with genuine delight . . .

Bone and muscle and scar tissue and an almost infinite variety of smiles. Ian Spencer, boy wonder. When he was working with his computers, all the carefully learned protective expressions faded and he looked half his age, a kid again, wholly absorbed in the very serious business of playing with the grown-ups' toys. He had a little of that look in sleep, too, like a small boy so intent on mischief that there were little crease lines of concentration between his brows. But all of the boy-look was misleading. He was younger than I in years, but not by much, and it had been a very long time since he had been a child . . . if he had ever been a child. Earther kids can grow up fast, too, when they have to; and from what I had learned and guessed of Ian's boyhood years, he had to.

I thought of him with that unexpected baby in his arms and realized with a start of something very like fear that the wrongness, the discomfort I'd been dodging that made me try to pick a fight with him, was there. What I'd told him, that not all women are maternal and that I had no desire to have or to hold or to tend a baby, was true: and yet . . . and yet. . . . For a moment I saw the hint of his expressions in the infant's unformed face. I saw her brown eyes transformed to silver-blue gemmed with amber. And I knew. I had no maternal instinct at all; but there is a related instinct, just as primitive and just as powerful. It makes one want to reproduce for a man: to guarantee him some kind of immortality, any way one can. It happens sometimes even to the least maternal of women . . . when they are in love.

I stopped my work right there, holding a metal plate in one hand and a welder in the other, and stared through the hole I had not yet mended at the darkness of space outside. In the far distance the reflected light of a tumbling asteroid crossed the narrow patch of black and was gone. It reminded me of Ian's eyes. I had been fooling myself, all right. I had been telling myself we were having a pleasurable little romp, nothing more. I had convinced myself that the fascination would pass: that I was attracted primarily to the novelty of him: that when the novelty wore off, so would the sex, and we would—with luck—be left with a good, strong friendship; nothing deeper than that.

I had convinced myself of lies. No wonder the presence of an infant threw me off balance. I did not care for infants . . . but I thought Ian did. And some-where in the back of my undisciplined outlaw-adventurer's mind there were images of ivy-covered cottages and white picket fences and rose gardens and rocking chairs for the sweet old couple who had spent their lives together in love. Earther images. Down deep, I was as Earther as Ian: I was born there. I spent the first ten years of my life there. In my formative years I had known those ivy-covered cottages, those white picket fences, and even a few of those sweet old couples.

When I left Earth I believed I was discarding all the Earther values. I suppose in a literal sense I did: it wasn't really an ivy-covered cottage I wanted, but a well-appointed rock with room to grow. Room for a family. Little tousle-haired, silver-blue-eyed Ians chasing through the chambers, meddling with the computers, practicing clever con jobs on their indul-gent parents. . . .

I shook my head so hard I banged my nose on the edge of my faceplate. *No*. I didn't want a family. That was a cozy, happily-ever-after fantasy that I could not endure in truth. But maybe I did want Ian Spencer. Maybe I wanted him in my life, not just for now, but forever.

Did he guess? Probably; he knew me too well. The expectable girlish question echoed unanswered and unanswerable in my mind: did he love me? It didn't matter. I finished the repair job mindlessly, my hands working with steady precision while my mind tum-bled through chaotic possibilities and I chose one without reason or intent or conscious awareness. When the job was completed and the atmosphere had begun to cycle back into the blocked corridor, I put down my tools and headed, still suited, for the other airlock: the other landing dock: the *Defiance*.

I would be leaving Ian without means of transportation, but he had weapons and supplies and the Comm Link on which he could call somebody for a ride. I don't know whether I thought it through that consciously. I don't know whether I would have gone, if it would have left him without one or more of those things. I don't know. I was going, and that was as clearly as I thought it out.

To get to *Defiance* I had to go through the cramped little airlock in the emergency bulkhead that blocked the other end of the breached corridor. By the time I had wedged myself in, cycled it through its paces, and clambered out again, Ian caught up with me; the breached section was up to pressure and the bulkhead on Ian's side had retracted first because nobody was using its airlock. The one on my side waited till I was out of the airlock and promptly began to retract. Ian was waiting in the section I had just left. I hadn't moved three paces toward *Defiance* before his hand on my arm stopped me.

He didn't exert any pressure. His touch was enough. We stood there a moment like that in the empty corridor. I had my back to him. The space suit insulated me from his touch; from the world; from reality. I didn't need the suit anymore, and they make me claustrophobic, but I didn't take it off. Finally Ian stepped around to reach the fittings and carefully removed the helmet while I just stood there, not even looking at him.

"It's not like you to run." His voice was very, very gentle and so soft I could barely hear it; with him, that was a sign of strong emotion, but it could have been anything from rage to bliss. Without looking at him I couldn't tell, and I could not force my gaze up to meet his.

I stared at his chest and said, in a voice almost as softly expressionless as his, "How long have you known?"

"That you would run away?"

I listened to that for a longer time than it took him to say it, and I tasted all the possible responses, and then I turned away from him and did my best to put my fist through the nearest wall. The effort was unsuccessful; the wall was a good deal tougher than my hand. It was made of rock, and I wasn't, and it seemed to me that was a graphic expression of exactly my problem, so naturally I tried again: I've seldom been accused of having a whole hell of a lot of sense.

He stopped me before I could hit it a third time. Like the wall, he was stronger than I. "Melacha—"

"Don't say it." I fumbled with the fastenings of my space suit, suddenly frantic to be out of it.

He released my arm, hesitated fractionally, then began to help me. "I wasn't—"

"Don't say *any*thing." I pushed his hands away and tore the suit off, hurling it to the floor beside the helmet he had dropped. My hand hurt. I looked at it, at the knuckles already going puffy and beginning to dimple, and suddenly the sheer idiocy of my behavior got through all the angst and made me grin at myself, probably a very sheepish grin. "What a rockhead I am. You're right: it's not like me to run away."

"Breaking your knuckles on walls is much more in character."

I looked at him then, but those strange blue-gray eyes revealed nothing. "I don't think they're broken."

"Well, you did your best."

"Yes." I looked away again. "Ian . . ."

He interrupted me. "Will you marry me, Melacha?"

I tilted my head, managed what I hoped was a mocking grin, and said, "But darling, this is so sudden!"

He shook his head impatiently. "I've wanted it for a long time. But I had to wait till you noticed you loved me, didn't I?"

"You're pretty confident of that, now?"

"Yes."

The alarms went off again before I could respond to that, which was probably as well for him; my mood was precarious. I might as easily have hit as hugged him. He knew it too; I could tell from his posture even though I couldn't read his eyes. The alarms broke the spell and sent us both flying toward the control chamber again, ready for another firefight. I was cursing under my breath. Three firefights before breakfast would have been too damn much even without a marriage proposal tossed in to add to the confusion. I was reminded of the ancient Chinese curse: "May you live in interesting times." Things were getting just a little too interesting for my taste.

Chapter Four

If I had been alone, I would probably have headed for *Defiance* instead of for the rock's controls; *Defiance* was defenseless, docked out there, and fond as I was of my rock I was fonder of my shuttle. But it would have been a close thing, cutting her loose in time to fight whatever had tripped my alarms; and with Ian and the baby to consider, I knew better than to try hotshot tricks like that when there was adequate weaponry closer to hand.

Of course with the two of us present and both good with the guns, it would have made sense to send Ian to the control chamber while I went for *Defiance*. That's called teamwork. It's not one of my better tricks. I'd been a loner for too many years: the possibility didn't even occur to me.

It didn't matter: we weren't under attack this time.

We were about to receive a message drone. Either somebody had got impatient when I ignored the Comm Link, as I had been doing for the past week or two, or somebody from very far away wanted to talk to me. Or so it seemed. I was feeling a little paranoid in the wake of my last two visitors, and one of the things about a message drone of the type I saw approaching is that it has to be brought aboard through an airlock, just like a human. Since *Defiance* was occupying one of my landing docks, that meant the drone should logically use the other. The one everybody had been so intent on destroying.

There were a couple of other, smaller airlocks here and there on my rock, meant mostly for maintenance work on exterior antennae and whatnot, but it would be easier to bring the drone on board through the landing dock. Therefore, when it got near enough my rock for my scanners to probe it, I let it engage synch systems with mine, but I didn't let it come straight on in. I held it out there at a nice, safe distance, and looked it over.

It looked like an ordinary message drone. It was properly blazoned with the emblem of the Postal Service, and carried no visible arms. I couldn't see a thing wrong with it.

"What are you waiting for?" asked Ian. "Aren't you going to let it in?"

"I don't know." I stared at it some more. The scanner probes showed nothing unusual about it. They would have detected some concealed dangers, but not all. For instance, if it were packed with explosives, depending on the type, I would probably have no means of knowing they were there.

29

"What's the problem?" Ian approached the scanner screens and studied them. "It's a Postal drone, isn't it? What are you worried about?"

I smiled wryly. "The simple faith of the innocent? Come *on*, Ian. If you wanted to make that little monster deadly, there are a good dozen undetectable ways you could do it, yeah?"

"Yeah, sure, but why would I?"

"Why would two unidentified shuttles try to destroy me before breakfast?"

"They weren't after you. They were after your airlock."

"Whatever."

"I think they were after the baby."

"You said that before, and it seems as improbable to me now as it did then."

He shrugged, his expression vaguely defensive. "It's still possible. We don't know who she is, or where she came from, or why."

"Don't you think she's a little young to've made such formidable enemies already?"

"Can you think of a better reason why anyone would have it in for that particular airlock on this particular rock? She had been put there very recently. They had no way of knowing we'd already retrieved her."

I looked back at the message drone. "Okay. So they *still* don't know it, so this thing could be all set to explode the minute it gets on board."

He looked enormously patient. "Obviously, even if it's as dangerous as you think, it's not going to explode as soon as it's on board. Not unless it carries a more powerful explosive than any I know of; it just isn't large enough to blow the whole rock, and how else could it be sure of getting the baby? Unless you think it's a miniature nuke?"

"I know it's not that; my scanners would have detected anything like that."

"Okay. So we're talking conventional explosives here, right? So if it's after the baby, it's got to be sure it's in range of the baby. So you bring it on board, and in the unlikely event that it refuses to divulge its message except in the presence of the baby, I'll have a little talk with it."

"I don't understand you. How can a person as devious as you be as essentially *trust*ing as you?"

He was beginning to smile. "What have I overlooked?"

"Just the fact that you're not infallible. Or omnipotent. Once it's on board, it could be set to seek out the brat regardless of any attempted interference. Or to explode if you fuss with it. You can't know."

"Oh, but I can. Look." He pointed to a readout screen. "You trust your own computer, don't you? Well, it says that thing has a Simpson Motivator, which—as even you should realize—can be programmed only for simple guidance and evasion. It found your rock and that's all it knows how to do. And here." His finger moved down the screen. "Murphy System. That's to retain and protect whatever message it's carrying, and it can't do anything more than that. The only other on-board computers it has are simpleminded operational and maintenance ones, most of them little smarter than a hand-held calculator. In fact, most of them not *that* smart. None of them can do what you're suggesting. The idea is too sophisticated for the equipment."

"So saith the computer expert. I still don't like it.

Do you seriously mean to tell me that you couldn't use those idiot brains you've named to make a lethal device if you wanted to?"

"Of course I could. But I'm brilliant."

He managed just the right tone to make me laugh and give in. "Okay. Okay. We'll bring the damn thing on board. And if it turns out you're wrong, I'll break your face."

"If it turns out I'm wrong, you won't have to; that drone will probably do it for you."

"There's that." I signaled it on board and we watched it maneuver gracefully toward the dock. Some of them are capable of transmitting their message once they have line-of-sight on their target, but they're more expensive. Whoever sent this one knew I could bring it on board. I began to wonder what its message would be if it did carry one. Who did I know who was so far away or so impatient with my cavalier attitude toward the Comm Link that he would send a message drone? Well, there were several people in that latter category, so maybe there would be a message. When the little drone was lined up with the dock and gently sliding in for contact, we left the control chamber and headed for the airlock. There was no hurry; the lock had to cycle in atmosphere before we could open the inner hatch cover.

By the time it signaled readiness, my nerves were in a state of ill repute. I don't know what I expected, but I was ready for damn near anything. And all we found, when we swung the hatch cover open, was an ordinary message drone humming electronically to itself and waiting for us to let it know it had reached its ultimate goal. If we were its ultimate goal. I was still half convinced that what it wanted was that abandoned brat asleep in my bedchamber.

I was wrong. We were ready to block any effort it might make to reach the brat, but it didn't try. It hummed to itself while Ian led it in out of the airlock, and it settled comfortably down on the rock floor for all the world like a satisfied puppy when he punched in my code to let it know it had truly arrived. It hummed a little longer, clicked to itself internally, burped a time or two, and began to speak in Jamin's voice.

"I wish you'd ever answer the Link, Skyrider. I know, I know, you're busy with something, no doubt illegal, but look, have you even been off your rock in the last month or so? D'you know what's going on out here? I didn't try to call you at first because I kept thinking we'd hear from you. And then I didn't try, because I heard you'd taken Ian Spencer out to your rock, and whatever the two of you might be cooking up together . . . Rumor has it you're just having an affair, but I know you two. I doubt if it's *just* an affair, if it's an affair at all. Criminal minds . . . Anyway, now it's got to the point where I think you'd better know what's going on. Have you been paying any attention to recent news? Do you even look at the newsfax? If you're kidding yourself the wars are over, you're in for a rude shock sooner or later, and I thought you'd rather have it sooner. Check out the newsfax. Then call me, okay? I think you'll guess why, once you've seen the news. I . . ." He cleared his throat, and the drone reproduced the sound as perfectly as an old-fashioned tape recorder would have done. "I might need some help." There was a pause, and I could imagine his face both arrogant and embarrassed as he tried to decide whether he needed to make the plea any stronger. Then the drone said, still in his voice but subdued, as though he hadn't really decided but was at a loss as to what more to say, "That's all."

The drone clicked internally again, hummed to itself, and then fell silent, its mission accomplished. Ian looked at me. "Do you want to hear any of that again?"

I shook my head. "No need."

"Okay." He wiped the drone's message-memory, punched in its return instructions, and put it back in the airlock. Once released in space again, it would make its way to the nearest Postal depot to be put to use wherever it was next needed.

"It's your turn to make breakfast," I said.

"Then you'll have to check on the baby; we shouldn't leave her unattended forever," he said.

"We'll both check on it. I'm sure it's fine. Then you can make breakfast."

"And if she's not fine?"

"Oh, hell. Then I'll make breakfast."

"Lucky for you I know how to tend a baby."

"Lucky for it." I looked at him. "Where did you acquire that esoteric skill, anyway?"

Sudden shadows darkened his eyes. I knew that look. I had touched some piece of his past he didn't want to acknowledge. There was a whole hell of a lot of his past he didn't talk about. I suspected he was ashamed of it, but I had no idea why, or what it was. Now he just looked at me and shrugged and said in a carefully indifferent tone, "Oh, around. You know."

I didn't know, but I knew better than to ask. "Well, good thing, anyway. It sure isn't one of my better tricks, and as long as we're stuck with the brat, somebody's got to tend it."

"What would you have done if she'd arrived when I wasn't here?"

"I don't know. Spaced her, I suppose." I wouldn't have, and we both knew it, but what else could I say?

"Have you given any thought to how you're going to get rid of her?"

"I'll look into the Company orphanage thing. There must be ones."

"Of course there are. I told you that."

"You never let me claim your ideas."

He wasn't in a bantering mood. "Listen, Melacha . . ."

"Okay, I'm listening."

"I don't think . . . I don't think that will be a very good idea. A government orphanage. I don't think that will work."

"Because the brat is a Faller? I can find out how much difference that will make. It might really not make any, you know. Not all government people are Earthers. Or at least, they don't all think like Earthers. They might treat the kid just fine."

He shook his head. "I don't think so." He hesitated. "Not because she's a Faller. Just . . . because."

"Because what?"

We had reached the bedchamber doorway, and the infant was inside still sleeping quite happily, velcroed to the retaining panel on the far wall. Ian stared at it almost speculatively while I reached inside to flip on the intercom and switch its signal to the galley, so we could hear if the infant woke up while we were having breakfast. When I turned away, Ian followed, but his mind was light years away.

I walked beside him in silence for a moment before I said gently, "Because what, Ian?"

He looked surprised to find himself not alone in the corridor. It took him a moment to rearrange his face in its customary amiably boyish lines. By then we'd reached the galley, and he could busy himself with the dispenser while we talked. "I forgot what we were talking about."

I didn't believe that, but I told him anyway. "Orphanages."

"Oh. Yeah. Um." He concentrated on his dispenser programming, then turned to operate the old-fashioned coffee maker I insist on using whenever there's gravity enough for it to work right. "Well . . . I know about orphanages. It's no good, that's all. We should try to find out where the baby really belongs, and give her back."

"The people at the orphanage would do that, surely."

"The people at the orphanage would do that, *may-be*." He had the coffee maker all organized and plugged in, and had nothing left to do with his hands. He stared at them for a long moment while I waited. Finally he shook his head briefly and turned to me, and I couldn't read his expression at all. There were shadows in the mirrored eyes, and a strange twist to his lips that I had never seen before. "She'd be just another kid to them. They wouldn't care. They'd follow procedure, I suppose, if it was convenient; but standard procedure for finding out where an abandoned baby belongs is a one-day ad in the newsfax. That's it. They don't waste money following it up in any way at all. So she'd be swallowed in the system in no time. Another faceless brat, underfed and unloved and valued only for whatever slave labor she could do when she got old enough."

"Slave labor?"

"Oh, the government pays them; but then they keep the money to pay for the kid's bed and board, such as it is. And the pay is never quite adequate to repay the fees owed for the early years. There's no way out. Except running."

"Is that what you did?" It was a guess. I half expected him to deny it, but he didn't. What I didn't notice at the time was that he didn't exactly confirm it, either.

He looked away from me. "They don't chase runaways. Most kids can't make it outside; you're not trained for any work that pays enough to live on, you have no place to go, nobody to turn to, no skills, no hope, no future. Most of them go back. Or die."

"But you didn't."

"No. I spent ten years surviving by my wits in places you can't even imagine." His mouth twisted. "They called us gutter rats. And that's exactly what we were."

"You made it out of that too. You're not a gutter rat now."

"Maybe." He glanced inadvertently toward the bedchamber. "But I am brilliant, and I got some damned lucky breaks. Do you want to take that kind of chance with her life?"

I sighed. "Okay. No orphanage. I think the coffee's ready. Now what do we do?"

His face relaxed. He almost grinned a spontaneous boy-grin. "We drink it."

Chapter Five

THE INFANT WOKE BEFORE WE WERE FINISHED WITH BREAK-fast. Ian didn't argue about it. He just glanced at the remainder of his breakfast with infinite regret, gulped the last of his coffee, and fled for the bedchamber with hardly even a reproving glance at me. I tried to look sympathetic till he was out the door, then went on eating.

We had been discussing various possible means of divesting ourselves of our unwelcome guest, and hadn't come up with any useful ideas except that we ought to reexamine its accoutrements to see if we'd missed any identifying markings. Ian had informed me that at its tender age, the infant would likely do little besides eat and sleep, mostly sleep. We had agreed on the desirability of that, Ian perhaps even more fervently than I since he was charged with its tending when it wasn't asleep; but perhaps we'd been premature. It seemed to me that it hadn't been very long at all since it went to sleep, and here it was awake again. Surely this was too soon for it to require additional sustenance already.

Whether I let him know it or not, I was profoundly grateful for Ian's presence during this crisis. I didn't even want to think about how I would have managed if I'd been alone when the baby arrived. In all probability I would have killed one or both of us out of sheer ignorance or panic. Certainly those attacking shuttles would have had a better chance at me, if I'd been juggling an infant during the firefights. Whoever left the creature here must either have had the same tender feelings toward me those pilots presumably had—and not much cared for the baby either—or been stark, staring mad.

Of course, if people really were trying to kill the infant, as those pilots seemed to have been . . . well, maybe its parents had listened a little too long and not too carefully to my legend. Maybe the idea of dumping the kid on me was for its own protection. Maybe somebody thought I could fight off its enemies successfully. As of course, so far, I had; but primarily because Ian was here to tend the brat.

Ian and I hadn't figured it out together, and I wasn't going to figure it out alone, so I gave up in disgust and turned on the newsfax to see what Jamin was getting excited about. I couldn't really imagine any circumstance in which it would be crucial that I have a ready grasp of world politics. He had intimated there would be another war, but it seemed to me there was always going to be another war. I'd had a hand in fighting the last one, and maybe even in making it end a little sooner than it might otherwise have done, but I didn't fool myself that the world couldn't have got along without me.

As for the idea of Jamin needing my help . . . it wasn't so much that the idea was farfetched, as it was that the concept of his deciding he needed my help and *asking* for it seemed highly improbable to me. Always before, when he needed my help, I'd had to browbeat him into accepting it. And now he was asking? I doubted it. He'd just thrown that in to pique my interest, because he had some personal reason for wanting to get me involved in the current political situation, whatever it was.

I misjudged him. I should have realized the idea that he would swallow his pride and ask for my help when he didn't have a real, serious need for it was ridiculous. Like me, Jamin didn't ask for things he needed. He earned them, took them, or did without. Except where Collis was concerned. The first newsfax reports I read didn't make the situation very clear to me at all; the Science News cycle was on, and all I could understand for sure was that a scientific discovery of some magnitude had been made: and that Collis was, or would be, or could be, involved. He was certainly affected. Not by the discovery, but by the thing that had been discovered: a new allele on the gravity determinant gene.

I wasn't sure what an allele was: my years of formal schooling were long behind me, and genetics was never one of my favorite subjects. I knew what the gravity-determinant gene was, of course. It was what made freefall mutants like Jamin. Originally all humankind had been Grounders, genetically adapted to gravity. Either they didn't have the gravity-determinant gene, or they all had two genes for gravity.

Sometime during early space colonization, the freefall mutation had developed: *Encyclopedia Terra* claimed the first Fallers occurred on Station Challenger in the middle of the twenty-first century. In the natural course of events, they mated and reproduced with Grounders, since Grounders were mostly what there were in those days. The offspring inherited one gravity-determinant gene from each parent. Two for gravity made a Grounder; two for freefall made a Faller; and one of each made a Floater, like me, who could live comfortably in either environment and move back and forth at will.

Grounders could live in either environment, too, if they kept up their exercises and ate the right dietary supplements and made sure they spent some time in gravity occasionally. If they never spent time in gravity, they would eventually lose the ability to return to gravity safely, and that was the biggest difference between them and Floaters. That and the fact that they thought of themselves as "pure" and "original strain" and "normal" and other supposedly superior things.

Freefall mutants couldn't live in gravity at all without constant medication that would keep them alive but could not eliminate the pain gravity caused them. Most of them didn't try. Maybe even Jamin would have had sense enough not to, if his adoptive son hadn't been a Grounder who became dangerously ill in freefall. We had always thought that was an inner-ear problem. Now the newsfax was telling me that the untreatable, unexplained cases of freefall allergy like Collis's had become more frequent in recent years, and that although it was usually diagnosed as an inner-ear problem, it was something else entirely.

It was a symptom of this new alele, whatever an alele was, on the gravity-determinant gene. A new quirk, anyway, on the freefall mutation; and quite possibly Collis had it, even though he wasn't a freefall mutant. The newsfax called the freefall allergy "a symptom of the Floater Factor in Grounder children." That's what they called the alele: the Floater Factor. Apparently Collis's symptoms could be expected to disappear in puberty . . . and he would begin to display Floater characteristics! He and his adoptive father would no longer be environmentally mismatched. Jamin wouldn't have to keep living in gravity to be with Collis. They could both move to freefall quarters. Unless, of course, they got killed by rabid racists in the meantime.

I was coming in on the middle of the story; even when the newsfax cycled onto World News it assumed I'd been keeping up with developments right along, so I got it in bits and pieces that I had to fit together myself to make any sense of it. For one thing, Grounder kids weren't the only ones who had this Floater Factor. Floaters could have it, though of course it wouldn't affect them personally, but only their offspring; Floaters didn't suffer from the symptoms Grounder kids did with it, but just acted like Floaters from birth. Freefall mutants, however, could have it too. The article said, "The Floater Factor is a dominant trait that can make even a genotypical Faller show the phenotype of a Floater." That was what upset the racists.

I had to dredge up memories of grade-school genetics to remember that a phenotype was what somebody looked like, and a genotype was what he *was*. With dominant genes like eye color, for instance, one could have a genotype for both blue and brown eyes, and one's phenotype would show brown eyes. I thought. Anyway, apparently with this Floater Factor, one could have the genotype of a Faller—both gravity-determinant genes for freefall—and still show the phenotype of a Floater if one of the freefall genes had this new allele.

Since Grounders and Floaters were virtually indistinguishable except after prolonged periods in freefall, the exact nature of what happened to freefall-allergic Grounder children at puberty had not been recognized at first; and since Faller children with the Floater Factor showed no early discomfort at either gravity or freefall, they were simply assumed to be Floaters. Or, if both their parents were Fallers, they were assumed to be Fallers and were never exposed to gravity.

When I went to Earth at the beginning of the Brief War to see the President of World, Inc., about some gross misbehavior being performed by the Belt branch of the government, the President had decided to instigate some scientific studies into the exact nature of the freefall mutation. She had since died, and I'd heard nothing more about such studies, so I had assumed the idea died with her. It hadn't. They just hadn't had anything momentous to report until recently.

Sometime in the last few months, a genotypical Faller braved the rigors of gravity in the interest of this study, only to discover that it caused him no discomfort whatsoever. Probably the same thing had happened any number of times before, in private, and had been kept very quiet indeed: the Faller, if both his parents were Fallers so that he could not possibly be a Floater, might well have wrongly assumed that his mother had been impregnated by someone other than his alleged father; and that's not the sort of thing most people are really anxious to discuss with their parents.

This time the Faller had witnesses, and he was a scientist, and instead of trying to hide and making wrong assumptions, he got curious. He checked. And yes, indeed, he was a Faller. But gravity didn't bother him one bit.

From there it must not have taken long to find the alele responsible, and I knew just enough genetics to be able to grasp that it must be dominant without knowing quite enough to explain why I thought so. Anyway, the scientists said so: it was dominant. Which meant two things (probably more, but two occurred to me at once): one, Fallers with the Floater Factor could "pass" for Floaters or Grounders; and two, the Factor was going to spread. The social ramifications of those two things were both obvious and scary.

It would no longer be possible to be at all certain that persons met in gravity were not freefall mutants. The only simple way to tell mutants from "normal" people was gone. And it would keep going. This wasn't just an isolated mutant who could "pass": this was a phenomenon that was going to spread and spread till eventually there might not be any clearly distinguishable Fallers left in the Solar System.

All this information had hit the news services in the last month or so. Maybe there was some scientific mention of it earlier than that, but if so, I hadn't noticed. It became a matter of public record, commonly discussed in laymen's terms all over the Solar System, sometime since I stopped answering my Comm Link because I was having such a good time with my new playmate.

According to the newsfax, a couple of weeks after it became a matter of public knowledge, it became a matter of public misinformation, confusion, fear, and dissatisfaction. Mothers Against Mutant Accession, the bigoted association that had once successfully defended the murder of a Faller child by claiming that since he was a Faller, he wasn't human so his death couldn't be called murder (the trial took place on Earth), had started a political hate campaign the moment the Floater Factor was made public.

Bigoted people everywhere were now suspicious of all strangers. Acts of violence against known and suspected mutants were increasing in number and severity throughout the Solar System, and it looked to me like the Patrol was turning a blind eye to it whenever possible. Not surprising; the Patrol, like the rest of the government, was Earth-based and Earth-bigoted.

Colonial disaffection with Earth rule was, naturally enough, on the increase again. Since the Brief War we'd won a number of concessions from Earth and I had really hoped things were going to smooth out at last, maybe to the point where we wouldn't have to fight any more wars. I hope a lot of things like that. I'm a very optimistic person. (Some people call me naive.)

A new bid for colonial independence had already been made politely, through legal channels. The newsfax didn't say so, but I could guess that if they'd gone that far, the colonists were also secretly and a good deal less legally beginning preparations for yet another civil war. And all the time I'd been playing house with an Earther.

He came back into the galley just then, and I don't know what my expression looked like, but it made him stop at the door with the oddest look on his face, like a small boy wrongfully accused but belligerently willing to defend whatever act it is he's supposed to have committed. It was the sort of look that usually made me giggle and lose all anger with him. It didn't work, this time.

After a moment he said softly, with the faintest hint of his wild warrior smile, "Skyrider? What is it? What's happened?"

I knew there was no reason to be angry with him. He was an Earther, yes, but I'd be as bigoted as they if I assumed that he therefore thought like an Earther. There was no reason to lump him in with the likes of MAMA. Hell, he was genuinely concerned for the welfare of the Faller infant on our hands. If he thought like most Earthers, he wouldn't care what happened to her and couldn't successfully pretend he did, even to please me. I knew that. I knew exactly how unreasonable I was being. And I went right ahead being unreasonable. I scowled at him and said shortly, "Read the newsfax. I have to go call Jamin."

He looked bewildered and turned to the newsfax printout I'd left lying on the table. I stalked off toward the control chamber to call Jamin, feeling vaguely guilty but unable to talk myself into making any more civil parting remarks. I always behave badly when I'm frightened, and I was very frightened just then for Jamin and Collis. They were both perfect targets for the likes of MAMA: Jamin because he was a Faller, and Collis because he apparently carried the dominant Floater Factor. And I hadn't been available when they needed me. I wasn't even readily available now. If my hand hadn't already been too swollen to make a fist, I probably would have hit another wall on my way to the Comm Link to call them.

Chapter Six

MAKING A CALL AT ANY APPRECIABLE DISTANCE OVER THE Comm Link is never easy. It has to be routed through relay stations, bounced off satellites, power-boosted, transformed back down, carrier-waved or occasionally fiber-opticked, and the gods only know what else. And at nearly every stage of the way there is opportunity for some officious Comm Link clerk or computer to put in its two credits' worth of interference, sometimes apparently just for the holy hell of it.

I wasn't in the best of moods to start with when I punched in the complex code for Home Base, then the shorter area code for pilot territory, and finally Jamin's personal quarters code. My mood didn't improve when the first thing I got in response was a tin-voiced computer telling me, "I'm sorry, but the number you have dialed is not in service at this time; please consult your directory and try again."

There's not much joy in arguing with computers, so I disconnected and tried again. I didn't need to consult my directory. I spent twenty years in pilot territory on Home Base, so I knew those numbers as well as I knew anything; and Jamin's personal code differed only by two digits from the one I'd had when I lived there, so I wasn't in any doubt of it either.

On the second try I got a human voice, but it was probably a recording. All it said was, "I'm sorry, we have a satellite overload in the eighth sector; please hold, and we will put your call through as soon as the overload is cleared." The voice clicked off and my Link unit began to emit the kind of noises Public Relations folk refer to as music: bland, expressionless melodic tones carefully calculated to offend nobody and to please only Public Relations folk. After thirty seconds of that, the voice clicked on again in the middle of a particularly tasteless sequence of notes to inform me in a nasally cheerful whine, "We have not forgotten you. Please continue to hold, and we will get to you as soon as possible."

I gave them another thirty seconds, after which a new voice came on to advise against disconnecting on grounds that it would only put me at the back of the line again, so to speak. I disconnected.

On the third try I got all the way to Home Base before I got interrupted by clerks. This time it was a live one, complete with visual image: a sly-faced little man with watery brown eyes and a mirthless and meaningless smile, who stared soulfully into the Comm Link camera and said unctuously, "Please be patient with us: our lines into pilot territory are all busy at this time, but if you will hold the line, we will connect you with the number you have dialed as soon as there are lines open to that area."

I said, "Hey!"

He looked startled, lifted his eyebrows, and peered nearsightedly at his screen. "Yes? You have a question? If you will please hold the line, your call will be put through as soon as possible. Please hold the line."

"Just don't—" I broke off; he had disconnected from my call, maybe to answer another, or maybe just for the hell of it. I'd intended to ask not to be given the standard waiting music, but I got it anyway. At least that established that he hadn't disconnected my call entirely.

After thirty seconds he came back on the line to say with infinite patience, as though I'd been nagging him the whole time he was gone, "*Please* be patient. We are undergoing considerable renovation in the systems here, and we regret very much that it has caused some delay in your call, but I assure you that you will be connected at the earliest possible moment."

I wanted to tell him that I was already pretty well connected, but he cut off again. He probably wouldn't have seen the joke, anyway. He didn't look like a man who understood the concept of *joke*. I waited, trying to ignore the soulless imitation of music that was being piped into my control chamber, for another thirty seconds. After that I didn't have to wait any longer: the line went dead. The little bastard had cut me off.

Well, that established that there was one useful purpose to the "music"; it let one know whether one was still on line. An innocuous beep, click, or buzz at five- or ten-second intervals would have done the job as well and caused fewer ulcers among innocent music lovers attempting long-distance Comm calls.

I tried again. And again. And, after some hearty cursing and kicking of furniture, again. On the sixth try I got through. Jamin's face smiled at me from the Comm Link screen . . . only it wasn't Jamin's face. I should have been ready for that. His old one had got shot off in the war, and the Diademan med-techs who had saved his life hadn't known what he looked like before, so they gave him a whole new face. He hadn't seen fit to have it altered once he got back to civilization. There was no real reason to; it was a perfectly good face, at least as handsome as the old one, capable of all the sardonic arrogance he had always displayed. But it was still a stranger's face to me. I opened my mouth to greet him, and nothing came out.

He knew why. The sardonic smile widened. "Hi, hotshot," he said comfortably.

I swallowed hard, and managed some sort of greeting. My voice squeaked. I cleared my throat and scowled at him.

"You want to break some furniture before we start talking," he asked, "or do you want to use the Link while we've got a line open?"

I couldn't hit him at that distance, and I'd had about enough of hitting walls and kicking furniture, so I relaxed and grinned at him. "You win. Let's talk."

I could see him relax too. I must have looked pretty fierce if it made him automatically get ready to defend himself when he knew damn well I couldn't touch him. "You've looked at the news?"

"I've looked. How are things at Home Base?"

"Not too bad yet; we've had a couple of incidents,

52

but nothing directed personally at Collis and me . . . so far."

"What kind of incidents?"

"We have our share of MAMA's Warriors for Decency at Home Base, same like most anyplace else. All of a sudden MAMA's membership seems to include about half the Earthers in the Belt, and at least half of those are Warriors for Decency."

"Warriors for crissake for Decency? What the hell is that when it's at home?"

He made a wry face. "If they were Fallers, the newsfax would call them terrorists."

"Oh. What fun. Jamin, for once in your life will you please damn it *listen* to me? You and Collis need to get the hell off Home Base. You could come to my rock. There's room. I'm maybe leaving, anyway. And there are separate controls for gravity in every chamber. I know you don't like to run from things, and maybe you have some commitments to the Company you feel like you have to keep, but you could work off my rock. You'd be hell of safer over here. Bring somebody to watch Collis when you're on a run, and just *live* here until we figure out what to do next. Please? You and Collis are just too damn good targets when something like this is going on—"

"Peace," he said.

I paused, the thread of my argument broken, and stared at him. "What?"

"Peace." He made a defensive gesture. "No more. You win." His look was half sheepish, half triumphant. It took me a moment to figure that out.

"Oh. You said you wanted help. Was that it? You *wanted* to come to my rock?"

"That was it. And by God, Skyrider, you're slipping. You came right out and offered what I wanted without bargaining or even trying to get me to agree to any kind of price—"

"Oh, there's a price," I told him.

His look turned sardonic. "You already offered what I wanted."

"Because I want the same thing, for a different reason. I told you to bring a sitter for Collis when you're out on runs, yeah?"

"Yeah, so?"

"So make sure it's somebody who knows a little something about infants. And can tolerate freefall. And can handle the big guns."

He was the only person I had ever known who could look bewildered without losing his essential look of arrogance: no mean trick. "What? Why?"

I hesitated. "I don't think I want to talk about it over an open Link. You'll see when you get here. Just don't come without somebody who fills those requirements. That's the current price for a stay on my rock. Is that quite clear?"

He nodded slowly. The bewilderment was gone, leaving only bemused arrogance. "It's clear. It's hell of clear. What are you and Spencer up to, Skyrider?"

"Nothing at all," I said innocently.

He shook his head. "What it *sounds* like is impossible; you haven't had time. And the next logical possibility, considering it's the two of you we're talking about here, is . . . *kid*napping?" He scowled at the screen. "Surely that's *too* illegal, even for you?"

I grinned with what I hoped was innocent good cheer. I wasn't feeling hell of cheerful just then, much less innocent, but it seemed the appropriate response. "How soon can you get here?"

He hesitated, still scowling at the screen, then said reluctantly, "We're all packed and ready; if you hadn't called, we were going to come uninvited."

"Things are that bad over there?"

"They're not good. I don't like leaving Collis here alone when I'm on a run."

"I don't like having either one of you there with this idiocy going on. Get over here as soon as you can . . . But don't forget the baby-sitter."

"He's ready too." He hesitated. "But I'll have to check whether he's willing to tackle an infant. How old?"

"Ian says about two months."

His eyebrows lifted. "How the hell . . . Never mind. A Faller?"

"Ian thinks so."

"Okay. I'll check with the sitter. If he's willing, we'll be there before you know it."

"Not quite."

"What?"

"You forget my perimeter alarms. I'll know it."

"Oh. Right." He looked exasperated. "Did anyone ever tell you you're too literal-minded for your own good?"

"Yes. Frequently. Say hi to Collis for me, okay?"

"Say it yourself, when we get there." He turned off his Link before I could answer that.

I stared at the blank screen for a while, thinking of absolutely nothing at all, till I noticed that Ian had come in and was watching me. Then I transferred my look to him, still thinking of nothing at all; I'd had too much thinking already for one day.

"How's Jamin?"

"He's okay."

"He coming here?"

I nodded. "Complete with baby-sitter for our Faller infant, as well as for Collis."

"Good. That was his problem? He needed someplace to hide?" He lifted his hands before I was all the way out of my chair. "Sorry, I didn't mean it that way." He backed off till he saw I'd had time to reconsider, then relaxed against the doorway, looking at me. "Okay. That's Jamin's problem solved. Now you want to talk about what's wrong between us?"

I settled back into my chair, suddenly infinitely weary. "I don't know what you mean." I did, of course, but making him state the problem gave me a brief respite before I had to answer the question.

"I think you do."

So much for brief respites. "Okay. So you already know what the problem is. So what did you want to discuss?"

"I didn't say I knew what the problem was. I said I thought you knew."

"Oh, hell. *Earther.*"

He looked at me for a long moment before he spoke again. When he did, his voice was very soft . . . and he was smiling. "So that's it."

"What's what?"

"Don't play games with me, Skyrider. We've had enough games for one morning."

"We sure as hell have."

His smile broadened. "Well?" With his baby face, and that wide, humorless smile, and the look in his silvered eyes, he looked as though he probably ate babies for breakfast.

"Well what?"

His voice got gentler. "I said no more games, Skyrider." If he'd been a stranger, I'd have killed him right then. The way he looked and sounded, it was the only safe thing to do. "I mean it. You're feeling guilty, right? Because a bunch of Earthers have been playing hell with the colonies, or with freefall mutants, or some other damn thing, and I'm an Earther, so now all of a sudden I'm the goddamn enemy. And you've been consorting with the enemy when you should've been out saving the universe." His strange eyes studied me. For a brief, mad instant, I thought they could see right through my soul. "That's it, isn't it?"

I shook my head. "I don't know. Ian—"

"The hell you don't know." He had moved imperceptibly away from the doorway, till he was standing in tense battle-readiness just far enough away from me that I could have leapt out of my chair in a flying tackle and reached him if I wanted to start one hell of a fight.

The odd thing was, I didn't want to. "Ian—"

"You goddamn bigot. I thought I knew you." He shook his head. "I never knew you at all, did I?"

"Ian, damn it—"

"Yes, I am an Earther." He saw I wasn't going to fight him, and he went right on smiling that deadly, implacable smile. "And if that's all I am to you, then you'd better figure out hell of fast how exactly to tend to a Faller infant once I'm gone, because I'm damn well going."

A curious, cold mixture of rage and despair swept through me, literally shaking me. I had to fight to keep my voice steady. "You'll have a bit of a problem with that, unless you intend to steal my shuttle."

"That's exactly what I intend to do," he said quietly. "And if you try to stop me, by God, I'll break you in half."

It wasn't worth it. Nothing was worth anything. I shook my head slowly. "I didn't ask for this, Ian. You're not even interacting with me, not really. You're just having a conversation with yourself, while I watch."

For a moment I thought he actually would try to break me in half, and I wondered without much interest whether I would have to kill him. I could have. Maybe I even would have. And maybe he realized that, because he shook his head suddenly, said *"Belters"* in a tone of terminal disgust, and walked away.

He did steal my shuttle. I didn't make any effort to stop him. I watched him hurtle across the monitor screens in my *Defiance*, tripping all the alarms like crazy, and I patiently turned them off one by one as he passed, turning them on again when he was out of range. When he was all the way out of sight, I went on staring at the starfield for a long time through the thick polarized glasteel viewport before I hit it. That time, I did break my hand.

Chapter Seven

THE BABY SLEPT WITHOUT COMMENT OR COMPLAINT WHILE I bound my hand as best I could and looked in to see how she was doing, then alternately paced and cursed in the corridor outside the bedchamber till I'd finally worn myself to such a frazzled state of exhaustion that the next time I looked in on her, the freefall hammock hanging next to her looked too attractive to resist. My hand hurt less in freefall. I was going to have to find a med-tech soon with equipment to mend it, and I hoped it wouldn't be the one who'd mended my broken hands before. They get so damned bossy about it after a while, as though it were something of theirs one kept breaking.

Anyway, that was for the future. Right now I just wanted to rest and stop thinking. I fastened myself into the hammock and closed my eyes, thinking sourly that no matter how determined I was to use sleep as a means of escape, I would probably accomplish nothing but greater vexation from hanging there however long I had the patience for it, unpleasantly wide awake.

The perimeter alarms woke me. They woke the brat, too, and made it howl, but I couldn't take time to worry about that: it might not be Jamin who had tripped them. I had a moment's difficulty, one-handed, with the hammock fastenings. Then they came loose, and I dived straight toward the door head-first. Luckily I had left both halves open. I was still dazed with sleep, and might have made that dive right *into* the door if it had been closed. As it was, I hit the corridor rolling and came up running. When I reached the control chamber, the intruder was still too far out to be readily identified on my screens.

I queried the computer, opened a Comm Link channel, got the big guns ready, and tried not to think of that poor frightened infant screaming to itself in red-faced, infuriated terror in the bedchamber. There was nothing I could do about it till I found out who had tripped the alarms; and not then, either, if the intruder turned out to be hostile. In that case I'd have to keep the kid alive first, and worry about comforting it later.

I had programmed my Comm Link to make an automatic querying hail on all channels, then home in on one for further communication if it got an answer, so I didn't have to do anything but turn it on. And the monitor screens were automatic, with manual override: I had only to tell the computer I wanted to see what had tripped the alarms, and I got those coordinates on close-up. But the big guns required hands on. Checking their charge one-handed was no problem, and altering them was even simpler; but tracking and firing with any degree of accuracy was a two-handed job. It had been difficult when my right hand was merely painfully swollen. It would be damn near impossible if, now that I'd broken it, I couldn't use that hand at all.

The immobilizing bandages I had used didn't prevent me from wrapping that hand around the guidance control. The big question was whether I would be able to pull the firing stud if I had to. Of course I would still be able to pull the left-hand stud; tracking and focusing was done in tandem, but firing was done independently. The trouble was that I might need both chances: inexperienced as I was with these guns, what I liked to do was get a moving target lined up, then pull the studs one after the other; it gave me more leeway in focusing since that way, in effect, I was firing at two targets very near each other in space, rather than using both shots on one target. If I could only pull the left-hand stud, I'd get only one chance at the target each time, so I'd have to be more accurate in my focusing.

Fortunately, it was a moot point after all; the intruder wasn't hostile. It was only Jamin. When he hailed me I called him on in, and theoretically I could have left the control chamber then and gone to see about the infant; but to do that, I'd have had to turn off the alarms Jamin hadn't already tripped and rely solely on the ones he was already past to warn us if anybody followed him in. I was feeling a damn sight too paranoid to do that.

Admittedly, I was reluctant to deal with the infant, but I really would have done it if I'd thought it safe to do so. I could still hear it squalling when I turned off the alarms Jamin had triggered, and I felt sorry for the little monster. I didn't feel sorry enough to leave my rock undefended for the time it took Jamin to come in.

Maybe I should have gone and got the kid, brought it back to the control chamber with me, and tried to comfort it while I watched the monitors and turned the alarms off and on again as Jamin passed them. But I would have had to do it in freefall, one-handed, and if anybody did show up on Jamin's tail, things could have got messy. I left the brat alone, tried not to listen to it howl, and waited for Jamin to get there.

Once he was in past the alarms, I set them on automatic again and went after the baby. Then I didn't know what the hell to do with it. What does one do with an infant when it cries? I was afraid to take it off the retaining panel. In freefall there wasn't much danger of dropping it, but for all I knew, just holding it wrong could hurt it. It looked so damned small and fragile. I tried patting it gently, and that helped some. Then I found one of its bottles, already loaded and ready to go, and that helped more. It wrapped its wrinkled little hands around it, shut up, and began to feed with cosmic satisfaction and greed.

That left me free to go meet Jamin and Collis at the airlock, which I did. When the lock cycled open, I was ready for one of Collis's whirlwind hugs, but apparently he had outgrown them. He sure had outgrown my memories. No more plump little Buddha-faced boy: he was taller and thinner, his face oddly intense, his bones elongated and frail-seeming with the baby fat gone. The only thing that hadn't changed at all was the summer-blue smile of his eyes. He looked at me uncertainly till I said, "Yup. Absolutely guaranteed, those eyes are going to break a lot of tender girlish hearts one day."

That made him grin and say, "Oh, *Sky*rider," with boyish severity.

I returned the grin and looked past him at his adoptive father. This time I thought I was ready for the new face, and it still took me by surprise. I'd meant to greet him casually. I didn't.

He grinned lazily. "Good to see you too," he said. "This is the baby-sitter you asked for: Chuck Dakine, expert on infants."

I looked past Jamin with difficulty, to find a mild-eyed, mustached young man with the gentle face of a monk grinning at me. "Pleased to meet you, sir. I've heard a lot about you." His voice was as mild as his eyes, with a soft Earther twang both unexpected and, in the circumstances, painful. He sounded altogether too much like Ian for comfort.

"Some of it good, I hope."

"Most of it from Collis," he said, "so I expect you can guess."

"Oh," I said. "The legend. Um. Well. I prob'ly won't live up to that, so don't expect it."

"Oh, I know," he said happily.

"You planning to invite us in anytime soon?" asked Jamin. If his grin got any more sardonic, I just might smash it.

"Oh. Sure. Come on in." I glanced at the empty airlock floor. "Where's your luggage?"

"Still on board *Challenger II*," said Jamin. "Where's your shuttle?"

"Ian stole it." Which shows how rattled I was by the whole situation: that was the truth, but it was also a damn-fool thing to say to Jamin.

His eyebrows lifted and the smile got so sardonic I almost did hit it. Only the refusal of my broken hand to make a fist stopped me. I could have hit him with my left, of course, but I didn't really *want* to hit him. I was just jumpy.

"And you *let* him?" asked Collis. Small boys rush in where their fathers know better than to tread.

I shrugged and said, in what I hoped was a casual tone, "It seemed the logical thing to do at the time." I was leading them toward the galley by force of habit; that was where guests gathered. "So, Chuck. You can handle the big guns?" His face was so sublimely innocent I had trouble believing he'd ever fired a weapon in his life.

He hesitated, thinking about it. "Depends on the guns, I guess. What kind you got?" I told him. He looked relieved. "Oh, hell yes. No problem. That's what I had on my rock." For just a second, as he said that, I saw a wholly unexpected light in those otherwise kindly eyes: the unholy pleasure of a warrior in battle handed his favorite weapon when he had thought it irretrievably lost. Then he smiled, and the look was gone. But I would not again mistake his gentleness for harmlessness. This man would make a dangerous and deadly enemy. And, if I was any judge, one hell of a steadfast friend.

"What happened to your rock?" I asked.

"Destroyed in the war," he said. "I wasn't on it."

"You went in to stake your claim?"

He nodded. "Me and all the other gullible dolts in the Belt. I guess I was lucky, at that. When I tried to get it back, it was destroyed in the battle. I wasn't."

Collis was still worrying about *Defiance*. "But Skyrider, why would you think it was logical to let *any*body steal your shuttle? I know you and Ian were, I mean, he's, I guess he's your boyfriend, but . . . why would you let him steal *Defiance*?"

"Well, kid, mostly 'cause I wanted rid of him, but not quite badly enough to kill him. Don't worry, I'll get *Defiance* back. He won't do her any harm, and he'll leave her at Home Base or somewhere for me to claim. She'll be all right." We'd reached the galley, and I led them inside with the brittle jollity of a nervous housewife. "Can I get you guys anything to drink? Or eat?"

"Can I have a soda?" asked Collis.

"Sure," I said, at the same time as Jamin said, "No." He and I glared at each other for a moment, till he gave in with an impatient shrug and said, "All right, *one*."

Collis grinned at me in triumph while I produced it. "Anybody else?" I asked.

"If you made some of your infamous coffee, I'd drink it," said Jamin. "I don't know what time it is for you, but for us it's just past breakfast."

Chuck looked alert. "I'd like to try your coffee."

"One pot of coffee, coming up." I was glad to have something to do that kept my back to them, just in case they started asking any more questions. "I don't know what time it is, but I know I haven't had enough coffee yet today."

"Can you manage, with your hand like that?" asked Chuck.

I could imagine the warning glance Jamin threw him for that, but it wasn't necessary. Their mere presence was jollying me out of the near-terminal angst I'd been feeling. "Sure, I think so. If not, I'll ask for help."

"That'll be the day," said Jamin. "What did you do, hit Spencer?"

"Never mind," I explained. I might not have got away with that if the infant hadn't elected just that moment to let its presence be known by means of a pitiful wail that progressed rapidly into the enraged bellow I was beginning to know and dislike so thoroughly.

"What's that?" said Collis.

The intercom was still on, carrying the infant's howls quite clearly to the galley. "That's Chuck's other charge," I said.

"Where?" asked Chuck.

"In the bedchamber. Here, I'll show you. Jamin, you know how to make the coffee, don't you?"

"Most people might say, 'Will you please?'"

I glared at him. "I'm not most people."

He grinned and rose from the table to deal with the coffee. "That's true enough."

I ignored him. "Come on, Chuck. She's in here." I led him silently to the bedchamber. The infant became steadily more audible as we approached. It had very healthy lungs for something so small.

I had left the door open and the warning light off, since I was alone on my rock, and I forgot to warn Chuck before he stepped into the bedchamber. He had good reflexes. He looked briefly startled when his first step inside bounced him halfway to the ceiling. Then he performed an elegant twisting movement that brought one foot in range of a wall, which he kicked just hard enough and at just the right angle to bring him up against the infant's retaining panel in one oddly dignified swoop. He was wearing ordinary

Belter clothes, but I could almost see a monk's robe swirling gracefully around him as he moved.

I said, "Sorry, I forgot to warn you," but I'm not sure he heard me. His whole attention was on the infant.

"She's lost her bottle," he said. "And she needs to be changed. You have fresh diapers?" He peeled her off the retaining panel and thrust her at me. "Here, hold her for a minute."

He didn't give me time or opportunity to refuse. I accepted her gingerly and stared at him in panic, afraid to move. She stopped wailing and looked at me with wet brown puppy eyes.

"There, see?" said Chuck, rooting ambitiously in the bundle of her belongings stuck to the next retaining panel. "She wanted to be held. Babies need a lot of attention." He found what he was looking for and turned back toward us . . . and exploded into laughter at the sight of my expression.

There was no way I could kill him with an infant in my arms, but I sure as hell had a strong inclination to try.

Chapter Eight

I SETTLED FOR HANDING HIM BACK THE INFANT. AND HE, realizing his laughter had vexed me, looked genuinely chagrined. "I'm sorry, Skyrider. I didn't mean to laugh at you. It was just that you looked so—"

I said, "Don't say it," at the same time as he said, "Frightened." We looked at each other. He was doing his very best not to laugh at me again. The impulse to kill him was gone. And, oddly, so was the deadly weariness that had dragged me down since Ian left. I managed a feeble grin and said in what I hoped was a reasonably cheerful tone, "Okay. You win. I *was* frightened."

He cocked his head. "Of an infant?"

"That I might hurt her."

"Or maybe partly that somebody might see you holding her?" He busied himself with diapers.

"Somebody's been talking about me."

"Only Collis."

"That's right, you told me that already. Well, just don't swallow the legend whole: it may contain a few minor exaggerations."

"I expect it does." He had deftly removed the infant's diaper, thrust it into the disposal, wiped her bottom with a premoistened paper towel, and administered a fresh diaper, all with the ease and dexterity of long practice. The infant chortled contentedly to itself during the process, and made an occasional awkward swipe at Chuck's face with both tiny fists when he bent into possible range. "What's her name?" he asked me.

"Oh . . . I don't know." I must have looked as startled as I felt: for some reason, the concept that it might have a name had simply not occurred to me.

Chuck gave me an odd look, but before he could say anything, Jamin floated into the room and across it to peer at my unwanted acquisition. "Where did you get her?" he asked, his tone clearly indicating preparedness to disbelieve whatever answer I gave.

"I don't know that either."

Both of them stared at me. "Come *on*," said Jamin. "She didn't just appear on your rock—"

"As if by magic? In a way, that's exactly what she did." I grinned with, I admit, a certain amount of triumph showing, and gave them a moment to try to frame a response to that before I relented and told them the truth. "Somebody dumped her in my airlock."

"Who?" They both spoke at once: Jamin was already familiar with my rock's complex alarm systems, and Chuck had seen them on the way in. They both knew how improbable it was that anyone could have got past all that without tripping a single alarm.

I shrugged—always a mistake in freefall; it bounced me off a wall and I had to grab a handhold to stay the same side up as both of them. "I don't know. I didn't see."

"How could you not *see*? What were you doing when the alarms went off?" Jamin realized the probable answer almost before his question was spoken, and looked embarrassed. "I mean . . ."

"It's okay: we weren't doing anything particularly private," I said. "We were just sleeping."

"You slept through the alarms?" He clearly didn't believe that.

"Whoever brought the brat didn't trip the alarms."

Chuck looked dubious. Jamin looked thoughtful. "And you say Spencer was with you?" His expression was a lot less arrogant after only a few minutes in freefall: most of the unpleasantness he usually displayed in gravity was just a defense against pain. In freefall he could be downright human when he chose to be. I decided I could learn to like his new face, given time.

"He was with me, and sound alseep, so for sure it wasn't he who brought her."

"He still could have been involved. Must have been."

Chuck was looking back and forth between us as we spoke, his expression sublimely innocent and interested. It was hard not to imagine him in flowing monk robes when he looked like that. "Why?"

We both looked at him in surprise. "Why what?" I asked.

"Why must this Spencer person have been involved?"

"Oh. He wasn't," I said.

Jamin said, almost but not quite simultaneously, "Because he's the only person I know who could get past all those alarms without tripping any."

"Why would he?" Chuck asked curiously.

"He wouldn't," I said.

"He's a con man," said Jamin. "A hustler."

I scowled at Jamin. "Look, he was just as surprised as I was."

"An ac*com*plished con man," said Jamin.

"Don't be silly, why would he? Where's the profit?" I shook my head. "Besides, you didn't see how he acted about the infant. He was concerned about it."

"Not very, or he wouldn't have left her in your care."

I didn't bother to argue with that; it was probably true enough. I just said, "He knew you were coming," and was surprised how sullen my voice sounded.

Jamin eyed me for a moment, then shrugged ineffably without losing his balance, and looked at the infant again. "So what do you plan to do with her?"

"I don't know."

"Why not take her to Home Base? An orphanage would take care of her for you, find her parents, or put her up for adoption or something."

"No!" My vehemence startled all of us. "I mean . . ." I hesitated, thinking of what Ian had told me. "I just don't think it's a good idea. I'd rather try to find her parents myself."

"And meantime you want Chuck to take care of her for you."

71

"That's right. It won't be for long. If I can't find her parents, I'll . . . I'll find a home for her, myself."

Jamin gave me an odd look, but didn't say anything. Chuck smiled beatifically and said, "Why the big guns?"

"What?"

"You wanted to make sure I was good with the guns. Why?" He hesitated, and a fleeting look of embarrassment dimmed the beatific smile. "I mean, I don't want to pry into your personal affairs, but I think I ought to know who I might be fighting."

"Oh, I don't know that either. Just somebody trying to kill the brat."

He stared at the infant in his arms. "Trying to kill *her*? This child? Why would anyone do that?" He lifted his gaze to me. The mild, dark eyes once again had that deep, half-hidden gleam of predatory ferocity.

"I don't know."

"There doesn't seem to be much you do know, does there?" Jamin eyed me dubiously. "Skyrider, if this is all some bizarre scam you and Spencer cooked up between you—"

"Damn you." I said it without force or conviction; it was a pretty unlikely story, and past friendship aside, he had no particular reason to believe me. "I'm telling the truth."

"Okay, let's say I believe you. What next?"

"That's another of the many things I don't know."

"Who was it who tried to kill her?" asked Chuck.

"I couldn't tell. They didn't identify themselves, and their shuttles bore no markings. The computer couldn't ID them. At a guess, they were modified Starbirds, but that's not much help."

"Did they say *why* they wanted to kill her?"

"They didn't say anything. They just attacked."

Jamin looked at me sharply. "Then how do you know it was the baby they were after?"

I sighed. "I don't, for sure. But they both tried to hit the airlock she'd been left in, and neither one made any particular effort to hit anything else. Oh, they both took potshots at the main viewport, but the airlock was their primary target."

"Spencer was already gone by this time?"

"No, he was still here. He tended the baby while I fought the shuttles. Why?"

"So *Defiance* was docked outside, and they didn't hit her? They just went for the empty dock?"

"That's right."

Jamin nodded reluctantly. "Sounds like it wasn't you they were after."

"I think that's what I *said*."

The baby had fallen asleep again. We watched Chuck fasten it gently to the retaining panel. When he was satisfied it was secure, he turned to me, looking more than ever bemused and innocent and, at the same time, mildly mischievous. "Would you let me take a look at the tapes of those shuttles, if you still have them?"

"Sure." I frowned at him. "Why? You think you can identify them?"

"It's possible." His voice was as innocently mischievous as his face. "I know a little something about shuttles. And it occurs to me that if you could identify her enemies, you'd be on the way to identifying her." He nodded toward the infant. "In the meantime, you ought to give her a name, you know."

I led the way toward the corridor. "Why?"

He dived past me and caught up against the door-frame to pause and look at me with cheerful earnestness. "Everybody ought to have a name."

"She probably has one. We just don't know what it is." Since I wasn't in a hurry, I went out the door right side up; and since I had an audience, I did it as gracefully as I could manage.

Chuck followed, much more gracefully, though he didn't seem to give it any attention; he was just stepping through a doorway, and the transition from freefall to gravity might as well not have existed. "She still ought to have a name now," he insisted. "Even just a nickname." He automatically paused again outside to reach a hand back through the doorway to steady Jamin's progress through.

"I'm not a damn cripple." Jamin hesitated, still in freefall, scowling at Chuck.

Startled, Chuck looked at him, lifted his eyebrows, said, "Oh, sure. Sorry," and turned to move on down the corridor as if there were no question of Jamin's ability to follow us easily into gravity.

I led him toward the control chamber to show him the battle tapes, so Jamin had no audience for his return to gravity. That left him free to concentrate more on getting it done than on making it look painless. But I think Chuck was listening just as tensely as I was while we walked away, as if by empathy alone we could ease the transition for him. We couldn't, of course. Nothing could. A Faller should never have to walk in gravity.

"Does Collis know about this new Floater Factor thing?"

Chuck glanced at me, clearly aware of the thought process that led to the question. "He knows. It's all I can do to keep him reminded that he may not have it. Not all Grounder kids who're allergic to gravity will ever outgrow it. Some of them really do have something wrong with their inner ears."

I nodded. "Besides, he's only seven. It'll be years before he outgrows it if he's going to."

"Two or three, anyway." Aware of Jamin's approach, Chuck smoothly diverted the conversation from anything to do with gravity, and the three of us talked random nonsense the rest of the way to the control chamber.

Chuck made me run the battle tapes three times before he would commit himself, but he seemed quite confident when he finally looked up and said with peaceful certainty, "Martian manufacture. Nobody else can build 'em quite like that. Sweet little shuttles, those two. Custom jobs, both of 'em. My guess is the Tanaka brothers, but there are some others who do nearly as good work. I can give you the names and addresses. It'll give you a starting point, anyway." I must have looked dubious, because he grinned suddenly and added, "I do know a little something about it, you know: used to be a shipbuilder myself."

"Oh?"

He nodded. "That was before I joined the monastery, of course."

"Which was, presumably, before you joined the Marines and went to war?"

He cocked his head at me, still grinning. "Actually, it was the Colonial Fleet I joined, and I'd been kicked out of the monastery a couple of years before that."

"Kicked out? What for?"

He laughed softly. "For having led too sheltered a life. All I'd ever done was work in my father's ship-

75

yard; which, being Martian, *was* pretty parochial, I guess. They said I needed to see more of the world before I made any major decisions. They were right."

I suppose I still looked doubtful. I know I sounded doubtful. "If you grew up on Mars, how come you sound like an Earther?"

"When I left the monastery, I didn't leave Earth right away. I took their injunction to see the world pretty seriously, you know. And where do you find better fleshpots and sinkholes of depravity than on Earth?"

"Are you serious?"

"Occasionally."

"And you decided not to return to the monastery?"

"I got married instead, and fathered some offspring, and that sort of thing spoiled me for the monastic life."

"Where are they now? Your family?"

For the first time, the mischievous grin faltered; but only for an instant, like a shadow passing across the sun. "They were killed in the First War. And now that you have my life history, do you want the names of these shipbuilders?"

I glanced at Jamin, who was watching us with amusement. "You trust this guy?"

Jamin shrugged. "I hired him to baby-sit Collis."

"Right. Okay, Chuck, tell me about shipbuilders."

Chapter Nine

J<small>AMIN GAVE ME A RIDE BACK TO</small> H<small>OME</small> B<small>ASE.</small> I<small>T HAD BEEN A</small> long time since I'd ridden shotgun in somebody else's shuttle. We didn't talk much. He seemed oddly subdued, and I suppose I was too; I kept wondering whether I could have prevented Ian's precipitous departure . . . and concluding that, given the circumstance and our two personalities, I couldn't have. It was not a comforting thought.

We were almost at Home Base when Jamin said suddenly, "They're building up the Fleet again. At Mars Station."

I looked at him. "You wonder why I haven't asked why you didn't go there."

He scowled at the controls. "I suppose you think you know why."

I looked out the viewport, at a large rock tumbling

lazily out of our path, its pitted surface constantly changing shape in the changing light. "I sat out the First War."

He shook his head. "That was different."

"Was it?"

"Obviously. That was a purely political war. You're not a political person."

"There are those who would disagree with you." I sighed more audibly than I intended, and looked at him again. "Jamin, Collis already nearly lost you once. Did lose you. When the Brief War was over, and he went down to Mars without you, thinking he would always be without you . . . thinking you were dead . . . " I cleared my throat. "Damn it, Jamin, if you have the courage to stay out of this one for his sake, I'm damn well not going to question it."

He looked at me for a long moment, then looked away and said in an unconvincingly indifferent voice, "Maybe it won't come to that. Maybe there won't be another war."

"Sure. Maybe the Earth will be sucked into a black hole tomorrow, never to be seen again."

He was silent for a long moment. "If there is a war, I'll fight it."

"I wish you wouldn't."

He went on as if he hadn't heard me. "But until there is . . . if there is . . . I want to keep Collis well out of the line of fire from these damned MAMA terrorists."

"You don't have to justify yourself to me."

"I know." Home Base came in sight and he played needlessly with the controls, finessing our approach. "Maybe I have to justify me to me."

I laughed: a harsher sound than I intended. "If you win that one, let me know."

He glanced at me, started to say something, and changed his mind. After a moment he shrugged and gave his whole attention to the controls. We didn't speak again till we were safely on the landing deck and he was opening the hatch for me while I collected my belongings. Then he said almost diffidently, "You'll be going to Mars?"

"Looks like." I hefted my tote bag and looked at him. "Why'd you ask?"

"No reason." He hesitated. "Don't forget you're a prime target for MAMA's terrorists too."

"Don't forget they're a prime target for me."

"Damn it, be careful."

"I always am." I swung down onto the flight deck and grinned back up at him. "Take your own advice, okay? Be careful."

"I always am." There was a wry note to his mimickry.

"And if that brat gives you any trouble . . ."

When I hesitated, he tilted his head with a knowing smile. "Yes?"

"Don't call me."

"That's what I thought you'd say."

"It always pleases me to be able to fulfill somebody's expectations." I gave him a mock salute and turned to scan the flight deck, looking for *Defiance*, while behind me Jamin closed the hatch and jockeyed *Challenger II* for liftoff.

Defiance was there, as I'd thought she would be, waiting for me. Before approaching her I made a brief side trip to Sick Bay to get my hand mended, and had to resist the impulse to risk breaking it again on the face of an officious med-tech who had mended my hands a few times before. I restrained myself and got out of Sick Bay quickly. I had nothing else to do on Home Base, so I headed straight for the flight deck and *Defiance*, and very carefully did not even wonder whether her presence meant Ian was still on Home Base. I didn't want to know. There was nothing I could say to him that would change what had already been said . . . and not said. No sense even thinking about it now. The thing to think about now was that infant; that was something I could *do* something about. I could find out who was trying to kill it, and where it belonged, and maybe even see that it got a chance to grow up to fight its own battles someday.

I would like to report that I spent some time figuring the angles, trying to find a prospect of profit for me in that enterprise: I'm aware what it may be doing to my reputation to announce that I hadn't even thought to wonder whether there might be anything in it for me. But the plain fact is that the good old hotshot Skyrider, who, according to the legend, might not *breathe* if nobody paid her (of course that wasn't true; who would pay me?), never even thought of trying to turn a profit that time.

It would be profit enough to get rid of the brat with a clean conscience. I don't say Chuck was right when he suggested I was afraid of her, or of what people would think of me for sheltering her. Of course I wasn't afraid of her. And as for what people thought . . . well, people are always going to think. You just can't stop them. My reputation had weathered worse than infants. But I sure did want to find a place to put that one comfortably out of my life.

Maybe I would have done the whole thing differently if Ian and I hadn't fought. Maybe I would have done the same things, but in a different way. Maybe it wouldn't have changed anything at all. "What if" can be a killing phrase. I did what I did. I left the infant with Chuck and Jamin and Collis, and I did not look for Ian on Home Base, and I fired up the *Defiance* and fled toward Mars as though I were pursued by demons.

Well, I was. They come in all sizes and shapes and colors, demons do. Some of them have jeweled mirror eyes and Earther accents. It gave me a lot of satisfaction to push *Defiance* to the limits of her abilities in that demented rush toward Mars. Ian had left her fully fueled and in good repair: there was no evidence he had ever even been on board her.

The Gypsies sang to me all the way in. *There are ghosts among the asteroids.* Ever since my first love, Django, died, in an accident I should have prevented and didn't, I had heard them: they sang to me. Especially the Gypsies. At first I had thought they sang to haunt me, to taunt me, to drag me down into the final starless darkness with them, but I was wrong. I was guilty, and I heard what I expected to hear. I should have known better: I knew Django well enough. He did not know how to hate. He certainly would not start with me.

Now I knew they sang for love. I would never have put it that way, of course, if I were telling anyone; but then, I seldom told anyone anymore. I had mentioned it, at first, before I realized how it sounded, and it had found its way into the legend. Everybody knew the Skyrider was crazy, anyway.

And a few people knew enough to believe it when

the Gypsies sang me warnings. But nobody knew they also sang me comfort, hope, and reassurance, when they could. That was what they sang on that trip to Mars, and it was what I needed. I arrived in a much better frame of mind than I'd been in when I left Home Base.

At Marstown I traded *Defiance* for a rental groundcar and was given directions to the first ship-builders on my list. They were easy enough to follow: take the only road straight thataway for about forty kilometers. When you come to a farm, that's it.

By the time I got there, I sure knew what Chuck had meant by isolation. From Marstown all the way to the Tanaka brothers' farm I didn't pass a single human dwelling, or any sign of habitation. It was a wild and desolate country where the Terraforming simply had not taken well. Oh, the atmosphere was breathable without a respirator, and the temperature was endurable with only a windbreaker to cut the chill, but the land itself was alien; and if it was not hostile, that was only because it did not deign to recognize my passage. Humankind did not belong in that land.

It was high desert country, vast and still and silent. Gaunt mountains thrust ragged teeth up out of savage plains to snare tattered little scraps of clouds down out of the dark and distance-shadowed sky. Mutated Terran desert herbs crouched frozen in obscene postures, their gnarled limbs angled wildly in mad efforts to reach across the red sand emptiness between them, as if in search of comfort or companionship. Only once in over an hour of driving did I see any sign of life other than those twisted, crippled plants: a rabrat that interrupted its cannibalistic carrion feast to stare at me over the moldering remains of one of its fellows so long dead I could not tell at first glance what it had once been.

The live rabrat lifted its twitching rabbit nose toward me, and flicked its long, soft rabbit ears, and stared at me with fierce red rat eyes like gleaming shards of garnet while its rat fangs dripped corruption from its feast and its long, hairless tail flicked back and forth in oddly catlike irritation. It put one pink rat hand on its meal in a defiant gesture of possessiveness, and the flesh of the half-eaten thing seemed to sink a little into the soil at its touch like a deflating balloon . . . or a mound of thin jelly on a porous surface.

Shuddering, I hurried past, and tried not to recognize the faint stench of decay carried into the groundcar by the skirling wind of my passage. I had seen rabrats before, in zoos, and was well aware of the important part they played in Terraforming and maintaining the Martian ecology. Nor was I a stranger to death and corruption: I had seen far uglier episodes than that played out by men, for whom it was not a natural and ecologically desirable way to behave. Yet that little scene shook me: and it stayed with me, long after I had left the rest of Mars behind.

Perhaps it was the recognition of the very human look in that creature's hot gemstone eyes that troubled me. Or perhaps I was just unnerved by distance and silence and the terrible, alien beauty of that land. At any rate, I was more relieved than I would have cared to admit when I topped the last rise and saw at last the Tanaka brothers' ranch spread out across a lush green valley below me. It was not the sort of place I would want for my own; I was a Belter, and could never call any planet home. But that ranch was a very welcome symbol of the survival of humanity in a land that had begun to look to me so inimical to my own kind that I could not hope to find any survivors there.

If that was the sort of place where Chuck grew up, in an island of sanity surrounded by such *alien*ness, I wasn't sure the monks had been right to call him "sheltered"—not if he had ever left the farm and rambled, as children will, over the surrounding countryside—but I could see why they thought his knowledge of the human world inadequate. It could hardly have been anything else.

Even the Terraformed high desert shrubs that grew on the hillside between me and the Tanaka farm seemed increasingly "normal" as I left that fearsome desert behind. I studied the farm ahead eagerly, as much in hope of seeing some actual humans, just to know they were there, as in an effort to find the shipbuilding area where I might, with luck, find the sister of the two matte-black shuttles that had attacked my rock.

At first I could see neither humans nor any shuttles at all. It seemed to be a working farm, complete with livestock and orderly, well-tended fields, but I could see no sign of the people who tended them, nor any indication that they did any shipbuilding, even as a hobby. Then my rental car's Comm phone emmitted a shrill whistle for attention: and at exactly that instant I realized that the big shrouded objects down by the farm's entrance gates, which I had taken for farm equipment, were massive guns.

They were tracking my car's progress down the hillside with the smooth and deadly silence of stalking cats.

Chapter Ten

I slowed the car and answered the Comm phone. It told me to identify myself. I did. It told me to state my business, and I did that too. There was a silence while I crept forward, toward the farm's big closed gates and out from under the farm's big guns. The voice on the Comm phone hadn't told me to stop, and I wasn't much inclined to do so while I was under those guns.

I was still in range of them when they abruptly stopped tracking me and turned lazily to aim at the crest of the hill again, where they must have picked me up when I first came over. Lest I get the wrong idea, the voice on the Comm phone told me where to look to see that I wasn't out of danger yet: I'd just come in range of smaller arms hand-held at the gate.

I stopped the groundcar with its nose almost against the gate and waited while the guards and, presumably, unseen holovision cameras looked me over at their leisure. The Comm phone remained silent. The first indication I had that I was to be allowed onto the farm was when the big gates began to open before me, apparently of their own accord: the guards hadn't moved a muscle, and I couldn't see anyone else controlling them. The guard's weapons were of the lethal persuasion, and they were aimed unerringly at my most vulnerable bodily parts. Not my favorite situation.

I edged the car forward and through the gates slowly. The guards' expressions were unreadable. They tracked me as smoothly as the big guns had done. I was careful not to make any sudden moves or unexpected gestures. These people seemed just a trifle paranoid. I have a healthy respect for armed paranoids. I was positively eager to do exactly what they wanted me to do, whatever that was, at least until I found out what was going on.

The guards stopped me just inside the gate, still without speaking, and we waited again. One of the guards, a young boy with golden hair and wide eyes startlingly dark in his pale, expressionless face, was beginning to sweat, despite the chilly wind that was making me shiver. I hoped it was the weight of the gun he held that caused it, not fear or nervousness. Fear or nervousness just might get me killed. I watched his trigger finger, wondering what I would do if he got the shakes. Of course the answer was obvious and the question downright silly: I would die. There wouldn't be time to do anything else.

After about an eternity, give or take a few minutes, the guards all lowered their weapons and turned away, their interest in me suddenly gone; all except the boy who had been sweating, who took time to wipe his brow and give me a sheepish grin before he walked away. I couldn't see their transceivers, but apparently they'd been told to let me pass.

Nobody had told me what I was supposed to do next, and I was just beginning to get cross about it when the Comm phone signaled again. I wasn't anxious to do anything unauthorized while I was still so near all those lethal weapons, but I would have if they'd left me unauthorized much longer. I answered the Comm phone and the same voice, made small and slightly tinny by the speaker, told me to drive slowly on down the road till I came to the nearest farm buildings, where I would be met.

I did as I was told, just as pleased to drive slowly so I had a chance to look around. The farm was a working farm all right: what I used to call a "bee-fanned airy farm" when I was small. There were plenty of "bee-fanned airy" cattle lining the fences along the road, all straining to reach the grass on the outside of the fence and ignoring that inside. Occasionally, one lifted its massive head to watch my passing, its big empty eyes staring without interest while it chewed thoughtfully on tufts of grass uprooted with soil still clinging to them.

They weren't the same as cattle I had seen on Earth. They were taller and broader and I had the uncomfortable impression that their teeth were longer, but perhaps that was only because this oversized rock was beginning to get on my nerves. In the distance I could see what I took to be sheep in another field, and they looked perfectly normal, or as normal as sheep can look: roundish blobs of wool with faces, their slender legs invisible from so far away. There were llamas, too, and a few gangly horses, and I saw a chattering cluster of the chimpanzees they breed for labor on Mars.

But it was shuttles I was looking for, and I finally found them, clustered on a landing field almost hidden behind tall rows of corn. By then I had nearly reached the farm buildings, where I was awaited by a welcoming committee not much more welcoming than the guards at the gate: a matched pair of tall Oriental gentlemen with rifles resting comfortably in the crooks of their arms, the barrels aimed casually but unmistakably at me.

I stopped admiring the farm and pulled the groundcar to a halt facing them. They bowed, Japanese-style, but one at a time so I was always oh-so-casually covered by one of the rifles. They were old-fashioned projectile weapons, but carefully tended and just as deadly as any laser in practiced hands, which I took these to be.

I bowed back at them, just to be polite, and said, "You must be the Tanaka brothers."

The taller of the two smiled formidably and bowed again. "Please pardon our seeming unfriendliness, Ms. Rendell. You understand, we do not receive a great many unannounced visitors in this isolated location."

It hadn't occurred to me to phone from Marstown, and I said so.

The smaller of the two shrugged ineffably and said in a voice at once deeper and gentler than his brother's, "It is of no great concern. We have communicated with Marstown since you arrived. You come highly recommended."

I looked at the rifle on his arm that was still pointed unfailingly at me. "Oh? And how do you greet those who come less highly recommended?"

Both brothers smiled amiably and ignored the question. "It is said that you seek a certain shipbuilder," said the taller of the two.

"That's right. I'm trying to track a couple of custom shuttles that a friend tells me were probably built on Mars, quite possibly by you."

"And what is your interest in these shuttles?"

The question was polite enough, but the eyes of both brothers gleamed dangerously as they awaited my answer. I considered lying, but there seemed no point to it. I didn't know that a lie would please them more than the truth. "I'm not much interested in them now; I destroyed them. What I'd like to know is who the hell was in them."

"Ah." Both brothers nodded sagely, and to my surprise both rifles were suddenly aimed away from me. Not by much: neither of them even visibly shifted position. Just one minute they were aimed at me and the next they weren't. "An unfortunate circumstance, when one is obliged to kill a stranger." They managed to look rather as if they meant that.

I almost giggled. Would it have been preferable to kill a friend? "I'm not real fond of killing anyone." That seemed a safer response.

Both brothers nodded again, this time with sympathy. "And you say you have reason to believe we may have built the shuttles you destroyed?"

I nodded. "Chuck Dakine thought so."

Suddenly both rifles were pointed very much away from me. "You are a friend of Chuck Dakine? Ms. Rendell, why did you not say so? Please, alight from

90

your vehicle, let us offer you refreshments. Come inside; the wind is harsh."

Bemused, I did as I was told. They ushered me into the little farmhouse with much bowing and smiling, and left their rifles in a rack by the door. From the outside the farmhouse had looked like any Martian farmhouse: a red adobe structure with flowers in the windows and a ginger cat cleaning its paws on the porch. The inside was a surprise: all pale, polished wood and open spaces; sparse, low furniture; shoji screens between the rooms; and no decorations at all on the whitewashed walls.

A tall Oriental woman with delicate hands and a solemn face seated us around a low table of beautiful yellow wood, and apologized to me in a small, sweet voice because she knew that "Westerners" were not always comfortable seated on cushions on the floor. She was dressed in bush jeans and a heavy woolen sweater, but managed to give the impression of flowered kimonos and painted fans. When we were seated, she disappeared into another room for a moment and returned with a tea tray, poured for the three of us, and disappeared again into another room, silently pulling a shoji screen closed behind her.

The brothers called me Skyrider-san and introduced themselves as Harold and Haruki. The taller one was Haruki. There were odd little cakes and candies and cookies on the tea tray, and Harold fussed anxiously until I had accepted a selection of them, tasted one, and expressed approval. Haruki watched with apparent amusement, absently nibbling a ginger-flavored pink sugar-frosted wafer and sipping his tea.

There was a brief silence while we all enjoyed our refreshments. Then Haruki cleared his throat and said tentatively, "You have known Chuck-san a long time?"

I shook my head, wondering whether the answer might cause them to recall the woman to whisk away the tea things and restore their rifles to their arms. "Not long. In fact, we only just met. I left him in charge of my rock and . . . and a friend's child, while I'm out looking for the owners of those shuttles."

They didn't whisk away the tea things. Harold nodded with polite disinterest and Haruki, still looking mildly amused, said comfortably, "So. You are from the asteroid belt. Yes, of course, I had forgotten." The look of amusement increased ever so slightly. "Isolated as we are, we have heard of you, Skyrider-san." He sobered. "And you have made a wise selection in one to guard your rock and . . . your friend's child. These shuttles you seek, did they attack your rock?"

"Yes. When Chuck looked at the battle tapes, he thought you might have built them."

Haruki ignored that for the moment. "Did they . . . forgive me, but did they express their reasons for the attack?"

Puzzled, I shook my head. "No. Why do you ask?"

He tilted his head, his expression speculative. "I see. And did you . . . But no." He stopped himself with a visible effort, looked blankly at the far wall for a moment, and shook his head. "No, it is best that I do not know." He inhaled deeply, exhaled slowly, looked at me again, and said brightly, "So. Tell me about these shuttles we may have built."

I wondered if he knew anything about the infant dumped on my rock. I couldn't think what else that withdrawn question might have been about. But I didn't ask. I don't quite know why not; only that something in his manner prevented it. Instead, I told him about the shuttles he might have built. I'd brought a hologram from the tapes, but even with it I wasn't sure anyone would be able to identify the black shadow it showed.

To my surprise, both Harold and Haruki recognized it at once. Haruki studied it first, then handed it to Harold, who glanced at it briefly, nodded, and returned it to me. "As we thought," he said.

Haruki looked at him and toyed idly with his empty teacup. "Perhaps. Perhaps not." He seemed about to say something, thought better of it, and closed his eyes. I looked at Harold, but he was watching Haruki. After a long moment Haruki said slowly, with his eyes still closed, "There is a strange story told of a woman who gave birth to a monster." He opened his eyes to see how I took that. I met his gaze, waiting. After a moment he sighed and lifted his teacup, looked into it, and put it back down on the table. "The woman believed that the monster could destroy her world, but those around her failed to recognize it for what it was."

I wanted to say I wasn't fond of bedtime stories, and besides, it wasn't bedtime, but I didn't. I lifted my tea and sipped it without much interest. It was good tea, but I had already had enough. When I put the little cup down, Harold filled it again.

"This woman," said Haruki, "would have destroyed the monster to prevent it from destroying her. She and her helpers set about to perform the deed, but they were overcome by their enemies and the monster . . . if monster it was . . . was stolen from them. These enemies of the woman believed the monster to be but a harmless child, you see, and they wished to protect it. So they took it to a place where they thought it might be safe. But the woman and her minions followed, and again attempted to destroy the monster."

"I'm sure this is all very interesting," I began.

Haruki ignored me. "The woman's enemies took up the child again, and carried it to another place where they thought it might be safe. And the woman followed. And the woman will follow, until the monster is destroyed. It is said . . ." He closed his eyes again, ruminating. "It is said she has lost track of the monster for the moment. It is not difficult to conceal a monster that looks like a child. But the woman who gave birth to it will find it. Believe that. She must, or it will destroy her."

"Look, Haruki-san . . ."

He smiled benevolently. "I understand, Skyrider-san. It was a story I thought you should know. Now we will talk of shuttles." And we did. He said that he and his brother had built the two shuttles I had destroyed. He said they had been commissioned by an Earther organization based in the artificial island cities off the coast of California. He said they had been painted bright yellow and orange, the company's colors, when they left Mars; and that was the last he or his brother had seen of them.

"If you seek them, you must seek them on Earth, Skyrider-san. We sold them to Ecology Now, Incorporated, and that is all we know of them."

"What would Ecology Now want with shuttles?"

His expression remained enigmatically benevolent. "I did not ask them."

I thanked them for the tea and cakes and information, and was ushered politely, formally, and very finally back to my groundcar; it was clear that Skyrider-san, even though she might be a friend of Chuck Dakine's, was welcome here once and only once. Bemused by the entire encounter, I didn't even wonder why. It seemed in keeping with the brothers' personalities.

I did ask, just before I turned the car to leave, about that myth of the woman who gave birth to a monster; the story had irritated me when he told it, but it stuck in my mind. When I asked, Haruki said gently, "It is not a myth, Skyrider-san," and carefully pointed the way back to Marstown as if there were some danger that I might otherwise take a wrong turning. There was none, of course. There were no wrong turnings to take. Just the one long, silent road through the barren and hostile desert in the cold, watery light of late afternoon sun.

Chapter Eleven

At Marstown I turned in my groundcar and thought of returning to *Defiance* for liftoff toward Earth, and suddenly the whole ridiculous quest seemed just too tedious to endure. I could not tolerate the thought of the long, silent shuttle ride alone with the winds of space, and eating a dispenser-processed meal or preparing anything more appealing from my stores, and going to bed in the darkened pilot's cabin with the monitors set to wake me in case of hazard.

The groundcar rental clerk directed me to a nearby hotel where, he said, I would find moderately priced rooms and an immoderately priced meal well worth what it cost me. He started to tell me about less expensive alternatives, but I told him it wasn't a problem and accepted his first suggestion. It was within walking distance from the rental agency, in the belt of hotels, rental agencies, souvenir shops, and massage parlors that circled the spaceport. The sun had gone down and the streets, artificially lighted an unholy orange color by permalanterns overhead, were crowded with tourists, spacers, and hustling locals of every race and description.

Prostitutes and preachers plied their trades side by side under the lights, in some cases virtually indistinguishable except that the preachers were on the whole less eloquent in extolling their wares. Tourists from Earth gaped and gawked and giggled: tourists from the asteroid belt stared and stumbled and shouted: tourists from other parts of Mars, its moons, or Mars Station tried very hard to look like they lived in Marstown and had only come out to the spaceport area to do some slumming. Most of them failed. They looked like farmers and miners and off-duty fliers, which they were.

Between the rental agency and the hotel, three real estate hawkers tried to sell me "beautiful, spacious farms fully stocked and ready to work" four prostitutes and two preachers tried to entice me to join them in bed or the love of a god, whichever was their personal preference; two Belters tried to pick fights with me and one succeeded (he was so drunk I only had to hit him once, and he stayed down); eight drug peddlers offered me everything from devil dust to codeine; and five off-duty fliers propositioned me with some very interesting sexual suggestions. All that, in a walk of maybe a hundred meters. It was, shall we say, interesting.

The lobby of the Downmars Hilton was an oasis of quiet elegance for anyone who had run that gauntlet. It was furnished for Earthers, with plush fabrics and furs and too much soft furniture for my taste, but it was both warm and silent, neither of which the street outside had been; and after a moment I noticed that there were, in the decorations, a few concessions to Belters' tastes. There were a couple of what the designer had probably called "conversational nooks" done entirely in rock and metal, for instance. Both were discreetly screened from the view of the main lobby by tricky lighting and indoor gardens, but they were there.

There was even a desk clerk who spoke pidgin. I noticed the desk clerks looking me over as I entered, and I wondered with amusement what they would make of me: I was dressed in standard Belters' tunic and stretch pants with a handgun strapped to one hip, but I knew that after the long ground car ride I was also sunburned and stained with the fine red Martian dust that had blown into the groundcar all through the desert. I had brought my tote bag with me when I left the *Defiance* for the Tanaka brothers' farm, and it was made of the best quality lightweight "spidersilk" imported from the Outer Rocks, but that could have meant anything; such fabric cost a fortune on Earth and was standard issue in the Belt.

I should have known what their estimation would be. As I approached the desk, one of the clerks stepped forward to greet me, his expression disdainful. He told me room prices in fluent pidgin, obviously expecting the information to scare me off.

It amused me. I told him, in the thickest pidgin I could manage, that I wanted the most expensive room he had to offer, and watched his face as I plunked a handful of gemstones onto the desk in payment. I'd got in the habit of carrying them as well as malite chips when my credit account was closed after the last

President died. Fortunately I'd had reason to do my best to clean out the account before she died; I had lost it in a bet to Ian Spencer, and he'd ended up with the worse deal since he gave me time to translate a lot of credit into durable goods before he took over the account, and then it was closed before he had much chance to spend it.

I'd have got a better exchange rate on the gemstones in the Belt, but I liked to use them in situations like this: it made the desk clerk's eyes pop. But the Downmars Hilton had a reputation to maintain, and he did his best to uphold it. He whipped the gemstones off the desk and into a little counting box in one swift motion, informed me there were no appraisers on duty at that time of night but that he would have the stones appraised and credited to my account by mid-morning, held the box out for me to put my prints on the seal, and dropped it into the desk safe. Either the box itself had assured him the stones were real, which was possible, or he had some other means of knowing; anyway, he didn't hesitate to register me, as requested, into the most expensive room he had.

When I'd filled out the registration form (which he had offered me dubiously, uncertain I would know how to read and write), he accepted it back from me and glanced at it with professional disinterest, just to see that I'd filled in all the little boxes. Something on it caught his attention, and he stared. Then he stared at me. Then he frowned, thought about it, smiled, and said in good Company English, "Welcome to the Downmars Hilton, Ms. Rendell."

"Ah, hell. You recognized my name."

He grinned. "I wasn't sure till you said that. You're the Skyrider, right?"

"'Ass why," I said, so disgruntled that I spoke pidgin without meaning to.

He said, his grin conspiratorial now, as if we shared a joke against the rest of the world, "Ho, da lucky, eh you, da kine bess room fo' stayeen. So what, you like go or stay? Get one muchi guru gourmet grine in the behind of you." He gestured toward a restaurant doorway set in the wall opposite the hotel desk. "Maybe you like scrubbeen firs' but." The odd Belter argot that was called pidgin or "Rock talk," was not really a pidgin at all, and was a good deal more complicated than I represent it here. It consisted of all the old languages brought out by the original pioneers who settled the Belt, and had been altered by time and circumstance till few of them were recognizable anymore except in the occasional word or inflection.

My desk clerk, clearly Martian-born, was so pleased with his mastery of it that I responded in kind, assuring him that I did want a meal in the "muchi guru gourmet grine," but, as he had suggested, would prefer to go to my room first and wash off some of the Martian sand that clung to my clothes and body and made even my teeth feel gritty. He snapped his fingers and a small older woman with broad shoulders and a broader grin came forward to try to wrest my tote bag from my grip.

I fought her off and managed to get my room key to myself by overtipping both her and the desk clerk with malite chips from my pocket. It wasn't hard to find my room without the old woman's guidance: the hotel was laid out in a standard boxy design and my room was one of the only four on its floor, the tenth, with a fine view through a glasteel window of the street below and the brightly lighted port beyond.

The window was unopenable, which might have vexed an Earther or a Martian but was just fine with me. The room was overdecorated with fabric hangings, fabric-covered furniture, and crowded, colorful old-fashioned paintings on the walls, but I was only going to stay there the night, not buy it, so I ignored it and tossed my bag on the too-soft bed while I stripped off my dusty clothing. I had locked the door carefully behind me, but out of habit I kept my handgun near me anyway, and carried it with me into the bathroom where I intended to take a shower and decided, when I saw the room, to take a bath instead; the tub was massive, the bath towels vast and soft, and the wall dispenser offered an alarming array of bubble baths, perfumes, lotions, oils, soaps, shampoos, creams, and powders.

The restaurant could wait. I was dirty and cross and tired and it wasn't often I had opportunity to pamper myself to such Earthly extremes. For that matter, it wasn't often I wanted to; but the idea had merit. I instructed the tub to fill itself with medium-hot water and placed my palm on the reader to commit myself to paying for every drop of it. The lotions, soaps, et cetera, were free; but the water, even though it would be recycled, was not. On Mars it was a far more precious commodity than any conceivable lotions, soaps, or et ceteras.

While I waited for the tub to fill, I wandered back into the main room and looked at the menu by the room dispenser. I considered ordering up a meal, but I'd get a much better one at the restaurant downstairs if I had a little patience, so I punched in a request for a glass of Martian brandy instead, and took it back to the bathroom with me.

The tub had been prompt in filling my order. I felt a moment's regret at not having specified some scented bubbles, but decided they were overrated anyway. It wasn't too late to add water softeners in the scent of my choice, and I asked for samples of Tea Rose and Snow Pea. Both were very pleasant, but the Tea Rose smelled a little too pink to suit me. Snow Pea was unabashed green, like crushed grass or broken leaves of some kind. I liked that. At my request, the dispenser dumped about a cupful of fine powder into my bath and the room suddenly smelled like a green summer pasture on Earth, or maybe a forest glade. . . .

I hung my handgun on the towel rack, put my brandy glass on the shelf provided within reach of the tub, and stepped into the water quickly, trying to distract my mind from some very pertinent questions like for instance why I, who had been devastatingly homesick for the Belt whenever I had visited Earth for any length of time at all, had just selected an Earther's idea of how to get clean, complete with Earth smells of a very unmistakable sort.

I just needed to relax, that was all. I just wanted to soak in the hot water and relax. Hell, I knew a lot of Belters who took baths instead of showers whenever they were on a rock big enough or rich enough to provide one. And when another glance at the dispenser informed me that I could have had rock-scented water to make me feel more at home, I told myself I had selected Earth scents because they were exotic. I was having an exotic experience, and I wanted exotic scents to go with it. I could smell rock anytime, just by going home.

I tell myself a lot of things like that. Lies, to put it bluntly. Sometimes I even believe them. I didn't believe them, that time. I knew damn well what I was doing. I was pampering myself, all right: with self-pity, because Ian Spencer had walked out of my life just when I had decided I wanted him to stay in my life forever.

Well, hell. Nobody's perfect. Life would probably be pretty damn boring if we were perfect. I slid down in the bath till only my head was above water, reached for my glass of brandy, sipped it, and tried to concentrate on the prospect of my proposed "muchi guru" meal in the restaurant downstairs.

I wondered whether Ian liked things that smelled green. Maybe he would have preferred the Tea Rose powder. Hell. I put the brandy back on the shelf and immersed my head too. For all I knew, he would have preferred the rock-scented powder. What the hell did I know about Ian Spencer besides that he was the best con man in the Belt, the most accomplished computer criminal I'd ever encountered, and more fun in or out of bed than any man I'd ever imagined. . . .

I ran out of breath and popped my head back up out of the water. Jamin was just as good in bed as Ian any day, and a hell of a lot easier to understand. I always knew where I was, with Jamin. If I felt I had to fall in love, he'd have been a hell of better choice than Ian. So why was I sitting in a Martian bathtub, mooning about Ian?

At my request, the bath dispenser produced a cake of green-scented soap and a chunk of loofah; the Downmars Hilton knew how to do luxury, all right. Which, considering the price of the room, was only reasonable. I used the soap and the loofah and green-scented shampoo and conditioner, and eventually a faintly green-scented shower to rinse in, and emerged from the bathroom at last with my brandy in one hand and my holster in the other, feeling much more human and not very much happier at all. What was the *matter* with me?

Rhetorical question. I knew damn well what was the matter with me, and I didn't like it. I'd fallen in love, and been spurned, and like any girl-child in the throes of adolescent fancy I was having a fit of dramatic misery. Whatever happened to the independent Skyrider of song and story, that risk-taker, lawbreaker, mercenary warrior with a heart of stone?

Hell with it. I found clean clothes in my bag and put them on, strapped my gun to my hip, finished my brandy, and departed my room in a green-scented miasma of self-indulgent rage.

Chapter Twelve

FORTUNATELY I DIDN'T PASS ANYONE IN THE CORRIDORS with whom to pick a fight, and by the time I got back downstairs to the lobby I had regained enough equilibrium that I wasn't even tempted to knock down any innocent passersby. The pidgin-speaking desk clerk winked at me as I passed him, a gesture that astonished me, but I managed a fairly creditable smile in response and went on to the restaurant door.

I had to pause there for a moment: like so many expensive restaurants, it was lighted about as effectively as a dungeon, and I had to wait a moment for my eyes to adjust to the gloom. The tables had actual candles on them, in glass chimneys, and that seemed to be the only source of light in the whole room. I've often wondered why restaurants do that. Maybe most people prefer not to see the food they're eating. Or, since it's only expensive restaurants that leave off normal lighting, maybe they think one wouldn't pay the outrageous prices required if one could see what one was paying for. I wasn't given a lot of time to ruminate about it; an obsequious little man in an undertaker's coal-black jumpsuit approached me the moment my eyes were well enough adjusted to make him out—he timed that perfectly, presumably from long practice—and inquired unctuously, "Table for" —his glance darted dubiously behind me—"one?"

I managed not to praise his counting ability. "Yes, please." I nodded, keeping my expression neutral.

"Right this way, please." He whirled and led me away at a breakneck pace, threading between tables in the gloom with unerring agility, as though he were equipped with radar. We went all the way across the room to a little table squashed awkwardly between the kitchen and bathroom doors, and I realized with a start of amusement that I certainly was on Mars.

"Excuse me," I said, before the little man had time to whirl and dash away. He had pulled out a chair at the isolated little table and gestured for me to sit in it, but I made no move to do so.

He frowned. I was interrupting the routine. "Yes?"

A waiter slammed through the swinging doors from the kitchen, knocking the chair out of the little man's hands. He stepped deftly aside, still frowning impatiently at me. Someone came out of the bathroom, bringing a strong whiff of industrial-strength disinfectant with him. I smiled cheerfully at the little man and said firmly, "I'd like that table over *there*." I pointed at one on the far side of the room beside a window that looked out onto the street.

"I'm sorry, that's a table for four," he said without looking. "If you'll just be seated . . . ?"

"You don't understand." I smiled benignly to let him know that was okay with me and he shouldn't feel too stupid just because he was. "I don't like this table."

He stared. He looked all around incredulously, as if seeking witnesses to my folly. He gestured expansively. "You don't *like* this *table*?"

I kept smiling. "No. If I can't have that one by the window, fine, but I won't take this one. Try again."

Another waiter bustled out of the kitchen, bumped into the little man, and didn't even take time to frown at him. "But what's wrong with this one?" asked the little man.

"If you like it so well, you eat here." I was losing patience. "I want a table that is not crammed in between the kitchen and the loo, and I'd prefer one with a view of something other than its own centerpiece. This is apparently not your busiest time of night: I can see several empty tables that would be acceptable to me. Choose one. Just not this one."

"My dear," he said, confident that a woman alone, even a Belter, wouldn't make a scene, "*this* is *your* table."

I studied him. "It is? This is my table?"

He nodded soberly. "Please be seated."

"You're sure this is my very own table?"

He nodded again with exaggerated patience. "Yes. Now if you'll just be seated . . ."

Smiling, I stepped forward and put my hand on the little table. He thought I was getting ready to sit down. What I was doing was making sure the table was made of wood. I didn't want to break my hand on a piece of plasteel. It was made of cheap Martian scrubwood. Still smiling, I lifted my arm and gave the table one quick, solid chop in the center with the heel of my hand. It split neatly down the middle and collapsed slowly with a rattle and crash as the place setting spilled onto the floor among splinters of wood. "Oh, dear," I said mildly, "how too bad. My table seems to have met with an accident. Obviously I can't sit there. I wonder if you could let me sit at someone else's table, just this once?" I looked at the mess on the floor between us. The candle, fortunately, had drowned in its own wax when its chimney shattered.

Diners all around us were staring. On Mars, women don't assert themselves much more than they do on Earth. Certainly not the way we do in the Belt. The little man was so flustered that the next waiter through the kitchen door almost knocked him off his feet. "I—I—you—"

I said patiently, "People are staring. Don't let's make a scene, shall we? Of course I'll pay for any damages to my table, but I'm really too hungry to wait for you to get it mended. Please either show me to another table or tell me where I might find the manager."

He hesitated, glanced at the neighboring diners, stared at the broken table, and gathered his dignity around him like a cloak. "Of course. If you'll just follow me . . ."

He didn't give me the table under the window that I'd asked for; that would have been too much for his self-esteem. I'd won, and we both knew it, but he was going to retain his pride. He gave me a pleasant little table beside a vine-shrouded pillar, screened from most of the other diners by a noisy little fountain filled with water lilies. Maybe the average Martian would have considered the table undesirable because it was so isolated, but I liked it. When the little man pulled out a chair for me this time, I surprised him by not only accepting it, but overtipping him as well. "Thanks very much: this is much more suitable."

He went away, shaking his head over the vagaries of Belter women.

A waitress materialized at my elbow and handed me a menu. "I saw what you did to the Dunce's Table." She spoke out of the corner of her mouth in a conspiratorial voice. "I've wished somebody would do that for ages. He always sticks single women back there. Maybe he'll think twice about it, after this."

I accepted the menu. "I hope so. But why didn't he just kick me out? I really thought he would."

She looked shocked. "Oh, no; aside from breaking the table, you were very quiet and well-behaved. If he'd tried to kick you out, you might have made a scene and really disrupted the place."

I grinned. "That was my plan."

She nodded. "Can I get you anything to drink while you decide?"

"No, and I don't need time to decide either. I want a big piece of beef, about half-cooked, and something green with it."

She looked sympathetic. "Just in from the Belt? How about rare prime rib? And a side of asparagus almondine?"

"Sold."

"Anything to drink?" When I hesitated, she said, "We have a wide selection of fruit juices. Fresh, not imported."

I selected a fruit juice and she went away satisfied. From my new table I could just see the one I had shattered. A cluster of uniformed maintenance workers was gathering up the debris. They were all very careful never to so much as glance my way. I smiled to myself, sipped the cold water provided, and stared absently into the water-lily-choked fountain beside me.

For the first time since I'd left the Tanaka brothers' farm I thought again of the myth Haruki-san had told me, of the woman who gave birth to a monster. Had that been a veiled way of telling me something about the baby that had been dumped on my rock? Some people did consider freefall mutants to be monsters, but he had said the woman feared her offspring would destroy her world. Nobody considered freefall mutants that kind of monster. That sounded like a bug-eyed monster with special powers, not a mutant with special limitations.

And yet, somebody had certainly tried to kill her. Somebody in Ecology Now, Inc., shuttles, which didn't make any damn sense at all. What would Ecology Now, Inc., want with an infant freefall mutant? She was hardly a threat to anybody's ecology. At her age, how could she be a threat to anybody's anything?

The waitress returned with my meal and I dismissed the problem of babies and monsters to give my full attention to the meat, which was excellent. A lot of Belters, born and raised on their rocks, don't care much for beef even when they can get it; but I spent the first ten years of my life on Earth, and developed a taste for some of its more exotic luxuries. Asparagus was another. Salads are plentiful in the Belt, but asparagus was neither cost-efficient nor space-efficient to grow even on the big rocks. My mother had always kept a patch of it going in our yard on Earth: when I was a child, I used to steal the new stalks when they first peeked out from their protective straw in the spring, and eat them raw.

Of course this was Martian beef and Martian asparagus, both different in subtle ways from their Earthly counterparts, but I was not gourmet enough to really notice. They tasted fine to me. I was so engrossed in the pleasure of eating them, and so isolated by the lily fountain from the rest of the dining room, that I didn't even notice the MAMA terrorists who had entered the dining room till my waitress came back to offer me after-dinner coffee, and pointed them out to me.

"We have to serve them," she said, "but thank God they're not at one of my tables. Some of the girls like them—they will leave a good tip if they're pleased with the meal—but they give me the willies."

I could see why: in their glittering golden costumes, bristling with more lethal weapons than a colonist would be allowed to carry, they looked rather like killer robots. Their faces were all identically arrogant, their eyes cold, their posture stiffly military. I wouldn't have hesitated to tackle one or two of them alone, but they always traveled in groups of at least four, and all that weaponry was just a trifle daunting.

I had seen groups of MAMAs dressed like that before the Brief War, but not often. They had been a minor hate faction then: a nasty little political outgrowth of the radical right that nobody took seriously, not so much because their views and behavior didn't merit it as because it was difficult to believe that anybody could be that insanely dedicated to such an illogical cause. There was a tendency to believe that they had to be joking.

These women were not joking. I doubted they knew how to joke. There was a look in their eyes that I had seen a time or two in the eyes of a *berserker* at war. A lust for violence: a killing rage. The waitress beside me shuddered, as if she were following my thoughts, and I glanced at her. "Why do you have to serve them?"

She shrugged. "Same law that protects everybody else: if they don't disturb the peace, they have a right. Hell, it's one of the laws they want rescinded. They'd still expect to get served, of course. They just want us to refuse service to known or suspected Floaters or Fallers."

"Which presumably means to all Belters, since how can you tell, these days, right?"

She nodded, still staring in morbid fascination at the MAMA members. "Mostly they're pretty well behaved, but there've been so many incidents lately. . . . I just like to stay out of their way when they come in, if I can."

"What kind of incidents?"

She looked at me in surprise. "What kind of . . . Oh." She let her gaze move back to the MAMAs, drawn there as if by a powerful magnet. "I forgot you're just in from the Belt. But don't you get the newsfax out there? There've been killings. Bombings. Assassinations." She shrugged. "You know how they think. 'If in doubt, kill it.' " Startled, she glanced at me again. "Listen, you'd better not let them see you. I mean, don't walk right past them on your way out, or anything, okay? You're obviously a Belter, and . . . you just never know. They're so damned *arrogant* these days. And even Ground Patrol won't stop them. Nothing stops them." She tore her gaze from them with an effort and smiled at me wearily. "I forgot. Did you say you wanted coffee?"

"Sure. Listen, don't worry: you're as obviously Martian as I am Belter. They won't bother you."

She pulled a wry face. "They're not above stomping on the occasional normie, especially a colonist. Off Earth, everybody's suspect: a normie's relatives might be muties. You can't tell by looking."

"And Ground Patrol wouldn't stop them?"

She shrugged. "They make a show of it. After the fact. You know, they let the MAMAs do their thing, and then the Patrol comes in and acts all officious and writes everything down and hustles the MAMAs away like they were arresting them, but an hour later they're back on the street and just as cocksure as ever. I'd better shut up. It's not even safe to talk about them. I'll get you that coffee."

"Wait a minute." I caught her arm to stop her. I wasn't really even sure why: but I'd been watching the MAMAs, too, and there was something going on over there that I didn't like one bit. They had settled at their table okay at first, and ordered drinks, and talked a little too loudly among themselves, but there was an edge to their voices that I recognized all too well. They were setting something up, and it wouldn't be long in coming.

It wasn't. One of them suddenly threw her glass at a table across the room and shouted, as if she'd just noticed it, "This damn restaurant servers *Belters!*" The tossed glass concentrated everybody's attention across the room from them, so nobody particularly noticed that they all rose swiftly as if on signal and exited the room at a half-run, suddenly silent. I noticed. And I noticed that one of them had left her purse behind. As they disappeared through the door into the lobby I jerked my waitress off her feet and hurled myself to the floor beside her.

We were just in time. I wasn't all the way down yet when the whole room seemed to explode with a bellowing *whoosh* and roar that must have buckled the walls. The floor seemed to roll beneath us like an ocean swell. Something crashed against the back of my head. I listened in dull, stunned confusion to other things falling all around us, seemingly for a very long time: heavy things, brittle things, hard things, wet things. A few of them hit us and I didn't even wonder what they were or whether either of us was hurt. There was a deep and dusty silence when things finally stopped falling.

Then the screams began.

Chapter Thirteen

THE IVY-COVERED PILLAR AND THE CONCRETE STRUCTURE of the lily fountain had protected us from the worst of the blast and from most of the debris. The room was pitch-dark: the blast had put out most of the candles, and thick clouds of dust shrouded the light that would otherwise have reached us from the hotel lobby. Beside me, the waitress sat up, coughing, and said in a choked and wondering voice, "What the hell *happened?*"

"A bomb. Are you all right? I've forgotten your name." I knew she was wearing a nametag that identified her, and I knew I had read it at some point, and it seemed oddly important now to know what it said. In the aftermath of violence the most trifling details of normality sometimes take on exaggerated importance, as if by clinging to them one might return to that safe time when disaster had not yet struck.

She giggled weakly. "Judy. My name is Judy. Very pleased to meet you, I'm sure." Her voice broke and she coughed again, not convincingly this time, but as if to cover tears. "Oh, God. Oh, God. We have to help them." I could just make out the shape of her against the settling clouds of dust as she rose beside me and stood unsteadily, one hand on the pillar for support. On this side it seemed to be still covered with ivy, but loosely; when her hand touched it, limp tendrils began to fall away, cut free when the blast destroyed the branches on the other side.

The screams had crescendoed as we spoke, then begun to die away as the hysterical were cajoled or cudgeled into silence and the wounded brought comfort by assistance or death. It was taking me a very long time to get moving, and I didn't quite understand why. Judy had not got past the pillar: she was standing there still, staring out into the room, one hand on the pillar and one on her stomach as if she were about to be sick. Perhaps she was. Someone had brought in portable lights, and the dust was settling. Visibility was increasing rapidly. There was a hand lying next to my right knee. It wasn't attached to anything. Just a hand: a woman's hand, with rings on its fingers.

I actually looked at both of my hands to make sure the loose one didn't belong to me. I wasn't wearing any rings, and the loose hand was the wrong color anyway, but never mind. Obviously I wasn't thinking quite clearly. Both my hands were still attached to me. I put one of them on the floor for support while I climbed to my feet, and it landed on something warm, soft, and wet. I looked down and instantly regretted the rare prime rib I'd just eaten.

Don't think about it. There's nothing wrong with

116

you. Get up. I got up. My legs almost refused to hold me. I couldn't understand it: I didn't usually react so badly to crises. People were still screaming. I might be able to help some of them, if I stopped wavering like an hysterical child. I willed unruly muscles to support me and joined Judy beside the pillar to survey the room, to see where we might best offer assistance.

One glance, and the struggle to retain my dinner was lost. The MAMAs had used a very powerful little bomb. There were pieces of people in unlikely places all over the room. A severed leg lay neatly in the center of a miraculously undamaged dinner table. A piece of an arm with the shirtsleeve still on it was tangled in the remains of a fallen crystal chandelier. A bloody hank of blond woman-hair filled an unbroken cup. A torso, headless and all but limbless, still sat at ease in a chair tilted crazily against the wall.

"Oh, God," said Judy. "Oh, God, they're still alive."

Having thoroughly tossed my cookies already, I felt somewhat steadier: still bewilderingly dizzy, but capable of rational thought. The light was brighter now. I looked where she was looking, and saw rescue workers digging mangled bodies out from under a fallen pillar not far from where the bomb had gone off. She was right: they were still alive.

"We have to help them." She started unsteadily forward and tripped heavily over a pile of rubble at her feet. It moaned.

"They've got help already," I said. "We're needed here."

She had figured it out already: on hands and knees where she had fallen, she was scrabbling among the rubble, trying to find the source of the moan. I bent

117

awkwardly to assist her and could not understand why I nearly toppled over onto the rubble I was trying to move. "Come *on*," she said impatiently. "There's someone here. I heard him."

"I'm *try*ing." My voice was querulous, like the voice of a sick child. Judy didn't notice: she'd found an arm and was following it, scattering huge stones and shards of crockery and bits of lumber in every direction.

"Damn it, *help* me," she said.

I helped her. And we found him. But it was too late: blind eyes stared at us from a damaged face, and crushed lips moved in an inaudible whisper, and he died. Judy kept trying to drag him out of the rubble. I had to pull her away. "It's too late for him. There may be others."

She stared at me for a moment, her eyes wide and feverish and possibly mad. "Oh." She looked around dazedly. "Oh." She didn't want to give up on the one she had worked so hard to uncover.

There was no shortage of others to choose from. More rescue workers were pouring in through the lobby door, carrying portable lights till the room was brighter than day and all its carnage clearly visible. Other diners and restaurant staff members who had escaped injury were joining in the rescue efforts. We soon learned not to waste time on lost causes. The room smelled like a slaughterhouse, now that the dust had settled. The fountain beside what was left of the table where I had eaten still tinkled merrily to itself, undamaged.

We found a small child, uninjured, in the arms of its mother under a shattered table. The mother was torn to ribbons, but her body had protected her child. It

118

wasn't even crying. It stared at us with enormous eyes and allowed itself to be led out of the restaurant, into the hotel lobby, without complaint.

We found three men splattered against a wall, a tangle of arms and legs and entrails, and would have left them there for dead if one of them had not blinked at us in silent entreaty. We dug him out of the rubble around them and sorted him out from the pieces of his companions and found him almost whole. He would live. Two dusty waiters with blood on their faces carried him away.

Once we found a waiter buried under a crumpled wall, and Judy cried the whole time we were digging him out. She kept saying his name over and over again in a shocked and agonized litany of hope and helplessness. When we had him half uncovered it was obvious we needn't waste any more time, but she wouldn't give up on that one. She cursed and cried and kept digging till I dragged her away by main force.

There were more like that. Too many like that. Once a pair of rescue workers tried to rescue us, but we fought them off and kept working. There were enough others there by then that we probably weren't needed, but neither of us was willing to quit. I don't know why. God knows I'd have been glad enough to get out of there, away from the screams and the moans and the dust and the blood and the overwhelming reek of death, but I didn't go. I couldn't see straight, and there was a peculiar roaring sound in my ears that nearly drowned the cries of the wounded waiting to be saved, and my body behaved very strangely, not always obediently doing what I told it to, but I wouldn't quit.

Maybe it was some kind of ego trip: the other rescue workers might miss somebody that we could save.

Maybe it was a morbid fascination: here's a foot with its shoe still on it, will I find a body to go with it if I dig here? Mostly, though, I think it was just a form of shock. We did what we did mindlessly, without thought and almost without emotion, simply because it was there to be done and we were there to do it. I don't think we really understood what we were doing, or that there were others to replace us if we quit. People needed help. We tried to help them.

Judy became increasingly impatient with me, and I didn't blame her. I could not understand why I was so slow and clumsy. It seemed to take minutes to make even the simplest motions, and a vast effort of will to understand anything that was said to me. I was impatient with myself. Hotshot Skyrider, indeed: I was behaving very badly for one whose reputation said she was so competent in a crisis.

Eventually we ended up with the majority of the rescue workers, trying to salvage mangled but still-living bodies from under the fallen pillar and section of roof that had collapsed near the center of the devastation where the bomb had gone off. The ones easiest to get at had already been rescued; now it was a seemingly hopeless business of shifting bloodied rubble and finding fragments of people, then shifting more rubble to see whether the fragments were attached to anything worth saving. Most of them were not.

We were all covered with dust and blood and soot, faces smudged with tears and filth, hands torn and bleeding from digging in shattered plasteel and concrete. It was not easy to tell the wounded from the well anymore: everybody was gruesomely stained, shocked and exhausted, trembling with the aftermath of horror and fear and a kind of mad and mindless rage that kept us searching for survivors long after there was any reasonable hope of finding any.

And we did find some. A woman deep in the rubble of the shattered ceiling lay in a pocket of clear space, sheltered by a massive section of pillar and a strong beam fallen crosswise over it, her pretty party dress barely smudged, her face white but undamaged, her body whole. She stared at us in silence as we uncovered her, and she had to be bullied and cajoled into climbing out under her own power when we'd excavated a safe exit for her.

When she was out we could hear a baby crying somewhere beyond where she had lain. It sounded fretful and peeved, but not injured. The workers all around me argued and hesitated and scowled at one another without going in after it, and I couldn't understand why. When I started in, somebody tried to stop me, but I shook off restraining hands and eeled in under that precariously balanced beam, following the sound of the baby's wailing.

It wasn't much deeper in than the woman had been. I had only to move some stones and one broad board, and I could see it. I could also see why the other workers had been hesitant to clamber in there after it. The only thing holding the ceiling beam, and half the ceiling with it, from falling onto the baby and me was God Herself, as far as I could see. I had known it was precariously balanced, but I hadn't realized quite how precariously.

It didn't matter. I was in there, and the baby was in there, and we needed to get out. I reached cautiously past a pile of rubble that looked as though it might be helping to balance the ceiling beam, and it shifted, and I held my breath while dust sifted down onto the baby and something huge and horrifying made grinding noises over my head. I had my hand on the baby's shirt. There was nothing to be gained by waiting, or by holding my breath. I tugged, and the baby flailed its arms and screamed when it banged its little fist against a rough shard of plasteel.

It didn't know what was happening to it, and there was no way I could tell it. I spoke to it anyway, hoping the sound of my voice might soothe it. It was about the same size and color as the one I had left behind on my rock, with the same wet puppy eyes and dark tousled curls. It was wearing dainty, ruffled things; maybe it was a girl too. But presumably not a Faller, or it wouldn't be on Mars. Unless it had the Floater Factor. That's the kind of idiot thoughts that fill a frightened mind trying not to think how near it is to dying. It didn't make a damn bit of difference to me whether the brat had the Floater Factor, or anything else about its genotype. I certainly didn't care what it was wearing. But I noticed with infinite attention to detail how beautifully made the lace was on its shirt front, and how delicately and yet sturdily sewn it was.

The sturdy part mattered: that shirt front was all of the baby I could reach, and I used it to drag the poor brat across the littered, stony floor to my side. It screamed at me, while I murmured meaningless soothing sounds, till I had it under one arm and could start trying to back out of that death trap into relative safety.

I couldn't get my knees under me, so I squirmed backward like a crippled snake, dragging the infant with me. The air inside that hole seemed stuffy and dank. I was gasping for breath as if I'd been running. Red stars danced before my eyes and I couldn't blink them away. I bumped into something and the world tilted crazily. I thought for a moment that I had dislodged the beam, and the ceiling was falling on us, but nothing happened. The roaring sound in my ears nearly drowned the baby's cries. My arms and legs felt curiously weak and limber, like wet spaghetti. I tried to squirm past the obstruction I had run into, and found I couldn't move.

After a long, puzzled moment of lying still and wondering dully what to do next, I remembered Judy. Maybe she could drag us out. I called her name, and couldn't tell whether I'd made a sound. My throat felt raw and dry, choked with dust, and it was all I could do to draw breath to try again. I tried squirming again instead, and the world nearly dissolved into a red-starred darkness. Movement was obviously not going to be one of my better tricks just now.

I think I had forgotten there was anyone outside besides Judy. I certainly didn't know whether I was visible to her or to anyone else. Maybe in order to save me, someone would have to crawl into the hole after me; and I did remember quite clearly that no one had been willing to do that before. That was why it was me in there with the brat. I said, "Judy?" and this time heard the hoarse, croaking sound I'd made.

She recognized it and answered. "What's the matter? Can I help you?"

I cleared my throat. "Can you reach my feet?"

"I can reach them."

I cleared my throat again, and spent a moment breathing, just for the sake of it. "If you wouldn't mind," I said with a curious diffidence, "would you just pull on them? I can't seem to move. Maybe you could drag us out."

"You got the baby?"

I nodded, forgetting she couldn't see me.

"Did you get the baby?" Her voice was demanding, impatient, and I wondered dully whether, if I said no, she would refuse to pull me out.

"I got the baby."

Someone took hold of my ankles and pulled. I tried to twist sideways, to keep the baby off the floor or at least to keep my weight off it, but wasn't at all sure the effort was successful. It was still screaming, and I thought I was still talking to it, but perhaps my voice wasn't working anymore.

And then we were out, into the relatively fresh air and safety of the charnel house that had been a restaurant, and somebody was lifting the screaming brat from my arms. Judy was kneeling beside me, saying something, but I couldn't understand her words. I said, "Thank you." I thought about it, and the world tilted dizzily, and I said, "Oh, sorry," and let the red-starred darkness carry me down.

Chapter Fourteen

THE BABY'S FRETFUL WAILING WOKE ME. I WONDERED BIT-
terly why neither Chuck nor Jamin did anything to
shut it up; my head hurt, my body was a mass of aches
and pains, and I wanted to sleep forever. I had a
dreamlike sense of remembered pity and horror that
my mind wanted to pursue, to find its cause, but I
wouldn't let it. I would sleep forever, and nothing bad
would ever happen or ever have happened, to anyone.

Right. I believe in Santa Claus and the Tooth Fairy
too. My mind went right ahead and supplied me with
memory, and I opened my eyes wide and suddenly, in
an effort to shut the memory out. It gave me something new to think about: I didn't know where I was.
Not on my rock, certainly, but I hadn't really expected
my rock. There was an object in my field of view that I
didn't recognize. I stared at it for what seemed like
minutes, forcing my mind back onto familiar path-

ways. A lamp. It was a table lamp. Lighted. And in the pool of yellow light it spilled, there was a shiny wooden tabletop. I felt smug at my powers of recognition.

"Are you awake?" The voice, raised slightly to be heard over the baby's incessant whining, was distantly familiar. I thought about turning my head to see if memory would supply me with a name, but the effort was too vast. Instead, I closed my eyes.

"Yes. Are you?"

There was a brief hesitation: then she chuckled. It was a dry, papery sound, barely audible, but it seemed to startle the baby into silence. Anyway it quit its thin, breathless complaints and I recognized new background sounds: the rustle of an air conditioner and the subdued roar of a toilet flushing somewhere beyond a wall. "I've *been* awake," she said.

I was sifting memories, searching for a name. A lot of unpleasant images cropped up first. I ignored them. There had been a nametag to go with that voice. I kept working on it till I found it: "Judy."

"You remember," she said. "The med-techs weren't sure you would. You had a concussion. The whole time I was bullying you to hurry up and help, you had a concussion and three broken ribs and you were bleeding, and I got impatient with you." She made it sound like the crime of the century.

"You didn't know."

"I should have." The baby was still silent. I could hear a rhythmic patting sound. When I finally forced my head to turn away from the lamp to look at the other side of the bed, I saw what it was: she was holding the baby in her arms and patting its bottom absently.

126

"How could you have? I didn't even know."

"You threw me on the floor and shielded me with your body," she said. "I might have guessed you got hurt in the process. Instead, I assumed that since I wasn't hurt, you weren't either. Dumb."

"Natural. Besides, you were in shock." I lifted my eyes from the baby-patting hand to her face, and could barely remember it. The waitress who had served me before the bomb went off had been a merry-eyed, smiling girl-child with nothing more serious to worry about than whether her boyfriend would show up for their date on time. This was a woman whose gaunt face and hollow eyes had been through Hell and come out the other side with the girl-smiles permanently dulled by horror.

"And you were in pain. You might have been dying. I'm sorry I bullied you. Honest to God I wouldn't've if I'd known."

"Oh, space." I lifted an arm to gesture and was surprised how heavy it felt. "I wasn't in any pain. I didn't even know I was hurt. Forget it." I peered at the infant in her arms. "Isn't that the brat I got out from under the rubble? I didn't know it was yours."

"It isn't." She grinned suddenly, the ghost of an impish girl-smile. "The thing is, I couldn't convince the med-techs it wasn't *yours*. That's why we're stuck with it." She sobered suddenly and eyed me uncertainly. "Look, I hope you don't mind, but I didn't have any money and the desk clerk said you had plenty of credit, so I charged some diapers and stuff to the room. I mean, she had to have them. Till we find out whose she is."

"Nobody claimed it? Somebody just left a whole infant offspring unclaimed?"

Her eyes darkened and she looked down at the infant, her face grim with remembered horror. She had one of the most expressive faces I'd ever seen. And one of the most transparent: she would never be much good at Planets or poker. Every brief emotion that flitted through her mind crossed her face just as clearly. "Probably her parents are . . . probably they didn't make it." She lifted agonized eyes to me. "So many people were, you know, so many . . ."

"Died? It's not a dirty word, Judy. One out of every one dies, and refusing to use the word won't stop that." I was attempting to sit up, testing my strength, easing past the sore points where newly-healed bones and muscles protested, so I didn't see her expression till her words made me look at her.

"How can you be so callous? How *can* you? You were there, you *saw* what happened. How could you talk about it like it was, I don't know, how *could* you?"

"Oh, space." I don't know what I sounded like. I just felt *old*.

"I'm sorry." There was real apology in her voice; and when I looked at her again, the dramatic look of stricken sensibilities was gone from her face, replaced by an odd, sheepish dignity. "I really am sorry. I don't know what gets into me. 'I've been acting like that ever since . . . since what happened. Oh, look, I've made her cry again. Ms. Rendell, I'm just a Martian farm girl, I've never been out in the world and seen much or done much, and I just don't always act right when things happen. I'm sorry."

I couldn't help grinning at her. "Seems to me you acted hell of right when things happened in the restaurant downstairs."

An involuntary shudder shook her and a spasm of

agony twisted that pretty, guileless face. "Don't remind me. I'm trying not to think about it."

"Sorry. That's probably a good idea, at that." The experiment in sitting up had been successful, so I swung my legs out of bed to try standing. The med-techs had healed all the broken bones, but it's not really the bones that hurt when you break them, it's the muscles and whatnot around the bones. Modern medical technology is very good at pasting muscles and whatnot back together as need be, but they haven't yet come up with a way to make the newly healed places feel anywhere near as good as they look. The med-techs say that's a good thing: it keeps us from straining things and tearing wounds open again. They aren't the ones in pain. If they were, they might talk a different story. I moved like an arthritic old woman. But I did move.

"Should you be doing that?" Judy stared at me, looking oddly frightened.

"I'm fine," I snapped, and was instantly sorry when I saw the hurt in her face; but I didn't apologize. She was doing her best to be friends. It wasn't my fault she chose a lousy person to try to be friends with. When I was sure my legs would support me, I began the long journey from my bed to the hotel window. It must have been all of three or four meters. I was so shaky that I didn't even notice till I had one hand on the window frame for support that not only was I dressed only in someone else's oversized shirt, but my handgun was nowhere in sight.

"Are you . . ." Judy paused and cleared her throat. "Are you really the Skyrider?"

"Where's my handgun?"

"Right there, beside the bed. I knew you'd want it

handy. Being a Belter and all." She cleared her throat again. "You never told me your name, but the desk clerk recognized you. That's how I knew what room to have them bring you to, and everything. Listen, are you really the Skyrider?"

I looked where she indicated, saw my holstered handgun hanging within easy reach of the bed, and scowled at her. "What if I am?"

She shrugged diffidently, blushing furiously. "Oh, nothing. Except . . . about the baby, you know. It was so strange. I mean, everybody's heard of the Skyrider. And who ever heard of the Skyrider having a baby, right? It just doesn't make sense. But it wasn't just 'cause you rescued this poor little mite that they decided she was yours. And it wasn't just 'cause nobody else claimed her. But there was this young guy . . . a Belter, and he acted like he knew you. . . . He'd been in the restaurant, I guess, or he came in to help clean up, anyway he helped rescue people, but nobody I knew had ever seen him before. Nobody knew who he was."

The scene outside the window looked just as it had before I'd gone to my ill-fated dinner. The artificially lit street was crowded with the same hawkers and hustlers, preachers and prostitutes, tourists and tramps. I felt obscurely grateful that at this distance, ten stories off the ground, I couldn't hear them. "So? There must be a million people in Marstown every day that nobody here knew before. So what about him?"

"Well, it was sort of weird. How he acted, I mean. I can't describe it, but he acted real strange about you and the baby. He insisted she was yours, and he made me promise to—" She blushed again, and looked sheepishly away when my gaze met hers. "I promised to take care of the two of you. Protect the baby till you were all right, and help you however you needed while you were on Mars." She lifted her chin and forced her eyes to meet my gaze, though it clearly wasn't easy. "He paid me a lot of money to do it, and I don't care how stupid you think it is, I know the baby isn't yours and you don't need anybody's protection if you're really the Skyrider, but this guy was *certain*, and I needed the money, and I took it."

"What did you need the money for?" It was an absentminded question, mostly just a sound I could make while I thought about her mysterious stranger and why he might pay somebody to protect me and a baby I'd never seen before. I wasn't really listening to her answer.

"To get off Mars."

It took a moment for that to register. "What? Why?"

She shrugged ineffably. "That's my business, isn't it?" She blushed again, but clearly wasn't going to back down. "He gave me enough money for it too. . . . I think."

"He said the baby was mine?"

"Well, not yours by birth. He said something like . . . that she had been left in your care. He wouldn't say by whom, or why, or anything. Just that she had been left in your care and I was to help till you got back on your feet." She looked thoughtful. "You know, it's funny, he made the med-techs check to see was she a Faller before he paid me. Like that proved she really was the right baby, or something."

I stared. "It can't be a Faller. It's on Mars. And it's not even crying. And if it didn't die of gravity shock on-planet, it would when it was lifted off. That's ridiculous. Nobody would bring a Faller baby to Mars."

She smiled maternally. "Oh, it's all right. She has that new Floater Factor that makes Fallers able to live in gravity just like anybody else. You know. It's what has the MAMAs so upset they go around throwing bombs and stuff." Pain darkened her eyes for a moment at the memory of "bombs and stuff," but she shoved the thought away and looked at me earnestly. "She'll be just fine, on Mars or anywhere else. She could even go to Earth. In fact, from the way that guy talked, I got the impression she might have been born on Earth. So I suppose they knew she was a Faller right away; hospitals routinely check infants' whole genotypes when they're born these days." She looked thoughtful. "Maybe that's why the poor kid's parents sent her—or brought her—off-Earth in the first place. Maybe they thought she'd be safer out here, farther from MAMA's base of operations."

I scowled at the brat. "Well, none of that is anything to do with me. I don't care what your mysterious stranger said, that brat is not mine and I don't want anything to do with it. In fact, I don't want it in my hotel room. Why don't you take it away and give it to somebody? Then they can get started finding who it belongs to."

"You can't, Skyrider."

"I can't what?"

"You can't abandon her. You'd be arrested. Listen, I tried to tell you. That guy was some kind of muckymuck or something. I don't know who he was, but he acted like he was important even though he was so young, and so did Ground Patrol and the med-techs and everybody. When he said this baby was yours, that made her *yours*."

"Nonsense. She *isn't* mine, and her parents will be looking for her. Or some other relatives. Somebody. She must have somebody. It only makes sense. Besides, she's got to have: she sure as hell doesn't have me."

Judy curved an arm protectively around the brat. "Maybe not, but you've got her, Skyrider. I'm telling you, you can't legally get rid of her now. She's yours."

"The hell she is." This was too much: two Faller infants dumped on me in the space of a couple of days. I don't even *like* infants. I sure as hell wasn't going to accept responsibility for another one.

Judy smiled at me shyly. "She's kind of sweet, really, when you get to know her."

I didn't break any furniture. I just didn't have the energy. I scowled till Judy lost courage and looked away from me. I said petulantly, "We'll see about *sweet*." And I went back to bed. It seemed the only logical option available to me at the time.

Chapter Fifteen

IT WAS LATE AFTERNOON WHEN I WOKE AGAIN. MY HOTEL room was blessedly empty this time, and I felt a lot better than I had when I woke in the night. Climbing out of bed wasn't even an ordeal, just difficult. Staying on my feet once I got upright was a little tricky; I was astonishingly weak. Just crossing the room to the dispenser wore me out. I let myself cautiously down into a chair next to it, punched up a meal almost at random, and realized I hadn't brought my handgun with me.

Sighing, I clambered to my feet and crossed the room again on trembling legs, got my handgun and strapped it on, and returned to the dispenser to see what it was producing. I wasn't feeling choosey. What I was feeling was hungry, as if I hadn't eaten in days. The dispenser produced a lot of steaming coffee that was hardly worth the name, some fruit juice that tasted like ambrosia, and an enormous plate of meat and eggs and potatoes. I'd have preferred rice, but Martians grow potatoes, not rice, so potatoes were what the dispenser offered.

I had eaten most of that and started on a second pot of bad coffee when I heard a key turning in the door. My response was entirely automatic: by the time the door came open, I was crouched in a defensive stance to one side of it, half-hidden by one of the hotel's big, soft chairs, my handgun balanced across its arm to cover the door.

Judy froze in the doorway, her eyes wide and startled, the baby clutched in one arm and a loaded paper bag in the other. She didn't say anything. She just stared while I sighed, straightened, and put my gun away. Then she stepped on inside and closed the door behind her, but warily, still watching me.

I returned to my breakfast. The food was cold, but I'd had about all I could eat anyway, and the coffee was still hot. I dumped the food into the disposal and poured a fresh cup of coffee, glanced at Judy, and said, "You want some?"

She was putting the baby down carefully on a big chair, with the back of another chair up against it so the kid couldn't fall out. When she had it settled to her satisfaction she turned to me, still clinging to her paper bag, and said in a small voice, "Yes, please. I'm sorry I startled you when I came in."

I almost laughed. "I think I startled you more. Sorry. Reflexes. I forgot you'd have a key, and I've had a little too much excitement lately. Here. This is supposed to be coffee, but it doesn't taste much like it. What d'you have in the bag?"

She looked down at it almost guiltily. "Oh, this?"

"Do you have other bags I don't know about?"

She glared at me. "I guess you're feeling better. You're getting meaner."

I did laugh, that time. A small, choked sound, but it was a laugh. "My reputation precedes me, as usual. I'm sorry, I didn't mean to be mean."

"This coffee tastes fine to me," she said.

I decided the contents of the bag must be a secret. "Did you get any sleep last night?"

She smiled. "And the night before. You must've left quite a deposit with the desk: they haven't even begun to worry about how long you're going to stay."

I stared. "How long *have* I stayed?"

"You mean how long have you been asleep? The bomb was night before last. You've been unconscious or asleep most of the time since then."

That was disconcerting. I stared around the room as if I might find my lost day lying in one of the corners. "No wonder I was so hungry."

"The med-techs said to just let you sleep, once they'd fixed you up as well as they could. How do you feel?"

"About as dangerous as that brat looks." For the first time since waking, I half remembered our conversation of the night before. Or of the night before that; I realized with a sense of disorientation that I didn't know which it had been. "What did the med-techs have to fix? I don't remember having been hurt."

She looked at me strangely. "You remember the bomb?"

"Of course I remember the bomb. And the mess afterward. And I sort of half remember some crazy conversation with you in the middle of the night. Something about being stuck with that damn brat because some Belter muckymuck told the authorities it was mine. But I don't remember what the hell was wrong with me."

"You had a concussion, several broken ribs, and a severe puncture wound in the left shoulder. In back. I'm afraid there's a scar: they were pretty busy that night and wouldn't take time to make it perfect. They said you had so many scars already you wouldn't notice." She glanced inadvertently at my legs, which were the only major part of me not concealed by the oversized shirt I was wearing, and which were both, admittedly, somewhat the worse for wear.

"They were right." I grinned. "Besides, I can't see my back, anyway."

"You saved me." She said it very seriously, with an earnest look of gratitude that embarrassed me.

I couldn't think of anything to say. "Um. More coffee?"

"You saw what was going to happen, and you threw me on the floor and protected me with your own body. That's why you were so hurt and I wasn't. Not even a scratch."

"Well . . . I didn't have time to think about it."

She blushed. "I'm sorry, I didn't mean to embarrass you. I just . . . I'm grateful. I wanted to say so."

I shrugged. "It was just instinct."

"It saved my life."

"Oh, piffle. The big deal is that I got between you and the explosion, right? And I'm not dead, so you wouldn't have been if I hadn't been there."

"I would have, though. I wouldn't have known to lie down. I wouldn't have known the bomb was going to go off. How did you know?"

"Instinct. One of the MAMAs left her purse behind,

and they all left in a hell of a hurry. Listen, it's no big deal."

"I owe you," she said earnestly. "I owe you my life."

"Piffle."

"No, really." She was avoiding my gaze. I wondered why. "So I was thinking . . ."

"Yes?"

"Well, you need somebody to help you take care of the baby, right?"

"What, you're really sure I can't get rid of it?"

"I don't see how. I've been checking, and still nobody else has claimed it, so if that guy was wrong and it *had*n't been left in your care, it is now. Its—jeez, you've got me doing it too—*her* parents must have died in the blast. So I think you're stuck with her. And I thought you'd need somebody to help take care of her." She glanced at me almost furtively. "'Specially when you go off-planet." She saw something in my face that made her gulp and look away and hurry on with her speech before she could lose her nerve: "I'm real good at taking care of babies. I have six younger brothers and eight younger sisters. I helped raise them all. In fact, I'd still be helping, if I hadn't left the farm. I really am good with kids, and I wouldn't get in your way or anything, I promise."

Her voice trailed away briefly; then she cleared her throat and forced herself to look me in the eye, blushing furiously. "I'm a good worker, and I'd charge just standard rates, nothing extra for having to go off-planet or anything like that."

This time my laugh sounded more like I meant it. "A woman after my own mercenary heart."

She blinked. "What?"

"I haven't forgotten as much as you hoped I would.

138

I remember very clearly being told you'd accepted a large sum of money from that muckymuck who stuck me with the baby. And I remember what you said you wanted the money for. You wanted to get off-planet. So it's real kind of you to volunteer not to charge me for giving you a free ride off. I appreciate that."

"Oh, hell." Her voice wavered and I thought for a moment she was going to cry, which would have embarrassed both of us; but she straightened her shoulders and looked me in the eye again and said firmly, "Okay. Okay, you're right, I want off-planet, and it looked to me like a chance for a free ride. It still does: you *do* need somebody to help you with the baby, and I *am* good at that. I'll do it in exchange for the ride."

"You don't even know where I'm going."

"I don't care. You're going off Mars. That's what I want."

"Space, don't be daft. I could be headed for the Outer Rocks—"

"I'd like that," she said sturdily, not quite meaning it and not about to let me know it.

"—or Earth. Would you really trade Mars for Earth?"

"If that's where you're going." She looked away, sighed, and said bitterly, "Oh, no, damn it, that isn't what I want, and you know it isn't; I want to go to the Belt, and that's where you're from so I thought that might be where you're going." She lifted her chin. "But you're the best chance I've got to get off-planet anywhere and have money left to live on when I get there, and I *will* take it—if you'll let me—even if you are going to Earth."

"Earth is even farther from the Belt than Mars is."

"I know. But it isn't Mars."

"What do you have against Mars, anyway?"

"I don't want to talk about it."

"You're in some kind of trouble."

"Not with the law, if that's what you mean. You don't have to worry about that."

"I never do." I studied her, puzzled and not a little impressed. I was beginning to like this woman. She held up well under stress, and had tried to get me to pay her when she should have been offering to pay me. As I said, a woman after my own mercenary heart. "You've got a deal, Judy. The brat's yours for the duration. Take good care of it."

"Her."

"What?"

"Her. The baby is a girl. A her, not an it."

"Oh. Yeah. I've heard that line of reasoning somewhere before."

"I tried to find out who that man was."

"What man?" I was thinking of the man who'd told me a baby was a her, not an it.

"The one that said the baby was yours. You know. That young Belter muckymuck. I couldn't find out anything about him, though. Well, hardly anything. I know what he looks like, of course; I saw him. And I found out he works for Ecology Now, Incorporated. Isn't that weird? I mean, not that he works for them, though I didn't know they had any employees in the Belt, but that somebody who works for them would care who ended up with a baby if it wasn't his. If any of them have babies. I suppose they do. They just seem like such freaks to me, I can't imagine anybody loving one of them and having a baby with him. I mean, they're always on about what kind of algae will do what with which chemicals in what-sized pond, and which variety of wheat yields best and provides the most nutrition, you know, and attacking industry for not spending all their profits finding ways to recycle their wastes, and . . . Oh, I am sorry, I always talk too much, sometimes I just can't seem to get myself to shut up, especially when I'm excited, and I'm really excited about finally getting to go off-planet, I've wanted off Mars for so long and now . . ." She stared at me in sudden panic. "You won't change your mind, will you? Listen, I could practice not talking too much, or I could lock myself in a room with the baby where you couldn't even see me, or something, I mean I really will try not to be a bother, honest, it's just that I . . . I'm . . . excited." Blushing, she let her voice trail away. "I'm sorry."

"There is one thing you'll have to learn if you travel with me." I tried to make my tone stern: and considering the look she gave me, I must have succeeded.

"What?" she asked in a very small, nervous voice.

"Stop apologizing."

"Oh." She thought about it. "Oh. I'm sorry. I mean . . ."

"Does it have a name?"

She stared. "What?"

"The baby. Does it have a name?"

"Oh. I don't know. I mean, I suppose it—*she* has, but I don't know what it is. Nobody knows where she came from. I've just been calling her Baby."

"That'll do, I guess." I wasn't really thinking about the baby. I was thinking about an important Belter who worked for Ecology Now, Inc., and thought I ought to have possession of a Faller baby. And of two black shuttles owned by Ecology Now, Inc., whose pilots thought I ought to be relieved of a Faller baby. This situation was getting weirder by the minute.

"I bought a stun gun," Judy said suddenly. "That's what's in the bag. My stun gun. And some clothes and stuff I thought I might need. If you let me go along. I know everybody in the Belt wears guns, so I thought . . . so I got one. Just in case."

I looked at her. "You know how to use it?"

"Well, naturally." She blushed. "Well, sort of. I used to have one on the farm. It was my older brother's, I mean, really. But he let me use it. I'd stun rabrats and stuff. Just for practice. And sometimes a groundhog or something. For food."

"So you're pretty good with it?"

"Well . . ." I couldn't tell if she was having an attack of honesty, or the sort of unconscious self-deprecation that makes an expert marksman say he's "fairly good" with a weapon. "I'm not *bad* with it."

I nodded. "I hope you won't have occasion to prove that."

She studied me for a moment. "Skyrider?"

"That's my name."

"Where *are* you—we—going?"

I grinned without humor. "As a matter of fact, we're leaving for Earth just as soon as I can get my act together."

"Oh. Earth."

"That's right. In just a few hours, probably." I intended, first, to check with the authorities and make sure Judy wasn't playing some game of her own about that baby: if I could get rid of it, I would. And I had a few other things I wanted to investigate on Mars before I left, plus possibly a few minor purchases to make. But I didn't see any reason to detail all that to Judy.

She was trying not to look crestfallen. "Earth." She forced a smile. "Well, I always wondered what it looked like. They say it's real pretty."

"I guess it is, if you like big rocks."

"I grew up on one . . . if you mean planets." She glanced at the window, though from where we were there was nothing visible beyond it but sky. "I guess I like them."

"But not this one."

She blinked. "I like Mars well enough. I just . . . I just want to leave, that's all. I just don't want to stay here . . . now."

"Well, cheer up. You'll be leaving soon enough."

"Yeah. For Earth." She was trying to sound excited.

I relented: she wasn't a bad kid, after all. "After that I'll be going back to the Belt, and if I haven't got rid of the brat by then I'll still need a baby-sitter."

The sudden sunshine smile she gave me for that reminded me sharply of Collis. For a loner outlaw queen, I sure seemed to be acquiring a lot of hostages to fortune these days. I scowled at her and left her in charge of the afternoon breakfast table and the baby while I went in search of clean clothing in which to tackle the Martian authorities.

Chapter Sixteen

UNFORTUNATELY, JUDY WAS RIGHT: I WAS STUCK WITH another baby. I couldn't get a line on the Ecology Now, Inc., fellow who had accomplished that, but he had done his job well. I might as well have been the kid's mother, for all the chance I had of getting rid of it with a minimum of fuss. If I'd been willing to hang around Mars and cope with half a lifetime's legal formalities, I could eventually have lost responsibility for the brat, but I didn't want to hang around Mars. I was still anxious to find out where the *other* Faller brat had come from, and why somebody wanted it dead.

Judy, the brat, and I lifted off-planet just as it was rotating Marstown past the terminator, onto the down-sun side. The streetlights winked on suddenly like strings of jewels below us, and moments later were lost in the haze of atmosphere and distance. Judy was strapped into the auxiliary control seat with the baby clutched in her arms, and for her sake I kept the gravity generators on full, at first to compensate in part for the excess gravities generated by liftoff, and later to give her a chance to get used to the concept of being in space before she had to deal with freefall too.

She stared at the aft screens with triumphant satisfaction till Mars was only an angry red star in the distance. The infant slept peacefully in her arms, oblivious to the forces both natural and political that shaped its world and its future. Judy patted it absently from time to time, the sort of unconscious gesture of affection that a mother would make: but I think she had really forgotten it was there.

At last she blinked, and sighed, and leaned back in her seat with a contented, catlike smile. "I don't think I really believed it till now." Her voice was dreamy, her eyes vague with pleasure. "I'm really off that damn planet. I'm free. I'm finally free. I told him I would go, and he laughed at me, and said I'd never make it, but by God I did."

"Who laughed at you?"

She had been talking to herself, or to the brat in her arms: the sound of my voice startled her. She stared at me in sudden consternation and said anxiously, "Oh, nobody. I mean—"

"Sure, kid." I was busy with the computer, calculating our course.

"I mean, of course it was somebody, I was talking about somebody, I was talking about . . . I, um, it's kind of a long story, you probably don't want to, I mean . . ."

I glanced at her and was surprised at the depth of pain and confusion in her eyes. "Look, kid, you don't have to justify yourself to me or anybody else. Okay?

You had your reasons to leave Mars, and you made it. You're off Mars. Whatever it is you left back there behind you, it can't reach you here."

"No. No, he can't." She said it wonderingly, with an awakening delight. "He really can't. Not ever."

The computer decided where Earth would be when we'd had time to get there, and told me how to match trajectories so we'd hit Earth orbit. "You're young to have something that bad to run from."

"I'm not as young as you think." She said it bitterly, not with a child's defiance but with a woman's infinite regret and sense of loss.

"I give up: how old are you, anyway?"

"Earth Standard?" I could see her calculating quickly. "About eighteen, I think." She smiled faintly, bitterly. "But age is only numbers."

"True enough." I punched in our course and unstrapped from the pilot's seat to go make a pot of coffee. By Marstown standards it might be early evening, but I wasn't on Marstown's schedule. For me it was still morning, and I hadn't yet had a cup of coffee worthy of the name.

Judy stared at me in sudden panic. "What are you doing? Where are you going? We're in *space*, you can't just get up and walk away, who'll fly us?"

"*Defiance* can manage on her own." I paused by my seat to look at her, resisting the impulse to grin. It wasn't her fault she'd never been to space before. "These shuttles are built to be run by one pilot, and some of the runs are hell of long. One person couldn't stay awake the whole time. There are sensors and alarms and computers and even automatic evasive maneuvers for small rocks. She'll let me know if she needs any help."

Her wide eyes stared at me, trying not to look frightened. "Who will?"

"*Defiance.* The shuttle. Come on, let's get the brat settled in your quarters and make some real coffee. I could use it."

"It flies all by itself?"

"She."

"What?"

"She. The shuttle's a she, not an it." I thought of Ian, with whom I'd had that identical exchange, as well as the one about the sexual designation of babies, and I did not hit or break anything.

"What's wrong?"

"Nothing." I heard the snarl in my voice and saw the vulnerability in her eyes and said crossly, "Sorry. Didn't mean to snap at you. We all have things we're running from . . . and that we don't want to talk about."

She had unfastened her shock webbing and risen, holding the baby in both arms and watching the controls as if she knew what they were for and was checking the computer's performance. Now she paused, and looked at me in almost childlike surprise, and said in a startled voice, "You? You have something to run from?"

"I'm only human." It wasn't a snarl, but it didn't sound really friendly either.

"I think I would like coffee." Judy's voice was small and uncertain, but courageous. She was facing down more demons than just a demented Skyrider. But being alone on an apparently unpiloted space shuttle with a demented Skyrider wasn't doing much to ease her discomfort. "And I'd like to put the baby down. Is there somewhere where she'll be safe?"

147

"We can rig something in your quarters."

"I have quarters?" She laughed at herself before I had a chance to. "I'm sorry, I don't mean to sound even stupider than I am. I guess I should have known . . . I mean, I'd have to sleep somewhere, and put my stuff . . . I just hadn't really thought."

"Relax, kid. I know this is all new to you. And I'm not half as mean as the legend says."

She gave me a dubious look for that, and didn't respond. We got the baby settled in her quarters by fastening it in a freefall hammock that would double as shock webbing in a crisis. Judy went back to the cockpit and got her paper bag full of belongings, and I showed her how to use the locker compartments to stow her things. The newly purchased handgun she strapped awkwardly to her hip with a look of sheepish defiance. "I never had a holster for my brother's gun. Is this how you do it?"

"You could draw quicker if you hung it a little lower."

"Oh. But then, doesn't it get in the way when you move around and sit down and stuff?"

"You tie it down. And you get used to it. Hell, I suppose it did get in my way when I first learned to wear one, but now I feel naked without it."

"Oh." She loosened the belt and let the holster drop, eyeing the way I wore mine, trying to match it. "You won't laugh at me?"

"Not unless you're funny."

"I meant—"

"I know. Look, kid, give yourself space. You're going to make some mistakes, and you'll probably get laughed at for some of them, if not by me then by somebody else. When that happens, you've got a couple of options: laugh with him, or kill him."

She stared, trying to figure me out. "*Kill* him?"

I shrugged. "You can always try."

"Oh, I don't think I could kill anyone. At least, not just for laughing at me."

"Then you'd better learn to laugh at yourself. Let's go make that coffee. Come on, the brat'll be all right."

She looked uncertain about that, but she followed me.

The strength of the coffee I made shocked her, but she tried to conceal it. I told her she didn't have to like it, and she assured me quite unconvincingly that she did. I think she thought it was part of the fierce Belter image she seemed to want to learn. I could have told her there were a lot of Belters who couldn't handle my coffee, but I decided she was confused enough already.

She hadn't shared my breakfast, and I wasn't sure how long it had been since she'd eaten, so I showed her how to work my dispenser, which was different enough from the standard model that she might have had trouble with it by herself. She watched my demonstration carefully, and eyed the results with evident hunger, and told me primly that she didn't need to eat between meals: she'd wait till I wanted lunch or dinner or whatever.

"Look, kid, we're not on the same schedule, and we don't have to be, for space sake. If you're hungry, eat."

"I can pay for it." She sounded defensive.

"No need. It's all part of the service."

"But I'm not paying for my ride or anything."

"Hell, you wanted *me* to pay for your ride. Come on, what is this, some kind of weird pride? You're paying for the ride, or you'd better be: I'm not going to take care of that brat in your quarters."

"Oh. Yeah." She ate the snack I'd ordered up without further argument, and even figured out how to request a sandwich and a drink. "Skyrider?"

"Judy?" I was leaning back in my chair, sipping my coffee, trying not to think of Ian. There was no point in thinking of Ian. Thinking wouldn't put him back in my life. Considering how easily he'd left my life, maybe I didn't want him back in it. But I could not forget the jeweled beauty of his eyes. . . .

"Why are we going to Earth?"

"What?"

"I mean . . . I don't know if I should ask . . . but I just wondered, why are we going to Earth?"

"Oh. Space, ask whatever you want to: I can always refuse to answer."

"Oh."

"I'm not sure why we're going to Earth."

She stared. "Oh."

"It's a long story."

"Does it have anything to do with Baby?"

"In a way, I guess. And maybe with a woman who gave birth to a monster."

"Baby isn't a monster!"

"Not apparently."

"She's not . . . oh. You didn't mean Baby?"

"I'm not sure I know what I meant. Or what it has to do with us, anyway." I repeated, briefly, the story Haruki-san had told me.

"And you think Baby is the woman's child? But how? . . . Why?"

"Actually, I hadn't thought of that. Could be your

brat *is* the woman's child. Could be that's why the MAMAs bombed the restaurant. To get that kid."

She shuddered. "They'd bomb a whole restaurant full of people just to get one baby?"

"They'd bomb it just for the hell of it. You should know that."

"I guess I do. But . . . Baby?" She shook her head. "Then what's the safe place they're supposed to have put her—the monster—in? It can't have been the restaurant. That was hardly safe."

"Maybe the 'safe place' was just with somebody they thought could keep her safe. Everybody has to eat."

She shook her head suddenly. "I don't believe it. Baby isn't a monster."

"Not apparently," I repeated. "But neither is the other brat I was recently stuck with, and somebody sure as space was trying to kill it."

"Somebody left *another* baby in your care?"

I made a wry face. "I seem to be first-choice caretaker for abandoned waifs, lately."

She thought about it. "Well . . . In your care would sure look like a safe place to me."

"If you had a spare monster lying around you wanted to protect?"

"A spare *baby*," she corrected, and unexpectedly grinned at me. "Your speech habits are contagious. Babies aren't *spare*. You don't have *extras*. They're people, not bits of luggage or cargo."

"They may grow up to be people. Or not. But they're not people yet, not when they're the size of that one in your quarters. Whatever else it may be, that ain't people."

"No, she's a person. Just one. You know what? I don't think you're half as tough as you want me to think."

I never had to answer that one: a warning klaxon startled me out of my chair before I had time even to scowl at her, which would otherwise have been my first reaction. I went out the galley door at a dead run, and only remembered at the last minute to shout back at her, "Strap in somewhere. Cockpit or quarters, I don't care. We're under attack. Move. Now!"

She moved. So did I.

Chapter Seventeen

THIS TIME IT WAS AN ORDINARY STARBIRD AFTER ME, painted only with standard registration numbers as legally required. She gleamed like a silver dagger against the cold black of space as she swooped across my scanner screens and tossed a shot at me the way you'd toss a ball to someone who wasn't expecting it: casually, almost aimlessly, without any apparent intent to harm. I hadn't seen where she came from, but her trajectory was not good for engaging me, and she was trying to alter that: the laser shot was just to distract me while she maneuvered.

Against most targets, it might have worked. I'm not most targets. The shot was wide, so I ignored it, and returned fire with equal carelessness while I queried the computer. It decided the Starbird had come from Phobos, one of the moons of Mars. If she'd meant to intercept me, she had misjudged my trajectory. At a guess, from the angle at which she had missed, she must have thought I'd be traveling faster than I was.

The logical thing to do about it was to start traveling faster: hell of faster. *Defiance* had Sunfinch engines and enormous fuel capacity. That made us at least twice as fast as the average Starbird and capable of sustaining speed for a good long while. There was no reason to stick around for a fight: I had nothing against that Starbird except that she was trying to kill me, and if I ran like hell she wouldn't get much of a chance at that.

I ran like hell. She got one more chance at me, but she had overcompensated for her initial error and her angle of fire the second time around wasn't much better. Apparently she had intended to come back in on my tail and ride it till she got in a shot that killed me; and ordinarily it might have worked. But she had too much inertia to overcome. I didn't even have to dodge her. Her path crossed mine close enough behind that she did get in one close shot, but then she was past and burning malite trying to kill inertia while I used mine for straight running.

She didn't have a chance after that, but I watched her in the aft screens anyway, just out of curiosity. She had a good pilot. She cut the corner shorter than I would have thought possible for a Starbird, and this time didn't overcompensate: when she straightened out she was exactly on my path. But she was too far behind by then, and losing ground fast. Her pilot didn't like to quit. There just wasn't any other choice.

I had told the Comm Link to hail her, not really expecting anything to come of it, but thinking it would be nice to talk to one of these would-be assassins if I could. When the Link signaled a frequency I just stared at it for seconds, so startled I almost didn't respond. She wasn't saying anything, but she had a frequency open for me if I wanted to talk.

I tried it: "You have any particular reason for wanting to kill me, or did you just need some target practice?"

Static: no answer.

"If it was target practice, you'd better get some more. You need it."

By then I didn't expect a response, so her voice startled the hell out of me. It might have, anyway: I'd seldom heard such venom . . . or such an impressively unprintable vocabulary.

I cut across it, trying to sound bored: we were getting out of range for standard channels, and if she had anything printable to say I might want to hear it. "Okay: that establishes that it was personal, not target practice. So, you want to tell me why?"

She continued in the same vein till I cut the connection. The signal was breaking up anyway, since I was leaving her behind so fast, and she wasn't even broadening my vocabulary. The only information I was able to sort out of her venomous diatribe was that she didn't much care for me and she liked my payload even less: Fallers were not her favorite.

I told the computer to track down her reg. numbers, and laughed at myself for habits of thought: so far, the chances didn't look good that this particular "payload" was going to pay very well: Judy was just along for the ride, and nobody seemed to want any Faller babies lately, any way but dead.

"Is it over?" Judy had found the intercom controls in her quarters.

I didn't laugh at her. As far as she was concerned,

that must have been a space battle: we had been fired on. The screen in her quarters would have told her that much. "It's over, such as it was. You can come forward now, if you want to."

"He won't come back?"

"He was a she. And she can't come back: she can't catch me."

She came forward and sat in the auxiliary seat very tentatively, watching the screens, trying not to look scared. "Why did she attack us?"

I shrugged. "Some people just don't like babies."

She stared. "She was after *Baby*? Really? Why?"

"That isn't clear. But I'm beginning to think the 'monster' in Haruki-san's little fable was a Faller, not a bug-eyed monster of the weird persuasion."

"MAMAs call Fallers monsters."

"Just so." I was watching the computer screen, waiting for a readout on the Starbird's reg. numbers. "But why anybody would think a Faller baby could destroy the world I don't quite see."

"Do you know who that was? Who attacked us?"

The computer found what it was looking for and printed the results on the screen. I read it aloud to Judy: "The Starbird is registered to a woman named Adrienne Martin. An Earther. There's no guarantee she was flying it herself . . . and no particular reason to suppose she wasn't. It's registered out of San Francisco. That's all I know."

"That isn't very much, is it?"

"No. That isn't very much." I asked the computer to look up Adrienne Martin, and after a moment's hesitation I instructed it to dig right into the CommNet if it had to: I could afford the distance charges, and I was damned curious. But I didn't really expect results, and I didn't get them. Even the CommNet had very little on Adrienne Martin. Aside from having once written a popular romance novel that the computer offered to show me (I declined), she had never done anything that got her into the CommNet. There were the standard references to schools and marriages (no offspring) and a list of ordinary office jobs she'd held at one time or another, plus a favorable credit report, and that was it. Nothing about Fallers, nothing about Ecology Now, Inc., nothing about babies. Nothing.

The rest of the trip to Earth was routine. No more attacks, no more adventures. Judy spent the time learning everything in sight, including how to function with reasonable agility in freefall and how to draw her handgun quickly enough that she might have a chance to use it should the need arise. I spent it housecleaning and performing general maintenance tasks for *Defiance* when Judy hadn't roped me into one kind of lesson or another. Baby spent it eating and sleeping. Ian had been right about that: babies that age apparently did little else than eat and sleep.

Judy was still very reserved about her reasons for leaving Mars so eagerly, but she chattered about anything and everything else with such naive friendliness that I, who ordinarily resent the loss of solitude inevitable when carrying passengers, found myself glad of her company. She also turned out to be pretty handy to have along for practical reasons. For one thing, she was taller than I by a considerable margin. There are some maintenance tasks that have to be performed in gravity, and the *Defiance*, like all the other shuttles I've ever flown, was built for people taller than I. Most people are. Judy could reach things

I'd have had to climb for, and she had such a quick and practical mind that she not only learned at a phenomenal rate, but was able to start improvising quite capably when most people would still have been uncertain about what was wanted.

Her chatter was contagious: I found myself talking more to her than I'd talked to anyone in years. She listened as well as she talked. And even outlaws get lonely. It scared me when I heard myself talking to her about Ian, including the final fight that had sent him packing. I stopped in the middle of a sentence, invented an excuse, and started to flee her.

She said, "Skyrider," and I stopped. I don't know why. There was a trusting gentleness in her voice that I could not walk away from. She waited a moment, and when I didn't speak again she said slowly, "It's natural to feel . . . vulnerable, the first time you tell someone something like that."

"Don't feed me psych-tender bullshit."

She smiled. She was being very patient with me. As patient as she always was with Baby. It should have irritated me. Instead, it made me feel curiously sad.

"I'm sorry," she said. "You're right, that was psych-tender bullshit . . . to an extent. It was also true."

"Okay, okay, big deal. We recognize that I feel vulnerable. So what?"

"So since we both know what it is and why it happens, why are you still running away?"

"From you?"

She sighed. Patiently. "Skyrider, I'm not going to use it against you in any way. Even if I could, I wouldn't. Besides, what's to use? Think about it. All you've told me is that you love someone, and you're hurting."

That did it. There were a lot of things she could have said that I could have listened to. That was not one of them. Outlaws do not hurt. "Listen, farm brat: I haven't told you a damn thing. You won't use anything against me because you don't know anything. You are an ignorant back-country farmer who's never been off-planet before. What the hell could you know about anything?"

That tone, when I first knew her, would have sent her shuddering into a corner. Now it dulled her smile, but that was all. She watched me steadily for a moment, to see if I would say anything else, or perhaps to see if I was going to explode; there was a readiness to her posture that said she was aware my mood might as easily have prompted me to hitting as to cursing. When I didn't say more, and didn't explode, she said very carefully, "You're right. There's not much I know anything about. There's not much opportunity to learn in the back country on Mars, and I hadn't been in Marstown very long when we met. But there is one thing about which I know about as much as anybody living: I know about pain. I sure as *hell* know it well enough to recognize it when I see it."

I felt my face twisting with mockery. I knew I was overdoing it, and I couldn't stop myself. "Oh?" My voice was politely cruel. "Did the neighboring farm clod reject your tender advances? Is that how you learned all about the terrible ravages of pain, back in your little sheltered farm world?"

The smile died. Sudden, deep emotion transformed her face: I had been mocking a simple farm girl whose sweet, pretty, patient smile had been born of endless Sunday dinners, family gatherings, recalcitrant children to be cajoled into behaving correctly, and all the peaceful summer nights when the children were safely in bed and the older folks gathered on the porch for a last cup of sweet herb tea before bed. That look was gone. Something deep in her eyes stared out at me from trapped distances: something fierce and private and badly wounded but unbroken. Hers wasn't a girl's face anymore. All the strength, all the simplicity, all the sadness of a pioneer woman driven to the edge of endurance was reflected in her suddenly austere face. This was a woman who had never known tamed land and quiet evenings. She had lived in the back of beyond, not in ignorance and peace, but in violence and pain. She had coped. She had triumphed. She had survived.

She brushed a wisp of her short hair away from her face and looked away from me, perhaps aware how much her expression had revealed. "You're right," she said softly. "I can't know . . . anything."

I shook my head impatiently, as much with myself as with her. "No, I wasn't right. Judy, what *did* happen to you back there?"

"Nothing." Her face twisted. She repeated it, more firmly: "Nothing. I'm sorry, Skyrider. I was intruding in your private business. I shouldn't have said anything."

I watched her, but she wasn't going to talk about it. "Okay. I can take a hint as well as the next guy . . . sometimes. I won't intrude in your private business. But if you ever want to talk . . ."

She shook her head violently. "There's nothing to talk about. Excuse me. I have to go see about Baby: she'll be waking soon."

Considering how recently she had fed the infant, I found that unlikely, but I didn't argue. She passed me

160

in the doorway carefully, eyes averted, and I couldn't read her expression at all.

We didn't speak again of back-country farmers, or of ill-fated love affairs; but once the initial discomfort had faded, we spoke more freely than ever of everything else. There was a palpable difference in our relationship. There was a new awareness between us: a new respect. We had not been equals. We had not been friends. That was changed.

I do not believe that a person's worth can be measured in the coin of her suffering: that wasn't why that little scene increased our mutual respect and drew us, albeit warily, so much closer together. I don't know what did that; I only know it happened. I had left Mars with a passenger. I arrived at Earth orbit with a friend.

Chapter Eighteen

IT HAD BEEN A LONG TIME SINCE I'D APPROACHED EARTH on a legal errand. When the Border Patrol hailed me my instinct was to keep silent and dodge them; but there was no reason to. Even an outlaw pilot from the Belt can land openly on Earth if she asks politely for clearance. I asked. They asked my business, and I told them it was a pleasure trip: I wanted to tour the artificial island cities off the coast of California. They told me the island cities had no public spaceport, and routed me to San Francisco. I thanked them politely and went where I was told.

The San Francisco spaceport was not, of course, really in San Francisco. It was in South San Francisco on landfill where there had once been a bay, and despite the air traffic control problems caused by their proximity, it immediately adjoined the San Francisco airport. For that reason if for no other, I did no hot-rodding on the way down: I was alert for instructions from the ATC computer and I followed them explicitly. The deeper we got in atmosphere, the more traffic we passed, till it was so thick I didn't know how even an ATC computer could keep track of it. I was grateful that San Francisco happened to be on the up-sun side at the time: I'd have been even more unnerved if we'd had to make that landing in the dark, where I'd have been aware of all the traffic around us, but able to see only ships' lights.

Earth landings are never my favorite. From space, it's a beautiful planet: but it's one hell of a gravity well to fall into by choice. And it is crowded. There are still places on Earth where a clandestine landing is possible, unobserved from either surface or space Patrol, and some of them are on the major landmasses and therefore useful to smugglers. But most of Earth is like San Francisco: swarming with residents on the surface; above it; and even below it, though fortunately that part isn't visible to the arriving visitor.

Busy following the ATC computer's instructions, I didn't have a lot of time to sightsee on the way down, but I was uncomfortably aware of the alien nature of the place. I was born on Earth, and spent the first ten years of my life there before I ran away from home in search of wider horizons and wilder adventures. Neither had turned out to be exactly what I had expected: but both had become a way of life for me. I no longer knew how to fit myself into the confines of Earth with anything resembling ease or even comfort.

I put *Defiance* in the parking space assigned to us and shut her down. Then I sat there and stared out the viewport till Judy finally asked me what was wrong. I had forgotten she was there. I stared at her in confusion for a moment before I figured out how to answer. "Oh . . . nothing, really. Just bemused by Earth. I don't much like it."

She looked out at the spaceport swarming with shuttles, ships, arriving and departing passengers and crew, groundcrews, and robot cargo haulers. "It isn't all like this, is it? It looked so pretty from space, all blue and white and . . . I don't know. Enchanted."

That wasn't a word I'd have used for any planet. They're just too damn big for words like that. "It's not all this crowded, but probably everywhere we're going will be. Unfortunately this isn't really a pleasure trip. Unless you want to jump ship here and enjoy the scenery. That would be fine, too, as long as you take the infant with you."

She shook her head quickly. "I'd like to see Earth, but you won't get out of giving me a ride to the Belt that easily." She grinned. "Besides, it's your infant."

"Not."

"According to Martian law it is. And I'll bet that'd hold up on Earth if you put it to the test."

I sighed. "Well, if you don't want to jump ship, I guess we won't be putting it to the test. Though I don't know what the hell we *will* do with it."

She grinned. "If you mean what we'll do with Baby, we'll take her with us, that's all."

"Great. She'll be a considerable help, I'm sure."

She patted the infant in her arms, which was feeding, and told me we needed to get more formula for it anyway. She thought about that, and her face clouded. "But, Skyrider?"

"Judy?"

"If somebody's trying to kill Baby . . . what will we do about that?"

"Discourage them."

"Oh." She tucked a fold of the infant's blanket closer around it. "That's it? Discourage them? That's the whole plan?"

"You know I don't like to be stuck with rigid schedules. It seems an adequate goal, and we'll just have to work out the specifics as they happen."

"Oh." She nodded. "Right. In other words, you don't know what we'll do about it."

I shrugged. "If you like to put it that way. Shall we get going? We've plenty of traveling yet to do today."

I had told her about the shuttles the Tanaka brothers had sold to Ecology Now, Inc., and why I was trying to track them down. Her response had been a dubious assurance that she would really like to see the island cities. She looked even more dubious now, but gamely gathered the infant and rose from the auxiliary seat to follow me outside.

"You know, you don't have to go," I told her. "You and the infant could stay on board *Defiance*. I could even have somebody deliver whatever it is you need to feed it, so you wouldn't have to go groundside for anything."

"No, I want to go with you." She hesitated. "If you don't mind. I mean, if we won't be in the way."

"How could that infant be anything else?" That made her expression so uncertain that I felt obliged to point out the truth: "Come on. It may be useful. I'm going after Ecology Now folks, and it was an Ecology Now person who stuck us with the infant. Maybe having it along when we see them will turn out useful."

"Or dangerous."

"You're learning."

"Nothing I really wanted to know."

"Life's like that." I grinned at her and popped the hatch so we could climb down onto the Earth. I had to help her with the baby's belongings, and I was quick to grab them so she wouldn't try to stick me with the baby instead. In gravity I might really do a baby damage if somebody thrust it unexpectedly into my arms.

We cleared Customs without any hassle despite the large sums of money I was carrying in various forms, mostly because the Customs people didn't see any of it. My ship isn't the only possession I own that's been modified for smuggling. Our first stop after Customs was a hock shop where I could turn some Belter goods into Earther credits. Spidersilk is lightweight enough that one can stuff quite a lot of it into a very small space. I'd picked up a bunch of it the last time I was in the Outer Rocks, and had been saving it for just such an occasion as this.

The credit that brought was more than we needed for the length of time I expected to be on Earth, but you can hardly have too much money. Judy wanted to pay her own way, but I talked her out of it pretty easily; she was working for me, and she didn't even want to go to the island cities. I told her to save what money she had till she got back out to the Belt and out of my employ.

We took the skytrain out to the cities. Judy seemed impressed with everything—the view, the weather, the people, and especially the ocean, which must have been quite a wonder to someone from Mars. I wouldn't say I was exactly impressed. At least, not in the same way as she. What I was, to put it mildly, was unnerved. Big rocks like Earth just don't make sense to me. When we were outside buildings and vehicles I kept wanting to dive for a space suit: when we were inside them, I kept wanting out of the crowds. I wanted to turn the gravity down. I wanted somebody to program better weather: we ran into fog halfway out to the islands, and from there on out, our skytrain car was an isolated envelope of crowded habitation in a strange white steamy world like the limbo of bad dreams.

The one good thing about the fog was that it made the island cities, when they came into view, look fairy-tale beautiful, with gossamer bridges and delicate towers in pastel colors; green park areas surrounded by fog-softened clusters of buildings, their windows glowing with warm light; and outdoor lights strung between them to light the walkways like jeweled spiderwebs. The ocean around the cities looked gray and forbidding, but that only served to intensify the cheerful colors of the cities.

The impression of beauty was a lie. As soon as the skytrain stopped and the doors opened, the stench of decay wafted inside like an aura of evil. From outside, shouts and occasional screams and the incessant rumble of machinery was an audible accompaniment to the stink, unnervingly well suited to it. We moved toward the door almost unwillingly. I could see that Judy was no more comfortable about it than I was, now that we were down on the surface where things weren't all fairylace pretty.

It would, however, have been difficult to decide not to exit the skytrain if we'd wanted to. The crowding passengers jostled us to and through the door whether we liked it or not. We had been gone over for weapons when we entered the train, so I was surprised that the first stop groundside was another weapons check: but they didn't take our handguns, so I didn't really mind. The check when we got on the train had been by train authorities seeking to avoid sabotage to the train. This check was by island officials seeking to avoid sabotage to the islands. If you want something done right, I guess you do it yourself.

The island cities were vulnerable, no question about that, and with MAMA on the rampage I suppose everyone was more anxious than usual about sabotage. The only thing I really objected to was the rudeness of those conducting the weapons search, and I managed (with difficulty) not to pick a fight with them about it. We didn't need a fight just then. But by the time we got out of the station I sure was ready for one.

I could have had it, too, from the looks of the people on the walkways. The universal expression was one of dissatisfaction: aggressive dissatisfaction. Belters who felt like these people looked would've been fighting already. I suspected it wouldn't take much to start at least a small fight if not a riot. But again I managed to control my whim: we weren't here for fights . . . I hoped.

From up close, the cheerful colors of the buildings were a good deal less cheerful. Rust was their primary component, at least in the area of the train station. The jeweled spiderwebs of lights were transformed into dim, sooty globes of sickening yellow strung on moldering wires overhead. The gossamer bridges were plasteel and concrete, grotesquely decorated with graffiti so thick little could be comprehended—if any of it had been meant to be comprehended. I picked out a few unsavory words here and there, and some anatomically absurd line drawings of sexual activities, but most of it was just a tangled mass of letters and lines and colors.

Even the green park areas turned out to be quite ratty when we got close to one: the shrubs were dying, the ground cover was dead, the overhead lights were all broken, and there were large signs warning against entry by unarmed individuals. The lights in the windows around us didn't seem warm anymore. From the skytrain they had made bright yellow patches of prettiness on the enveloping fog. From down here they looked gloomy, helpless against the pervading atmosphere of evil and decay.

Fortunately, the Ecology Now, Inc., complex was not far from the train station, so we didn't have to wander those filthy walkways for long. The ENI complex didn't look any more inviting than the surrounding buildings, but at least it was a goal. It provided the illusion of positive action. And it provided haven, however illusory, from the grim reality of the dying city.

We were provided access without question, and granted an interview with an ENI official without much difficulty or a very long wait. Things were beginning to look up, I thought. I should have known better.

Chapter Nineteen

THE OFFICIAL TO WHOM WE WERE GRANTED ACCESS WAS A
middle-aged man with a goatee that looked entirely
artificial on his round, cheerful, childlike face. He was
dressed conservatively for an Earther, in a crimson
suit of raw silk with a brocade vest and generously
ruffled black shirt. When we entered his office he half
rose from behind his desk and smiled meaninglessly,
an expression that did not in any way affect his
glittering dark eyes. "Ms. Rendell, Ms. Cavanagh," he
said, nodding to each of us in turn. "I'm Victory
Rajamanapua. Please be seated." He gestured toward
straight wooden chairs facing his desk and slid back
down into his own chair with an explosive sigh. "How
may I serve you?"

Judy took the chair nearest the wall and fussed
quietly with the baby. I took the other chair and
smiled amiably at Rajamanapua. "We're trying to

track a couple of shuttles," I said. "They were made by the Tanaka brothers, who sold them to ENI."

Rajamanapua put his elbows on his desk and steepled his fingers, nodding thoughtfully, as though he had nothing in the world to do but consider shuttles made by the Tanaka brothers. "I believe most of our shuttles are made by Martian firms, though I'm not certain what proportion of them are constructed by the Tanaka brothers per se," he said earnestly. "As you may know, it is only recently that we have owned shuttles at all as a company, having previously had few business dealings beyond Mars. . . ." He tilted his head to study us. "Tell me, what is your interest in these particular shuttles, if I might ask?"

"I might be interested in buying one of them. They're modified Starbirds." I told him a few identifying details of their modifications as described to me by the Tanaka brothers. "That's very much what I had in mind, and I learned from a friend that Ecology Now had purchased two shuttles like that from the Tanaka brothers."

He tapped his fingers against each other. "So then, you did not have a specific pair of shuttles in mind, but only the possibility that such shuttles existed, is it not? Or is it as you now say that you know of these shuttles?"

Cute. "I've seen them. I tracked them as far as the Tanaka brothers, who directed me to you."

He nodded soberly. "And might I inquire why you did not simply request that the Tanaka brothers build such a shuttle to your specifications? In that manner, you might acquire a shuttle even more perfectly suited to your individual needs, is it not?"

"Price is a factor." His speech patterns were contagious. "I had hoped to acquire a used shuttle more inexpensively than I might a new one."

He nodded again, his expression wholly enigmatic. "I see. An ecologically sound practice as well, this is, is it not?"

I nodded almost as earnestly as he. "So I wonder if you could check your records, and see whether these two shuttles are still owned by ENI?"

He still had his fingers steepled: now he pressed the index fingers against his chin under the goatee and separated the third and fourth fingers briefly, then tapped them against each other. "There would be no guarantee, you understand, that ENI would wish to part with the shuttles if we have not already done so."

"I understand."

He nodded absently, staring at me thoughtfully. After a long moment he shifted positions abruptly, put his fingers on the edge of his desk as though about to rise, then shook his head and punched a button on the desk surface. A computer console rose obligingly through a sliding trapdoor in the surface. He punched in a request, studied the screen, frowned, and punched in a further request. The computer's response seemed to displease him. He swiveled his chair to face a window beside his desk and stared pensively out into the fog for a long, silent moment. Baby made a fretful sound and Judy patted her absently. Rajamanapua swiveled abruptly back to face us and stared suspiciously at the bundle in Judy's arms, frowned, and caused his computer console to retract itself back into the desk. "Well," he said. "Well."

"Did you find the shuttles?" I asked.

He scowled at me. "If you will excuse me, I must investigate something elsewhere at this moment." He punched another button on his desk and a newsfax screen appeared as if by magic on the wall behind him: polarized glass had until then cleverly disguised it as an abstract hologram. "Please entertain yourselves with the news if you so wish." We had little choice but to watch it or leave the room, since it was by far too large to conveniently ignore. "I shall return momentarily." He rose abruptly and strode purposefully from the room.

Judy looked at me. "What a peculiar little man."

"And dangerous. I wonder what his computer told him." I would have asked it, but the newsfax caught my attention just then with a headline about MAMA: its founder, one Millicent B. Primm (a name any normal person would surely have changed the moment she reached the age of reason), had recently returned to the public eye after a year's seclusion for the purpose, according to MAMA, of a much-needed rest. Once back in the news, she seemed intent on monopolizing it. Her behavior, which had always been questionable, had graduated to bizarre. Most non-MAMAs agreed the woman was irretrievably insane, but that didn't slow the MAMAs any.

The headline that caught my eye did not, however, refer to Ms. Primm's insane behavior "per se" (as Mr. Rajamanapua might have said): it announced her engagement to Alexander Bone, the president of Ecology Now, Inc. That sort of behavior is not necessarily insane. In the circumstances, however, it certainly was interesting. The article beneath the headline was all about her wedding plans, with a footnote to the effect that neither she nor her fiancé expected the marriage to have any effect whatsoever on either MAMA or ENI and that neither wished at this time to make any public comment on the other's organization. I didn't blame them.

"My God," said Judy.

"Just so," I said.

"ENI has always been so . . ."

"Prissy?"

She nodded. "Exactly. What will it do to their image to be married to the mother of MAMA?"

Rajamanapua returned before I could answer that. He closed the door carefully behind him and returned to his desk, glanced at the newsfax screen, frowned, turned it off, and looked at us. "I am so sorry to have kept you waiting." He didn't look sorry.

"Did you find record of the shuttles I want?"

He tugged pensively at his goatee. "Perhaps. Perhaps."

When he didn't continue, I said impatiently, "Would you care to share the information with us?"

He looked startled, as though he had forgotten we were there, although he had been staring right at us. "Oh. I see. Well." He used both hands to caress the goatee into a neat point beneath his chin, though it had not been disarrayed by his tugging. "I can see no harm in it. No. None whatever, in the—in the circumstance."

Baby began to complain in a thin, nasal tone that I knew would soon work its way to an intolerable decibel level. I glanced at Judy. "Your brat is becoming audible."

She grinned at me and patted Baby's backside. I looked back at Rajamanapua to find him staring in shock at Judy and the infant. "Is that," he said, and cleared his throat. "Is that *your* offspring?" He looked almost frightened.

"What business is that of yours?" I said, at the same time as Judy said, "No." Unfortunately, he heard both of us. His relief was transparent.

"Ah." He looked at me with evident satisfaction. "Yes, of course, Sky—Ms. Rendell, you are most correct in your inquiry. It is not to do with me whose offspring your companion attends. Now, about your earlier inquiry."

"The shuttles," I suggested.

"The shuttles." He nodded, pleased with my powers of perception. "I find they have both been sold to a previous employee of ours, one Brenda Barraconda by name. I can provide you with her last known address, if you are still interested?" I was still interested. He provided us with an address in San Francisco and ushered us hastily out of his office without further delay.

"That," Judy said in the corridor as soon as we were alone, "was too easy. Wasn't it?"

"We'll see."

"Aren't you even suspicious?"

"I'm probably the most suspicious person you'll ever meet." I smiled cheerfully at the receptionist in the outer office and said nothing more while we walked past the museum of ecological horrors depicted in photos, holos, paintings, and sculptures that formed the entry corridor to the ENI offices. When the big front doors closed behind us and we were once again alone on the grim and gloomy walkway outside, I said, "For instance, there's no particular reason to believe he was telling us the truth."

Judy glanced around at the stark buildings and mysterious foggy shadows of the city as we walked. She shuddered. "Their museum of ecological disasters isn't half as effective as this is for showing how bad things can get."

"Reality has an unfortunate tendency to outdo art."

"I didn't even see a picture of these cities in that gallery of horrors."

"Perhaps this isn't considered an ecological disaster."

"Well, it's sure as hell a disaster." She hugged the infant against her chest and stared nervously at an approaching group of teenagers whose naked forms, caught briefly in the light of a passing roboservant, cast towering shadows across a graffiti-encrusted wall.

The roboservant turned off the walkway through the service chute of an office building. The teenagers, their bodies glistening with moisture from the fog, laughed too loudly and clustered briefly, then broke apart as they approached us. One of them was wearing a leather loincloth, but the rest wore only streaked black and red body paint and the inevitable bandoliers that Earther teenagers of both sexes, clothed or unclothed, all seemed to wear. None carried visible weapons, but quite aside from what might be concealed on or in the bandoliers, there were any number of small but quite lethal weapons they might be carrying concealed in their hands. I had even heard of Earther teen groups that went in for the surgically implanted weapons of professional assassins. Colonists were forbidden by law to carry lethal weapons, but Earthers could carry damn near anything they wanted to.

For the most part, Earthers didn't carry weapons except when they went off-planet: Earth was a very civilized place where, except in the worst slums, even the lawbreakers tended toward polite nonviolence. But teenagers have always been exceptions to social customs of every sort. Most of them are harmless. Some are not. Judy shifted Baby to free her right hand for her weapon if she needed it. I moved enough away from her to clear my right hand too.

Two of the teenagers, both male and muscular, smiled at us savagely. The other four just looked at us with varying degrees of interest from dull-witted to predatory. They all had the top halves of their faces from hairline to just under their eyes painted thick, glistening red exactly the color of blood. Their mouths were lipsticked black, their finger- and toenails painted black, and their bodies streaked in primitive patterns of black with occasional blotches of the same blood-red as that on their faces. I smiled at them, quite possibly as savagely as the two of them who were smiling, and said, "Good morning."

The smilers scowled suddenly. They all seemed to hesitate, judging us. It occurred to me that Raja-manapua, while he was out of the room, could very well have been calling assassins to deal with us: that could explain what he meant by saying there would be no harm in giving us the information "in the circumstance." As Judy had said, it had seemed too easy. Maybe this was why. Assassins come in all sizes and ages, and on Earth they could hardly choose a better cover than as a group of rebellious but essentially innocent teenagers.

One of the girls in the middle of the group smiled suddenly and quite cheerfully. "Good morning." Her voice had a musical quality, friendly and gentle. As if on signal, all the rest of them smiled, and I felt the tension going out of my body; they were genuinely friendly smiles. These were ordinary teenagers after all.

Beside me, Judy released her breath explosively and returned their greeting. They all nodded and smiled and said "Good morning" and walked on by, giggling and chattering again like teenagers anywhere. Perhaps they had been as much frightened by us as we had been by them: we were, now that I thought of it, probably as alien and dangerous-looking to them as they were to us. I had seen very few people in this city dressed like Belters and wearing sidearms.

"I'm getting paranoid," said Judy. "I thought Rajamanapua had called out a bunch of assassins for us."

"So did I." We looked at each other and grinned with the absurd good humor of survivors in the aftermath of disaster.

"Remember how startled he looked when he thought for a moment that Baby was mine?"

"I do indeed. You're too honest for your own good, you know."

She looked chastened. "I know. I realized it as soon as I said it: I should have said she was mine, yeah?"

"It wouldn't be a bad plan. Just in case somebody is trying to kill her. Make them think she's not the one they want. Which she probably isn't, anyway. And all babies look pretty much alike, so how can they tell?" I was feeling downright jolly. The walkway seemed brighter, the fog less enveloping, the graffiti on the walls less grim. We hadn't been in any danger at all, and I felt as though we'd just survived a battle.

"Not," said Judy.

I stared. "Not what?"

"Babies don't look so much alike. They're all different, just like anybody else. You only say that because you've never really looked at them, because you think you don't like them."

"I *know* I don't like them. And this one looks exactly like the one on my rock."

"How could you know? They *all* look alike to you."

We laughed together, delighted with ourselves and with having so fortuitously survived an illusory danger. That was when the real assassins struck.

Chapter Twenty

THERE WAS NO WARNING. WE DIDN'T EVEN SEE THEM COM-
ing. One minute we were alone on the walkway, and
the next we were surrounded by half a dozen men and
women who, in any other circumstance, would have
looked like ordinary businesspeople. Their clothing
was a little more streamlined than average for
Earthers: fewer ruffles to get in their way or to be
grasped by an opponent in hand-to-hand combat. But
it wasn't obviously designed for combat. They could
have gone shopping, or to work in an office, dressed as
they were, without exciting comment.

They probably came out of the office building we
had just passed; they did come from behind us, and I
had been trying to keep an eye on the walkway back
there just in case. Of course, the teenagers had dis-
tracted us; and the assassins moved very swiftly and

silently. They could have come from anywhere. It didn't matter: they were there.

I don't know why they didn't elect to laser us from concealment, or even point-blank once they were around us. It would have been a sure kill. Some assassins like hands-on work, of course, and almost all have preferred weapons they work with. None of these carried lasers, or at least none used them. Maybe a sure kill wouldn't have been macho enough for them. I didn't feel like complaining about it: this way, we had a chance.

Judy moved with the instincts of a born fighter. My impulse in her place might have been to put the baby down somewhere, to free my hands; but she knew the baby might be their specific target, and she wasn't taking any chances. She had already, when we confronted the teenagers, tucked the baby protectively under one arm to free her other hand, and she kept it that way now. There wasn't time for her to draw her weapon before the first assassin was upon her, so she slugged him instead. It didn't stop him entirely, but it gave her room to get her back to me before anyone could get between us.

That worked for the first three: neither of us had a chance to draw a weapon, but the assassins weren't using any either. I suppose they thought we were an easy mark, and wanted to practice their skills or display their superiority or something. If the six of them had tackled us at once, or if any of them had begun the fight with weapons, we would have lost it in very short order. As it was, Judy stopped one with a punch to the jaw and another with a kick to the crotch (that one was a man, and they're very vulnerable, and there wasn't much point in worrying about whether to use low blows: we weren't going to win this one on points). I killed one by breaking her larynx with the side of my hand, and did my best to put out another's eyes with stiffened fingers, but I missed that one.

The one Judy had punched in the jaw came back for more and she broke his nose for him with a punch that had so much follow-through it probably drove bone splinters into his brain. In any event he was out of the fight, as was the one she had kicked; and that left us with two men and one woman still intent on killing us.

They got serious about it. One of the men acquired a force blade from somewhere about his person and used it to chop a hole in the baby's blankets. By then, Judy had apparently had time to draw her weapon, because that was all the damage the force blade did before its owner slumped to the ground in a boneless heap and began to snore. The other man and woman were keeping me too busy to draw my gun: the woman had unsheathed a set of surgically implanted cat claws with which she was doing her best to shred my face, while the man sliced at my arms with a six-inch steel blade that he wielded with a butcher's dedication.

I couldn't hold them off. Not only had they gone *berserker,* but they were doing it with weapons that rank high among my least favorite. I find knives extraordinarily unpleasant: and the cat claws, which were an innovation I'd never run across before, were perhaps less lethal but nonetheless psychologically even more effective. I do not like sharp things. I particularly do not like them when they are being used to make unnecessary holes in my body. I've come close to freezing up when faced with a knife alone: a knife and cat claws both at once came hell of close to killing me.

Judy stunned them both and for a long moment all I could do was stand there bleeding, staring at them, and breathing. Breathing was a good plan. I think I had forgot to do quite enough of it when all those sharp things came at me with intent to do grievous bodily harm. I do not like grievous bodily harm. Particularly not when the body in question is mine.

"We'd better get out of here," said Judy.

"Yes." I stood where I was, still staring at the would-be assassins and practicing my breathing.

"There'll be Ground Patrol all over this place in a few minutes," said Judy. "I don't want to explain this scene to them. Do you?"

I looked at her. She still had the baby clutched under one arm and her stun gun in the other hand. There was nothing particularly funny about it, but I was in a mood: easily amused. I laughed.

She looked startled, looked down at herself, remembered the handgun and put it away, and cradled the baby in both arms. "Come on," she said patiently. "You know somebody will have seen this and called it in by now. Let's get the hell out of here."

We went. With no particular goal in mind, we just got the hell out of there, leaving the walkway strewn with bodies in various states of incapacitation. We turned the first corner we came to, and I glanced back at the scene of devastation before we stepped out of sight. The guy Judy had kicked in the crotch was still rolling on the ground, making a thin keening noise and clutching himself. None of the others moved.

We'd gone another half-block before I realized I was

leaving a tenuous but definite trail: the woman's cat claws had not done any damage to my face, because I'd managed to fend her off, but I hadn't fended the knife quite so well. My forearms were slashed in several places and dripping blood onto the concrete walkway. I said, "Oh, space," and stopped walking.

"What is it?" asked Judy.

I felt oddly disoriented and vague. It took me a long moment to figure out what to do about the blood. Concentrating on that, it didn't even occur to me to answer Judy; but she saw the problem, and hit on the solution at the same time I did. I reached for the diaper bag over her shoulder just as she reached into it and produced two disposable diapers, one for each of my arms.

I wrapped them tight and pulled my damaged jacket sleeves down over them to hold them in place, and quit leaving a trail. We moved again, still with no more goal than to put distance between ourselves and the fight scene. We hadn't started it, so maybe Ground Patrol wouldn't have hassled us much if we'd stayed: but we'd done a hell of a job of finishing it, and I felt confident Ground Patrol wouldn't approve. Now that we'd started running, they certainly wouldn't approve. And we couldn't prove we hadn't started the whole thing, anyway.

Getting thrown in jail for brutally attacking a bunch of respectable businesspeople would have stopped us almost as surely as getting killed. Besides, I don't like jails. And it doesn't do a smuggler's reputation any good to spend time in them. Maybe running was just an outlaw Belter habit, but if so, Judy shared it with me; and old habits are hard to break. We ran.

Neither of us was paying the smallest attention to

where we ran, or at least not consciously; but we ended up at the train station anyway, perhaps by instinct. When we began to see more people around us, Judy hit on the way to conceal my mangled arms: she gave me the baby to carry. She was right, it was the best thing we could do for the moment, but I didn't have to like it. I cradled it gingerly and tried to look affectionate and hoped, in idiot panic, that I wouldn't drop it or get it upside down or break it in any way. It seemed frightfully fragile, but she had it bundled in great swaths of blanket that helped shelter it from my clumsiness as much as from the chilly sea wind, and fortuitously helped conceal my arms as well.

The biggest problem then was getting past the security search undiscovered. We didn't know that the assassins had been found yet, and even if they had, it was perfectly possible we were not being sought by Ground Patrol, but it was equally possible that the security people would stop an obviously fight-wounded passenger just on general principles till they found out what was going on. It seemed wiser not to take the chance.

The station itself was built with an inescapable bottleneck through which every potential passenger had to pass to get to the ticket counter. From there one climbed a flight of stairs or ascended a creaking escalator to the platform, and that was where the weak link was in the security system: the platform could, conceivably, be entered by other means that did not include going through the ticket area. They did include some precarious climbing of girders and other obstacles, and possibly the security police had decided that was impossible. I decided it wasn't.

We went to the restroom first, where luck provided

us with enough time in private to put the baby down and get my arms cleaned up enough that the visible damage was only wet, torn sleeves. One of the baby's smaller, thinner blankets torn in strips provided bandages that, carefully wound and tied by Judy, partially closed the worst of the knife slashes and should keep them from bleeding much more. At a casual glance, once she had them tied in place, it looked like I had on a flannel undergarment beneath my torn tunic. It wasn't comfortable, and the muscles of both arms were damaged enough that I wasn't quite sure they'd do what I wanted them to when I started climbing: but at least the damage wasn't readily visible. I could get to the point from which I wanted to climb without being stopped for bleeding all over the walkways.

Exiting the restroom, Judy carried the baby and went through the security area to get our tickets. I went back out of the station and walked back the way we had come till I found what I was looking for: a maintenance door. I'd seen it when we passed it before, and guessed where it must lead. Somebody had to maintain that rusting structure to some extent, or the whole skytrain platform would erode till it fell on the walkways below. Obviously maintenance wasn't taken quite as seriously as it might have been, but some of it was being done: no structure built of that much metal could survive in the salt sea air for long without some attention.

Picking the lock was very little problem: that was one of a great many interesting new skills Ian had taught me. Once inside the maintenance area beneath the station, my biggest initial problem was not getting lost. I was in a maze of corridors, dimly lighted and blessedly deserted, with no clear idea where any of them went.

What I wanted was to get on the painters' catwalks outside. If they didn't provide access all the way up to the platform, the girders themselves would. I picked three more locks in three different corridors before I found the one that let onto the first level of catwalks above the island city's man-built "ground." I was outside again: I could see where I was going. The catwalk, like the corridors, was blessedly deserted: and the fog that enshrouded the entire city helped hide me from anyone on other levels, including the ground.

I had become so accustomed to the stench of the city that I no longer noticed it: now I smelled only wet, rusting metal that reminded me sharply of the asteroids despite the clear scent of sea and salt that went with it. I was a ghost in a place of ghosts: the sounds of the city were not muffled by the fog, but oddly distorted, distanced, as if they were not of my world but only the sound track of a HoVee drama. It wasn't a drama I would have wanted to see, even merely on a HoVee platform. Holovision is too real to me. I *know* it's only actors playing their parts, and I still can't handle the heavy-duty dramas. This would have been a horror show. Screams, shouts, whispers, and the rumble of machinery . . . oddly, I hadn't noticed the sounds so much when we were out there on the walkways, but I sure noticed them here in my ghost world on the catwalks.

I chose a direction and ran. If I'd guessed right, I'd find passage to the next level up through one of the main pylons. Maybe even passage all the way up to the platform. I'd guessed right: the passage was exactly where I expected it to be. But it was an elevator that had to be activated from the ground. I couldn't use it. I could get inside the pylon, where I found a little storage room full of abandoned tools, but I couldn't get into the elevator itself.

The abandoned tools included some painters' climbing belts and a lot of aging rope. I liberated some of that, and a belt that wasn't much too large for me, and went back out onto the catwalk. Carrying my new tools, I ran back the way I had come, looking for a girder near enough the catwalk that I could get to it. The sooner I got off the catwalk, the better: I'd been lucky so far, but I couldn't count on that forever. If a maintenance crew came along now, I was caught for sure: there was no way off the catwalks that wouldn't lead me into the arms of the security police if a maintenance crew radioed for them, which they would.

No way, except by climbing girders. Once I got off the catwalks onto the girders I might even be able to evade the security police if they were called. I preferred not to test it. In this fog, once I was off the catwalks I would not be seen. A maintenance crew could pass within meters of me and not notice. I put on the belt while I ran, and didn't choose my girder with any real care. I took the first one I could reach, tossed my rope over it, hooked the belt to the rope, and swung out over fog-whitened space and onto the girder. And very nearly off it again: my injured arms supported my weight all right for the swing, but my hands were clumsy and nearly missed their grip when I landed. And I still had three levels to climb to reach even relative safety.

Chapter Twenty-one

THE DETAILS OF THAT CLIMB WERE NOT CLEAR IN MY MIND at the time: they certainly are not clear to me now. Once I got onto the girders from the catwalks I was able to do most of the climbing along slanted steel beams, using the rope and belt only as a safety device. Once or twice I had to swing from one beam to another, and that was no fun at all. I remember once swinging in a perfect arc that put me on exactly the girder I wanted, from which I promptly fell because my hands wouldn't grasp it. I had wound the rope around my wrists, and that plus the belt saved me so I could try again. The second time, I caught the girder and clung to it for a long time before I even thought about the next move.

I passed a couple more catwalks on the long climb, but never did see a maintenance crew or anybody else: I was alone in the enshrouding fog with only the sounds of the city below and of my own labored breathing for company.

Once a skytrain passed overhead, shaking the whole structure so badly that I had to cling to the girder I was on while I waited for it to pass. The thrum of its electronic engines vibrated through the steel and through my bones. I didn't move for several moments after it was gone.

Eventually, somehow, I reached the platform level and paused long enough to remove the belt and leave it and the rope behind. There were no further barriers of any consequence: a low railing guarded the end of the platform, and that was all. On a clear day I would have been seen climbing over it, but here again the fog protected me. I swung my legs over it and was standing safely on the platform like any other passenger, with nothing to show I had got there by illicit means.

I found Judy at our appointed meeting place on the platform, and she had tickets for both of us, and the skytrain back to San Francisco arrived within minutes. We jostled onto it with the rest of the crowd, found seats in a back corner of the car, and were safely settled into them before I had time to really think about what I'd just done, much less react to it. By the time I got the shakes, it didn't matter: I was seated, pretty much concealed from most of the other passengers, and relatively safe, or at least as safe as I was going to get on Earth.

Judy knew me well enough by then to ignore it when I started shaking. She didn't want a fight with me, and would have got one if she'd commented. The last thing we needed just then was a fight to call attention to ourselves, but I don't always behave wisely. Judy tended the baby and kept quiet. I stared past her, out the window, and tried not to think about wet, rusted steel and frayed rope and long falls in full Earth gravity.

The fact that the whole climb might have been totally unnecessary, prompted by unreasonable paranoia, was something else I preferred not to think about. I didn't have to worry about that one for long: each skytrain car had a giant newsfax screen at the front and a coin-operated printout slot between every two seats. Judy watched the screen and, when we were almost all the way back to San Francisco, suddenly dug in her pockets for coins and used the printout slot between us to order up a hard copy on one article, which she handed me with a grin.

Not only had my paranoid climb to the skytrain been necessary, it had been successful: the article reported the brutal mugging of several prominent businesspeople, two of whom had been killed, by "person or persons unknown" and stated that Ground Patrol was confident of catching the killers soon since it was known that one was wounded, and the cooperation of skytrain and surface-vessel authorities had established that no person bearing recent fight injuries had left the island city where the two murders occurred. Ground Patrol was quoted in a lot of extravagant rhetoric about how impossible it would be for the miscreants to evade capture for long. I grinned at Judy and stuffed the printout in the disposal. It was good to know my efforts hadn't been wasted.

We didn't talk about what we were going to do next. Rajamanapua had given us Brenda Barraconda's address in San Francisco, and the CommNet had earlier given us the address of Adrienne Martin, the woman whose shuttle had attacked us on the way in from Mars. A quick study of the city map on the station wall as we exited the skytrain in San Francisco showed Brenda Barraconda's address to be nearer the station than Adrienne Martin's, so that's where we went.

I have read that in the old days, when San Francisco was still a major seaport, it was a beautiful city. There have been several earthquakes and a lot of landfill since then. There's not much bay left: the Golden Gate Bridge spans a salt marsh, and whatever additional bridges there once were have long since vanished, unneeded. Treasure Island is still called an island, but it's only a military reserve in the middle of a flat expanse of slumland that once was a muddy bay. The hill beside it, called Yerba Buena, was where Brenda Barraconda lived. It was an island, in a sense: an island of wealth in an ocean of poverty.

The flatlands between the skytrain platform and Yerba Buena were scummier even than the island cities we had so recently left. Here there were no towers to look gossamer in the thinning fog, and no tall pastel buildings to look beautiful in the distance. The whole area was covered with one- and two-story apartment complexes, most of them built of scaling stucco, and none of them recently painted or even properly mended where roofs and walls had fallen in. The residents patched the broken places with dull olive sheets of plastic if they patched them at all, and the whole place seemed to sigh and quiver in the wind that howled in through the Golden Gate. When queried, the taxi informed us that the flatlands had once been covered with towering condominiums and office buildings, but that such structures were not suited to landfill areas in earthquake country. It didn't say what had happened to them, but it wasn't hard to guess.

Now, naked children played in the cold, windy streets, listlessly batting frayed balls at each other or racing motorized skateboards against passing taxis. The taxis always won. Even electronic minds have their pride, I suppose. Ours invariably slowed to let the skateboards get even with us, then put on killing bursts of speed to outrun them. Several times it nearly ran down innocent bystanders in the process; but, just to even things out, several times the innocent bystanders weren't so innocent. We were shot at with everything from peashooters to one vintage rifle grenade that did no harm at all to our taxi but struck a couple of nearby kids with fragments of shrapnel. Our taxi called in a report and went on without hesitation, leaving the children screaming in the scarred street behind us.

Yerba Buena and Treasure Island were both very effectively fenced against the squalor around them. The Treasure Island perimeter was guarded by sturdily armor-clad soldiers and patrolling minitanks. The Yerba Buena perimeter was patrolled by armored private cop cars bristling with heavy armaments. The gate was overseen by robots, computers, cameras, big guns, and two lonely private cops wearing body armor even inside their little glasteel guardhouse.

To be permitted inside the gate, since we were not known to the cops, we had to submit to a thorough search of our persons and our belongings. We paid the taxi to wait and let the robots, computers, and cameras have their way with us. There were a few tense moments while one of the guards inside the guardhouse surveyed the camera's view of my mangled forearms and I had wild paranoid visions of somehow being identified as the escaped killer from the island cities, but after a few moments' hesitation the guard merely said quietly over the audio system, "How did that happen?" When I told him I'd been mugged in San Francisco earlier in the day he nodded, told me I should see a med-tech about those wounds and be more careful walking the streets alone, and dismissed the topic.

They made us leave our handguns with a robot outside the gate, which made me a little nervous, but what the hell? If they were this thorough with everybody who entered, we shouldn't need weapons inside. The taxi wasn't allowed through the gate, but Yerba Buena was a small hill and Brenda Barraconda's address was near the gate where we were searched, so the walk was no big deal.

It was, however, an almost total waste of time. Her estate boasted walls as heavily defended as the main Yerba Buena fence, and we were never allowed inside. We spoke over a staticky audio system to someone on the other side of the walls who told us crossly that Ms. Barraconda was not on the premises and would not be returning that day. Asked when she would be back, the voice admitted ignorance and added peevishly that Ms. Barraconda was not in the habit of admitting strangers to her estate in any event.

"I'm not sure we're strangers," I said. "If you have any way of getting in touch with her, please tell Ms. Barraconda that the Skyrider is looking for her."

"The Skyrider?" The voice sounded nasally unimpressed. "No name, just a bizarre title?"

"It will be adequate, I think. If Ms. Barraconda

doesn't recognize it, my business probably isn't really with her, anyway."

"Perhaps you should state the nature of your business. In case Ms. Barraconda asks."

"I'm looking for a pair of shuttles Ms. Barraconda purchased from ENI. Modified Starbirds."

"What is your interest in these shuttles?"

"I might like to buy them."

"Ms. Barraconda no longer owns any private shuttles. Since she joined Mothers Against Mutant Accession she has donated all her personal wealth to the cause."

"All of it?" I stared at the long wall around the estate, which was well constructed and very well maintained. "Doesn't she own this residence?"

"Well, this," said the voice. "And perhaps one or two other small things. You said it was shuttles you were after?"

"That's right. Two modified Starbirds. Originally commissioned by ENI when Ms. Barraconda still worked there."

"Ah." The voice had taken on a new quality, but I couldn't quite identify it. Whatever it was, I didn't like it. "Those. Yes. I believe I recall the shuttles you have in mind. Ms. Barraconda sold those shortly before she joined Mothers Against Mutant Accession. I assure you, if they have been used in the commission of any crime, Ms. Barraconda can establish to satisfaction that she no longer has any interest in or legal responsibility for them."

"I'm sure she can. Do you happen to know to whom she sold them?"

The voice sounded deliberately vague. "Ah, no indeed. I believe they went to someone in the Outer

Rocks of the asteroid belt, but I'm just not sure, and I certainly couldn't give you a name even if I knew it. Not without Ms. Barraconda's permission, I couldn't."

"Of course not. And you've no idea when Ms. Barraconda will be returning here?"

"I believe I stated that. None whatsoever." The voice cleared itself. "I am extremely sorry to have been of so little assistance," it said insincerely, "but I'm afraid I'm not privy to all of Ms. Barraconda's affairs. And now, if there's nothing else . . . ?"

"One more thing," I said quickly, before it could disconnect the audio system.

"What is it?"

"Can you tell me what position Ms. Barraconda holds with MAMA?"

"I assume you mean with Mothers Against Mutant Accession," the voice said primly. "No. I cannot divulge that information. Good day."

I didn't wish it a good day. It wouldn't have heard me, anyway: it had already cut the connection.

Judy, who had listened to this exchange in silence, gave me a quizzical look. "Now what?"

"Adrienne Martin," I said. "What else?"

"What, indeed?" We went back to the gate to see whether the taxi had waited for us as instructed. We were in luck: it had.

Chapter Twenty-two

On the way to Adrienne Martin's address, I paid the taxi to let me use its CommNet console, and learned that Brenda Barraconda, who had no recorded offspring, was personal secretary to Ms. Milicent B. Primm, the founder of MAMA. For the record, Milicent B. Primm also had no recorded offspring. It was unlikely that I would find the parents of either of "my" infants among the membership of MAMA, but I thought it was worth checking. If one of them had given birth to a freefall mutant, she would consider it a monster: perhaps even a monster that could destroy her personal world, since members of MAMA were supposed to be "pure" original-strain humans with two genes for gravity and therefore incapable of producing Faller offspring.

If either Barraconda or Primm had produced any

offspring at all in their lives, the CommNet held no record of it. There was no indication that either had ever even been pregnant, which I found a trifle odd since the name of their organization was *Mothers Against Mutant Accession*, but what the hell? The titles of organizations don't always reflect any truths about their memberships or goals.

"Ask about the president of ENI, what's-his-name," said Judy. "See if he's had any kids."

"Alexander Bone? Okay, but why?" I punched in the query and CommNet responded with a negative.

Judy shrugged. "Just curious. If he had a Faller baby, Ms. Primm might want to kill it so as not to cast an unfavorable light on her beloved."

"More likely she'd kill him," I said. "Not so much because he was capable of producing a Faller brat as because he'd so recently been toying with the fancy of another woman. Both these brats are pretty young. Couple of months old, yeah? That means their parents were pretty cozy just about a year ago. Primm might not insist that her future husband be a virgin—at her age, she'd better not—but she would certainly insist that he be able to make a convincing show of recent celibacy. They are Earthers, don't forget."

"All the more reason," said Judy. "Suppose he made it with a prostitute or something. I mean, hell, a year is a long time without sex, at least for most healthy adults. It would be unrealistic to feel sure he hasn't done it with *any*one. So maybe he did, and she got pregnant, and Primm found out and wants to destroy the evidence."

I shook my head. "The ENI guy on Mars made sure this kid was a Faller before he stuck me with it, remember? So whatever it is that's so important about it, it's not just that it proves somebody's been up to some hanky-panky in the last year or so. It makes more sense to think the important part is that it proves somebody isn't a 'pure' Grounder."

"Okay, then, who? The CommNet says it isn't Primm, and who else cares so much?"

"Most any member of MAMA, I suppose."

"You can't run a check on all of them. There must be thousands."

"There's still Adrienne Martin; I haven't asked about her." But the CommNet gave me a negative about Adrienne Martin too. "Oh well, it was worth a try. Let's see if we can find out who Barraconda sold those shuttles to."

The CommNet gave us the name of a mining firm in the Outer Rocks. I could find no connection between it and either MAMA or ENI, but that didn't mean anything. Of all the things that can be successfully concealed from the CommNet, business connections are reputedly the most difficult and are probably, in truth, the easiest. At least it gave us another place to look if Adrienne Martin didn't prove to be informative.

She didn't. Like Brenda Barraconda, she wasn't home and it wasn't known when she would return. Her residence was in a classier neighborhood, but for all that, it had probably cost less than Barraconda's, and it was less well defended. I could have got inside if I'd really wanted to. I couldn't see much reason to. She wasn't there, her shuttle obviously wasn't there, and records of her recent activities were probably not there. I would find nothing inside but a woman's home. I'd seen women's homes before.

When we returned to the spaceport, I asked around

and learned that Adrienne Martin and her shuttle had not been seen there for months. We bought supplies for ourselves and the baby at the Port Exchange. I had left instructions for the refueling of *Defiance,* and found they'd been followed in our absence, so that was fine. We were ready to go where we wanted and do what we wanted. All we had to do first was decide what we wanted.

I checked one other thing by CommNet while Judy was putting Baby to bed on board *Defiance.* Ian Spencer's present whereabouts were not a matter of public record. He had taken his shuttle *Lady Luck* off Home Base without any more flight plan than was required to get him out of Company space. From there he could have gone anywhere. As far as I knew or could learn from the CommNet, he didn't own a rock: but of all people, Ian Spencer was most adept at concealing his personal affairs from the Comm-Net. I wasn't going to learn anything he didn't want me to know, and it seemed he didn't want me to know much.

I spent a few minutes studying the flight plan he had filed, but it didn't tell me much. He'd gone straight out of the plane of the ecliptic, the quicker to get out of Company space, and from there he could have gone anywhere—Earth, Mars, the Outer Rocks, anywhere —without a trace. I tried to figure angles and flight paths, gravity wells and planetary orbits, wondering if one goal might have been easier than another from where he left the plane of the ecliptic, but I couldn't see any pattern. There was a hell of a big rock near his path: if he'd swung around it in a parabola, back into the plane of the ecliptic, he'd have been headed for

Mars. Depending on his speed. Of course, if he took it slower he might have got a good course for Earth. Faster, and he might have made the Outer Rocks without much fuel wasted. I couldn't guess, and I wasn't sure why I was trying. Ian Spencer had nothing to do with me. He had walked away. He didn't want me, and I damn well didn't need him.

"Who are you checking on now?"

I hadn't heard Judy come back into the cockpit, and her query made me jump. I wiped the CommNet screen almost furtively and turned to face her with what I imagined to be an innocent expression. Judging from the nervous grin she produced as a result, I guess I missed innocence by a considerable margin, but I don't know what I produced instead. Aloud, I said only, "Nobody. Nothing important. I'm fresh out of ideas: you have any?"

She shrugged. "The Outer Rocks, I guess. Only . . . that ENI guy on Mars thought Baby was born on Earth."

"She may have been, but the brat Chuck's taking care of on my rock wasn't. She's a Faller, same like Baby, but I don't think she has the Floater Factor. She seems uncomfortable in gravity."

She looked thoughtful. "That's probably really the baby everyone's interested in. . . . This one was probably just an innocent bystander at the restaurant. But if that's true, why did the guy think she was born on Earth? I mean, he must have mistaken her for your baby—"

"Chuck's baby," I said quickly.

"Whatever. And you say that one couldn't have been born on Earth."

201

"I don't think so. I don't know. Hell, come to that, I don't know a damn thing about either of them except that somebody's trying to kill one of them—or both —and somebody else seems to think either that I can prevent it or that it would be nice if I got mine along with the baby when it happens."

"Probably whoever it is thinks you can prevent it," she said almost patiently. "You know, I still think the idea that she's the kid of some MAMA is a good explanation for that monster story."

"You're right. Unfortunately, you're also right about the impossibility of tracking down the possible offspring of some thousands of MAMAs."

"Yeah." Sighing, she sat down next to me in the auxiliary control seat and stared pensively out the viewport at a shuttle coming in for a landing nearby. "Look, punch up Ms. Primm's history again, why don't you?"

"Why should I?" But I did it, and we stared blankly at the information the CommNet produced as a result. I asked for hard copy on the last three or four years, and we pored over that for a while.

"She disappeared for that rest period at just the right time and just long enough to conceal a pregnancy right up through delivery," said Judy.

"Or to conceal a budding romance with Alexander Bone, which seems a lot more likely, since she didn't come out of the rest period with a baby, she came out of it with a fiancé."

"Yeah. Well, she did know him before she disappeared. What if it's his kid? Hers and his?"

"The genetically pure pair produce a monster? That's science fiction. I've read his history too, you know. He's as proud of his pure heritage as she is: it's probably one of the things they talk about when they're alone together. The wonderfulness of themselves and their genes."

She sighed again. "It couldn't happen, could it? I mean, to get a Faller, they'd both have to be Floaters, yeah?"

"Or one Floater and one Faller. Or two Fallers. Certainly two Grounders couldn't do it: they don't have genes for anything but gravity."

"They could produce a kid with the Floater Factor, though, couldn't they?"

"I suppose they could, which would make it more comfortable in freefall than either of them, but it wouldn't make it a Faller. And that's one thing we do know about the baby we've got, and can pretty well guess about the one Chuck has: ours is for sure a Faller; she was genotyped on Mars, right? And his probably is, both because she's uncomfortable in gravity and because the guy who genotyped this one thought he was proving she was that one."

She shook her head. "It's all too confusing. I don't understand any of it." She looked at me curiously. "And I don't understand why you haven't devoted your energies to getting rid of both of them any way you could, instead of trying to track down their parents. I mean, everything I've heard about you . . ."

"I know. The legend. Look, I can't always live up to it, okay? I'm not a legend in my own mind, not really. I'm just another idiot Belter doing the best she can to look tough without actually having to *be* tough. The fact is, I don't want to hand either brat over to somebody who doesn't know what

danger it's in—or wouldn't take the danger seriously—
and might let it get killed. Besides, I'm hell of curious."

"The curious part I believe."

"You'd better believe it all. I ain't half the hero
some folks say I am."

She grinned mischievously. "It wasn't 'hero' *I've*
heard you called."

"Well, I'm about as outlaw as they come, if that's
what you've heard. But I don't eat babies for breakfast, and when it comes right down to it, I don't much
like anybody who does."

She stared in visible alarm. "Surely nobody
would?"

"Figure of speech, my innocent."

She looked sheepish. "Oh. Oh. Well. Um. So what
will we do next?"

"Head for the Outer Rocks, I guess. It's the only real
lead we have, at this point."

She looked relieved. "I thought we might stay and
look for that Adrienne Martin some more, and I have
to admit I don't much want to. I'll be glad to get off
Earth again."

"You don't like it here?"

"It's not just that. I've been reading the newsfax:
I've always heard Earth is really civilized, but it sure
doesn't seem like it to me."

"It's real civilized, most places. The big cities like
this are jungly, but even so, they're jungly in a
civilized way, if you see what I mean."

"Not frontier like the Belt, right?"

"Right."

"Well, I think the uncivilizedness of the Belt is
safer. At least, if it's more like Mars."

"Most Martians consider us pretty uncivilized in the Belt. Look at you: to learn to be a Belter you started wearing a handgun. Is that civilized?"

"But I never thought I'd have to use it."

"And you probably won't . . . in the Belt."

"But I did, on Earth."

"Yeah. I'll be glad to get off-Earth too."

"Besides, there are fewer MAMAs out there."

"They bother you?"

"I told you, I've been reading the newsfax. That bombing at the Downmars Hilton was nothing compared with some of the stuff they've been doing on Earth. It doesn't make sense, if what they really want to kill is mutants, because there aren't any—or at least not many; I suppose with the Floater Factor there are *some*—on Earth. But they're doing way more damage here than they are in the Belt, according to the newsfax."

"It's Earther politicians they want to influence, that's why," I said. "At least, that's my guess. Also they'd have a harder time getting away with some of this stuff in the Belt: we do all wear handguns, and we're very conscious of our environmental safety. The tolerances are not as great as they are on Earth."

"You mean they can do more damage with less force?"

"Exactly. Here, if you put a hole in somebody's wall, all you let in is a little rain. Out there, that wall may be the only thing between a community and a vacuum."

She shuddered. "That's scary."

I shrugged. "It's a fact. And one you'll have to learn to live with, if you're going to be a Belter."

205

She produced an excellent imitation of a devil-may-care outlaw grin. "Well, I'm going to be, so how soon do we leave?"

"Right now."

That turned out to be an optimistic estimate: whoever was tracking either baby, they'd found us again.

Chapter Twenty-three

OF COURSE OUR ATTACKERS WEREN'T PRESENT IN PERSON: that would have been too easy. I could have fought them off, even restricted as I would have been by Earther spaceport laws about the use of weapons groundside. Or I could have called Ground Patrol and had *them* fight off whoever was after me. That was what Ground Patrol was for, theoretically. That and catching miscreants like me, but I wasn't doing any miscreanting just then that they could know about, so I was safe enough from them for now.

What the would-be baby killers had done was to booby-trap *Defiance*, and they'd done a good enough job that it probably would have worked with anybody else. *Defiance* would have become an explosion of burning shrapnel and MAMA would have had another terrorist attack to brag about to the newsfax. But I'm not anybody else, and *Defiance* isn't just any shuttle. When I got the first *Defiance*, which was later destroyed in a battle with pirates, she had come to me loaded with booby traps that I had spent hours tracking down and removing by hand. Since then, I had developed the habit of checking for booby traps before liftoff no matter where I'd parked her. And that was another thing Ian Spencer had been useful for: when I'd lost the first *Defiance* and gone over this one to make sure she was properly modified for my purposes, Ian had added some innovations I hadn't known how to build into the first one. I've said he was a computer expert. I probably had the only shuttle in the Solar System fully equipped to inspect every centimeter of herself in search of unwanted alterations. Or perhaps one of the only two: Ian might have outfitted *Lady Luck* in the same way, though he had less cause, since he had fewer enemies.

Activating the sabotage-search before firing up the engines was so automatic I was hardly aware of doing it. I was already reaching for the controls when the search alarm went off and I froze, staring at it. They hadn't left me anything fancy or hard to find, but it sure as hell would have been lethal if I hadn't thought to look for it.

I took my hands away from the controls and told Judy, "Go get Baby."

She stared, but she didn't ask questions: she went to get Baby. I considered my options and called Ground Patrol. I probably could have dealt with the booby trap myself, and I admit I was tempted to, but I'd have had to explain my activities to Port Control and I'd have ended up with Ground Patrol on my hands anyway. Why not let them do all the work while Judy and I sat back in safety and watched from a distance?

Ordinarily it might have taken a while to convince them I was serious, and that my shuttle really was in danger, but MAMA's recent activities had them on edge. They ordered us off *Defiance* and had already begun to swarm around her before we were clear of the hatch. They showed up by the dozens, all wearing body armor and face guards and carrying so much equipment it looked as though they were going to open a warehouse. I told them where the bomb was, but sensibly enough they took that with a grain of salt and began their own search. I wouldn't have relied on somebody else's report about something like that either.

We were shuffled aside, into a bunker not far from our parking place, given a screen on which to observe Ground Patrol's efforts, and offered refreshments while we waited. That last was an unexpected treat, and one we had taken full advantage of by the time Ground Patrol was finally through with *Defiance*. It took them hours to remove the bomb I could have dealt with in minutes, but of course they were using the time to good purpose, examining the entire *Defiance* centimeter by centimeter, supposedly to make sure there weren't any additional bombs. I wasn't much worried about what they would find: her secrets were well and truly hidden. There were no more bombs, and as far as Ground Patrol could tell there was nothing illegal about *Defiance*, so eventually they were forced to take our report and let us go.

The report took another needless hour, during which we were questioned by six different officers, not all of whom seemed to understand that we had been the potential victims, not the saboteurs. I managed not to hit any of them, so we were grudgingly released when it became clear that we weren't going to produce any useful information.

I hadn't told them the problems I was having with babies. I didn't want to get them started on that. Following my lead, Judy had claimed Baby as her own, and I called them both passengers, to explain our presence on Earth and our filed flight plan back out to the Belt. Judy, I told them, had wanted to see Earth and was now curious about the Belt: your typical aimlessly wealthy tourist, looking for excitement.

"Well, you found it," one of the Ground Patrolmen told her. "Any idea why MAMA would want to kill you?"

Judy shook her head. "We've been over that and over it," she said. "The only thing I can think of is that my baby is a Faller, and I don't see how any MAMAs could know about that, or why they'd particularly care. I mean, what with the Floater Factor, there must be a lot of Faller babies on Earth by now."

The Patrolman glared at Baby with distaste and said with obvious disapproval, "I wouldn't know about that." Earthers will be Earthers. None of them much liked the idea that Baby was not only a Faller, but one who carried the dominant Floater Factor that would eventually disrupt the social structure of the entire Solar System; but there was nothing they could legally do about it, so at length they let us go.

I'm suspicious by nature: I activated the sabotage-search again before I started up the engines. It wouldn't have surprised me much if some bigoted member of Ground Patrol had decided MAMA had the right idea about us. But the bomb had been dismantled and removed, and no new ones had been put in its place.

Earth had rotated San Francisco onto the down-sun side by then, and Judy and I were both exhausted from the long day of gravity and adventure. It might have been sensible to spend the night groundside and lift off when San Francisco rotated up-sun again. We didn't do that. As soon as we were cleared, we jumped off-Earth at such speed that the unexpected gravity forces made Baby squeal.

"Sorry." I said it under my breath, slowing just a little to relieve the gravities, but not enough to delay us much in our flight out of Earth space. I wanted clear of Earth and of Earthers for a while: I'd had more than enough of them.

Once safely out of range of Earth, I altered our flight path slightly from the one we'd filed: no sense making it too easy for anyone following us. The new path would bring us to the Outer Rocks just as surely but a bit more slowly. We weren't really in a hurry. The extra time would let us study the CommNet and the facts we'd already gathered, and try to make some sense of them.

Before we studied anything, though, we needed sleep. Judy went to bed as soon as we were safely off-planet. I waited till we'd been on our altered flight path long enough to be sure nobody had followed us out from Earth, and that nobody was waiting for us in space, at least not where they would find us. Then I set the alarms so *Defiance* would wake me if so much as a wild rock crossed our path, and gratefully went to bed.

It seemed only moments later that Judy woke me with coffee and the offer of breakfast. The computer informed me it had been hours, and that our flight path had been clear the whole way so far. My slashed arms had stiffened so much during sleep that I could

211

hardly hold an eating utensil. Judy watched me struggle with breakfast for a while before she said diffidently, "There'd be no harm in stopping somewhere in the Belt where you could get those knife cuts seen to."

"They have med-techs in the Outer Rocks."

She shrugged. "There are nearer facilities, yeah? But it's up to you, if you have something to prove, I guess."

Once I would have hit her for saying something like that, and she knew it. She wasn't quite sure I wouldn't hit her for it, now: I could see her tensing, wondering how successfully she could fight back. It was an interesting question, but not one that needed to be resolved right then. "I don't have anything to prove. If you think it's so important, we'll stop at my rock; I've a small healer there that can take care of little cuts like this, and it's not too far out of our way. I guess I'd like to see how Chuck and Jamin are doing, anyway."

"Chuck is the one you hired to watch the other baby, yeah? Who's Jamin?"

"My best friend." I said it without thinking, and heard myself say it, and stopped with my fork halfway to my mouth. It was true: Jamin was my best friend. He was and always had been a better friend than Ian knew how to be. So why was I in love with Ian? Or *was* I in love with Ian? What had love and friendship to do with each other?

I knew the answer to that, of course. I loved Jamin and Collis. But I wasn't *in love with* Jamin. I'd never thought of him that way. We'd been to bed a few times, and it was fun enough, but there was no romance, no fireworks, no sudden beating of my heart at the thought of him, no eager excitement in his presence;

212

just the steady certainty of affection. We were just friends.

"What's the matter?" asked Judy.

I stared at her without really seeing her. What *was* the matter? What had happened with Ian and me? One minute we were talking forever, and the next he was walking away. Was that love? What had I felt when he went? Grief? Or relief? Suddenly I wasn't half sure, and I wasn't even sure I wanted to know. I'd felt a hollow ache of regret at the loss of him, but what had I done about it? I'd gone running off to Mars and then to Earth, that's what, on business that probably could have been done by CommNet from my rock. Judy had asked why I was trying to find these babies' parents instead of just trying to get rid of them, and I'd told her I did it for their sakes, but did I? Or did I do it so I wouldn't have to do anything about Ian's departure from my life?

Judy frowned at me. "Skyrider, what's the matter?"

I shook my head. "I just thought of something."

"Something about the babies?"

"Something about me."

"Oh." She looked at her breakfast. "Do you want to talk about it?"

"I don't even want to think about it."

"Oh." I could see her deciding whether to say anything more. "Are you in love with Jamin?"

If she had asked me that ten minutes earlier, I would have thought I knew the answer. "Hotshot outlaw queens don't fall in love."

"Right. Does he know?"

"I just said I'm not in love with him."

"Did you?"

"Leave me alone," I explained.

She looked pensive. "I never told you why I was so anxious to leave Mars, did I?"

"No reason to: it's none of my business."

She might not have heard me. "There were two reasons. A man I loved. And a man who loved me."

I was curious in spite of myself. "Not the same man?"

She shook her head. "No. Not the same man. The one who loved me . . ." Her face twisted. "He's a wealthy and powerful man on Mars. God only knows what he saw in me; I don't. I'm not his kind. I've never been rich, I'm not very pretty, I'm a social disgrace. Back-country trash. It would have been the scandal of the century if he'd married me." She shook her head. "Maybe he thought with his money and power he could live it down. Or . . . I don't know. Maybe the scandal was part of the attraction. He's . . . a very strange man. Not a pleasant one. He hurt me."

"He didn't want to take no for an answer?"

She managed a wry, half-embarrassed smile. "That would be putting it mildly. He was in love with a woman once before . . . that I know of. Maybe it's happened more often. I don't know."

"What's happened more often?"

She looked away from me. "The woman he loved . . . she was prettier than I. She was beautiful."

"Was? What, did he kill her?"

"Nothing so kind."

"Oh. And what about the man you loved? Couldn't he help you?"

"Perhaps. I didn't ask."

"Why not?"

"He was married."

I must have looked as puzzled as I felt. "So?

Everybody marries everybody else on Mars. My cousin Michael must have at least half a dozen wives and husbands. He wouldn't balk at one more: why would your friend?"

"That's just it: he was my *friend*. He only has one wife, but I suppose he would have taken on another if I'd asked. I didn't ask. I didn't want it, that way. I loved him and his wife both. I wanted to be part of their family. I think his wife might have wanted me to marry them, I'm not sure. But he didn't. It just didn't occur to him. I was his friend. He loved me, but not like a lover, do you see?"

I scowled at her in sudden, unreasoning rage. "Is there a moral to this story?"

"I don't know." She shrugged helplessly. "Maybe that . . . that friendship and romance shouldn't be mutually exclusive?"

The rage disappeared as quickly as it had come, and I was left with an overwhelming sense of weariness, almost like grief. "Maybe they shouldn't be," I said, "but sometimes they are."

Chapter Twenty-four

WE LOOKED UP FACTS THROUGH THE COMMNET AND DIS-
cussed possibilities all the way out to my rock, and
didn't come up with anything useful. No idea who
would have dumped a baby on my rock: no idea who
would then have tried to kill it: no idea who the man
had been on Mars who had stuck us with the second
baby, or where it had come from: no idea what the hell
was going on at all, in fact. Judy still liked the idea that
the original baby on my rock was the offspring of
Milicent B. Primm, who naturally wouldn't want
anyone to know she was capable of producing a Faller
child, but that didn't explain how it got to my rock.
Nor, really, who would be trying to kill it, unless
Primm had turned the MAMAs loose against it, in
which case why bother? If they knew she wasn't a
"pure" Grounder, what more did she have to lose?"

216

"The MAMAs might accept it and want to keep it their secret," said Judy.

"You're assuming MAMA is a political organization. It's not. From what I've seen of them and their Warriors for Decency, if they knew Primm had produced a Faller kid they'd kill her quicker than anything. They sure as hell wouldn't try to protect her secret."

"They're not all as rabid as the Warriors for Decency, though, are they?" she asked. "I mean, I kind of thought MAMA had some more sensible members; people who're just prejudiced but not . . . well, not so militant about it."

I shrugged. "I still don't think they'd protect Primm. They'd be as prejudiced against her as against any other Floater or Faller. They wouldn't want to keep a genetically 'impure' specimen in charge of their sacred organization."

"Okay, but maybe they don't *all* know it's her kid. Maybe she has just a few special friends who know, and they're trying to help her kill the baby."

"Then who brought it to my rock? Who's trying to protect it from her and her few special friends?"

"You are, for one." She grinned.

"Besides me. I got roped into this by accident, more or less. I certainly didn't choose my role as baby-defender of the year."

"Say Primm had a baby, and found out it was a Faller."

"Wait a minute. If the baby on my rock is hers, how did she even give birth to it? It doesn't have the Floater Factor. It couldn't have been born on Earth."

"No, and the guy who gave us Baby didn't know

that. I mean, he knew Baby had the Floater Factor, and he still thought she was the other baby. He thought the one somebody wants to kill was born on Earth. Maybe because nobody knows Primm left Earth during her restful little seclusion?"

"And what makes you think she did?"

"The fact that the baby on your rock couldn't have been born on Earth."

"That's backward thinking. Your logic is circular: the fact that the brat wasn't born on Earth more likely proves it isn't Primm's than that Primm spent time off-Earth."

"Where better could she go to hide an unwanted pregnancy and childbirth?"

"If she wanted to hide it that much, why not have an abortion? Quicker, easier, and no danger of producing any 'monster' offspring."

"Easier to conceal, too, than nine months of pregnancy followed by childbirth." She shrugged. "I don't know. Maybe she doesn't believe in abortions."

"But she does believe in killing babies?"

"It's not as illogical as it sounds: an abortion might kill a Grounder kid, which she would consider human. Once it turned out to be a Faller, she wouldn't consider it to be human and wouldn't hesitate to kill it."

"So why not kill it on the spot and be done with it? Or better yet, get the fetus genotyped and abort if it's a Faller or Floater, and carry it to term if it's a Grounder."

"Maybe she didn't know it *might* be a Faller. Maybe she really thought she was a 'pure' Grounder."

That possibility hadn't occurred to me, and it was a good one. "Okay. I like that. And I'll buy that she doesn't believe in abortion, and meant to give the kid up for adoption or something. But there's still a problem: she has to have known soon after it was born that it was a Faller. As *soon* as it was born, if the birth took place in gravity. I don't know if you could carry a Faller to term in gravity, but if she did, and then found out, why not kill it on the spot?"

"Maybe she tried. Maybe the med-techs stopped her."

"You're assuming they weren't MAMAs."

"They probably wouldn't have been: if she was really trying to conceal the pregnancy and the kid, she would have gone somewhere where nobody knew her."

"Not easy for a woman as well-known as Primm."

"Not easy on Earth, but she could have done it off-Earth. Which would explain why the kid was born off-Earth."

"I think your logic is going in circles again, but I'm not sure: I know my head is."

"Going in circles?"

"Spinning. This whole damn mess is ridiculous. And I keep coming back to the bottom line: why did somebody dump either of these brats on me?"

"To protect it."

"The wonderfulness of myself."

"Well, if I wanted something protected, you're one of the first people I'd think of to do it."

"Why not the Patrol? They're set up for that sort of thing. I'm not."

"They're Earthers. You saw how those Ground Patrolmen looked at Baby when they knew she was a Faller. Would you trust the Patrol to protect a Faller baby?"

"Okay, why not an orphanage? An anonymous donation, as it were. One Faller baby left in their airlock, just the way she was left in mine."

She looked pensive. "Maybe they don't like orphanages. Or maybe protecting the baby isn't all they wanted from you."

"What else would they want?"

"Maybe they hoped Primm would be exposed."

"Assuming Primm is its mother."

"Well, I am assuming that. It makes sense."

"So somebody thought I'd protect the kid and track down its mother. But you said yourself you would have expected me to get rid of it instead of tracking down anybody. You were surprised I kept it."

"Maybe whoever it was knows you better than I did."

"In that case, he'd have to know me better than *I* did."

She grinned. "People often know us better than we know ourselves."

"Oh, hell." Unfortunately, she might be right about that. "Okay. Assume the baby on my rock is Primm's. Where did Baby come from?"

"Just an innocent bystander."

"So why did we get stuck with it?"

"Because that guy on Mars—the guy from ENI—thought you'd brought Primm's baby with you, and when he checked and found out Baby was a Faller, he thought she was it."

"You've just run us into another snag. Why would anybody from ENI care what happened to Primm's baby? How would he even know she *had* one?"

"He could have been a close associate of Alexander

Bone. That would even explain why he wanted Primm exposed."

"Hold it. Bone is presumably the person from whom Primm would most want to hide her pregnancy. So how did one of his associates find out about it?"

She shrugged. "Is that really important? Just say he did. That would answer so many of the other questions."

"It wouldn't explain why he didn't just expose Primm and be done with it. I mean, he could have called in the newsfax reporters—"

"Not if she was trying to get rid of the baby on the spot, he couldn't. He had to snatch the baby—the evidence—and then how could he prove she was Primm's?"

"How did he think I was going to prove it?"

"I don't know." She sighed. "I don't know. How *are* you going to prove it?"

"I don't know that I am. I don't even know there's anything to prove."

And that, unfortunately, put us right back where we started. We hadn't learned a damn thing, and guesses weren't getting us anywhere. Nor was it really likely that a trip to the Outer Rocks would get us anywhere except to the Outer Rocks. So far, the most useful thing I had learned by dashing all over the Solar System was that Haruki Tanaka told a good story. Well, I had altered course to stop by my rock: maybe we would learn something there. Maybe somebody would have left a message, or something. Maybe Chuck and Jamin would have had better luck by CommNet than I was having . . . If they were looking for their brat's antecedents by CommNet. I didn't know that they were; they might be relying on the wonderfulness of my detecting abilities.

They might not be concerned about the problem at all. Chuck had seemed pleased with that baby. Maybe he'd be just as glad if I didn't find out where it came from, so he could keep it. But in that case, he'd have to protect it. And not on my rock. I was tired of fighting unidentified enemies for unknown reasons.

Tired or not, though, I wasn't finished with it: my rock was under attack when we got there. At least this time it wasn't unidentified enemies: the shuttles were clearly marked with the stylized Madonna with which MAMA's Warriors for Decency identified themselves. There were six of them. And there had been more: the space around my rock was littered with the debris of destroyed shuttles.

I punched in my private CommLink code and was not much surprised when it was Collis who answered: Chuck was obviously busy with the big guns, and if Jamin were there he would be helping with that, not answering the CommLink.

Collis looked relieved to see me. "Skyrider! Where have you been? We *need* you! These guys keep attacking us. Chuckie says they're trying to kill Sandy, so you better kill them, okay?"

Chuckie? Sandy? "Sure, kid. Have they said anything?" I was still far enough out that they hadn't noticed me yet, but they would soon.

"Nothing repeatable." Collis's expression was comically sober. "Just bad words about Fallers, and that sort of thing."

"Well, we'll take care of them." I said it with more confidence than I felt: I'd taken on equally dangerous enemies in greater numbers in my day, but I'd usually been in better physical condition when I did it.

The MAMAs noticed me then, and there was no more time for talking. I told Collis to hang loose and broke the connection. The MAMAs promptly opened a line to me; and Collis was right: most of what they said was unrepeatable. MAMA was an organization of pathologically prejudiced people, and the Warriors for Decency were the worst of a bad lot. They usually stuck to terrorist sneak attacks, sabotage, and bad press: methods that endangered their enemies without putting themselves at risk. But they knew how to fight when they chose to. The talk was just to distract me: four of them were still concentrating on my rock, but two of them had peeled off to come after me, and they damn near made it. My slashed arms made me awkward and slow.

Their lasers glared across my shields while I was still trying to line them up in my sights. Behind them, I saw the fire from the big guns connect with one of the other four, turning it into a brief ball of fire quickly snuffed by the vacuum of space. There wasn't time to think about that, or about whether Chuck needed help with the remaining three. I had my own problems.

I got one of the two after me lined up perfectly, and she slipped out from under my laser fire like it wasn't there. Meantime the other one tried to put a hole through my starboard shield. I rolled out from under that and came up firing, not because I really hoped to hit anything, just to keep them occupied. Neither of them even bothered to dodge. There was no need; my fire was off by a wide margin. Most pilots would have been edgy enough to jump anyway, but not these two.

Obviously, they weren't most pilots. The next thing I knew one of them had me on her laser screens and I could not get out from under. All the dodging and rolling and turning I did was a waste of effort: she clung to me like a magnet, and my screens sheeted yellow that all too soon turned sickening green as they began to burn out.

Chapter Twenty-five

Fortunately for me, Chuck was as good with the big guns as he claimed to be. I never did get an angle on either of the two shuttles after me. I didn't have to: Chuck maneuvered the big guns as easily as I maneuvered a shuttle. Better than I did with a shuttle when my arms were acting as though they were made out of wood. He took care of both the shuttles chasing me, one after the other in quick succession, before they had a chance to realize they were still in his range.

That left the three nearer my rock free to go after him, but that was okay, since it freed me to go after them. They'd got in close to my rock where it was hard for Chuck to get an angle on them, even as competent as he was with the big guns, but it was simplicity itself for me to hurl *Defiance* in a tight parabola around my rock that gave me shots at two of them on my way past. I made good use of them. I was moving so fast that none of them got a shot at me, or at least no shots worth firing, and I got both the ones I aimed for. The third and final one wasn't so easy. She was too close in for Chuck to hit, and she dodged me with the swift grace of a freefall dancer.

What she didn't know was that my rock had small guns too. And Jamin, apparently, was there: she kept out of range of Chuck and me, and took potshots at my rock that would eventually have just plain worn their way through even if she didn't hit any vulnerable spots in the process, but while we were busy trying to get an angle on her, the little lasers on my rock came unexpectedly to life. The big guns were still tracking, which meant Chuck was still with them. Not unreasonable: he didn't know, either, that my rock had smaller exterior arms. Jamin did. He used them to excellent advantage. Scratch one more terrorist shuttle. She never knew what hit her.

Afterward, Jamin opened the CommLink to gloat. "You're hell of slow today, Skyrider. Whatsamattah you?"

Maybe it wasn't really gloating. He seldom spoke pidgin except by accident, under stress. It was the unofficial "language" of the Belt: most of us spoke it some, and there were Belters who spoke no other language, but Jamin could and usually did speak flawless Company English. I think he wanted to make sure that Collis, if he spoke pidgin at all, would learn it as a second language, not a first. Which was a sensible goal: theoretically one could get any work one wanted no matter what language one spoke, if one was otherwise qualified and could make oneself understood by word and gesture, which most pidgin speakers could. In practice, however, Company English-speakers got first choice of the best jobs.

"I'm fine," I said sullenly. "Engage the synch system, will you?"

He did that without comment, connecting my on-board computers with those on my rock, so that catching and matching was done for me and all I had to do was sit back and watch. Obviously my rock was not impossible to dock with in the absence of a synch system: somebody had done it to deposit Chuck's baby in my airlock. I did it myself when I came in alone and there was nobody home. The synch system could be set to respond to the presence of *Defiance* and switch itself on, but I seldom bothered with that: dead dockings were good practice.

Today I didn't need any practice. The synch system coordinated the approach speed of my shuttle with the orbital velocity of my rock, and set us spinning in graceful imitation of my rock's rotation, then pulled us in. I rested my arms and thought about terrorists. And babies. And new friends who were hell of good with big guns.

Collis met us at the airlock, but he didn't bound into my arms with his old overwhelming exuberance: he stood where he was and eyed me dubiously. "Are you all right, Skyrider?" His voice was hesitant.

"You've been listening to your father." I reached for him and couldn't lift him, so I settled for hugging, despite Judy's presence: she knew me well enough by now, anyway. I hadn't much reputation left to maintain with her. "I'm just fine."

"Then what's wrong with your arms?" he demanded suspiciously.

"Just a few knife cuts, easily healed. I'll see to it in a minute. How are you guys doing?"

Reassured, he put his arm around me and led us toward the galley, talking so fast it made Judy giggle. At least, I chose to believe that was what amused her, and not the sight of the great Skyrider reduced to defenseless obedience by a blue-eyed boy. I didn't want a fight with her. If she hadn't expected this, she would just have to get used to it. "We're fine," said Collis. "Sandy's growing so fast you can almost see it, and Chuckie's taught me how to change her diapers, but mostly I can't because she doesn't like to be in gravity and I can't go in freefall; we practiced in light gravity and it made both of us uncomfortable but I wanted to know how, and Papa's switching back on all the alarms now but he'll be along in a minute, he doesn't have to go out on a run for a little while, he just got back. I guess you saw *Challenger II* at the other landing dock. He was just about to take her out after those MAMAs when you came back—"

"Slow down," I said.

He promptly slowed his walking pace and glanced at me worriedly. "I thought you said you were okay."

"I meant slow down verbally, Toad. I can't always keep up."

"Oh. That. Papa says I get too excited." He glanced shyly at Judy. "I got so excited I wasn't even very polite, was I? Pleased to meet you, I'm Collis, who are you?" His eyes widened as he realized what she was holding in her arms. "Is that another *baby*?"

Judy grinned at him. "I'm afraid it is. My name's Judy, and I'm very pleased to meet you. I've heard a lot about you and your dad."

Collis glanced at me. "Good stuff?"

"Of course."

"Mostly," said Judy, her voice overlapping mine. She and I glanced at each other and grinned while Collis looked nervous, whether about what I had told her or about whether Judy and I might fight each other, I don't know.

Assuming it was the latter (since he, too, knew me rather too well), I said, "It's okay. Judy and I have agreed to disagree about a few things."

He stared at Judy in complete awe and said in a hushed voice, "You mean you can outfight the Skyrider?"

Judy laughed out loud. "I don't know: I haven't had to try."

I smiled at him. "I don't make all my friends by fighting."

"Oh, I know *that*," he said impatiently. "But . . ."

"I know. Usually I do all my disagreeing with my fists. Well, not this time. Maybe I'm growing up."

He looked scornful. "You can't; you're already a grown-up."

"You're never too old to learn."

"Besides, what about how your hand was broken when we got here? That's how you disagreed with Ian."

"Never mind," I explained.

"And what about your arms, now? That was a fight, wasn't it?"

"Not my choice. We were set on by assassins."

"Really?" He sounded pleased. In spite of the years of war and near-war during which he'd done his growing up so far, he still had some illusions about the romance of adventure and assassins.

229

"Really. Hi, Chuck." We'd reached the galley, and Chuck greeted us with my coffeepot in his hand.

"You want some coffee?" Like Collis, he took a moment to notice Judy; she was being very quiet and hanging back with unaccustomed shyness. Unlike Collis, when he noticed her he forgot everything else and, after a breathless moment during which he stared like a religious supplicant suddenly granted a vision of his god, he very politely introduced himself and offered to shake hands: an enterprise doomed to failure since she had her hands full of Baby and the hand he was extending held a coffeepot. "Oh, sorry." He looked briefly disconcerted, put the coffeepot down on the table, and forgot to extend his hand again. As well, since she wasn't free to take it. "Um. Oh."

When he had introduced himself, she was busy staring at him with much the same expression of stunned pleasure he had worn when he first saw her, so I wasn't half sure she'd heard his name. Nonetheless she produced her own in a voice that was suddenly gentler and less self-assured than I had heard it before.

"There's something going on here, and I'm not sure what it is," I said. I've never been much for subtlety, I'm afraid.

Both of them stared at me as if startled to discover themselves not alone in the room. Chuck glanced back at Judy, wiped his hands on the front of his shirt like a boy, and said distantly, "Oh, Skyrider. You want some coffee?" He looked in confusion at the coffeepot on the table and back at Judy. "Would you like to sit down?"

"If Baby's asleep," I said, "maybe you want to get rid of her first. Collis could show you where the bedchamber is. Maybe the two infants will keep each other company."

Judy looked down at the baby in her arms in evident surprise. "Oh. Yes, she's asleep."

Chuck still didn't seem to notice the baby, though he understood the general meaning of my suggestion, since he was quick to offer himself as a guide in place of Collis. Judy accepted, and the two of them exited the galley in a youthful fluster of smiles and stares and unintentional bodily contacts to which they reacted as to unexpected contact with electricity.

"If I believed in love at first sight," I told Collis, "I'd say those two just got a bad case of it."

He looked after the pair with evident concern. "I've never seen Chuckie like that. Will he be all right?"

"I think so." My tone was unexpectedly wry. "Listen, would you pour me some coffee while I dig out the healer and get these arms mended? I'm tired of having hands that act like they're made out of cardboard."

"Sure." He became busy with the coffeepot and cups while I searched the cupboards for the portable healer. Once found, it made quick work of the knife slashes on my arms. It couldn't heal them as adequately as proper med-tech equipment, of course; it was only meant as a stopgap measure till one could get medical attention. But it cleaned the wounds and numbed them and got the healing process started, encased my arms in synthetic flesh that would protect them well if I didn't do any heavy work (or fighting) till healing was well underway, and reassured me that no tendons or major blood vessels had been damaged past the healer's capacity to mend.

Jamin came in during that process and lifted a mocking brow at the healer, but didn't say anything about it. "You didn't tell me, when I asked for sanctuary, that I might be putting myself in a worse position than I was already in on Home Base," he said. Collis poured coffee for him too.

"I didn't think you would be. Has it been pretty bad?"

"Those MAMAs were the only bad thing that's happened," said Collis.

Jamin lifted a brow at him. I grinned. "You're raising an honest son."

"Innocent, is more like. Naive."

"What's naive?" asked Collis.

"Somebody who doesn't try to badger me with the implication that I've seriously endangered him," I said.

"Not exactly that," said Jamin.

"Not exactly what?" I asked. "You mean that's not a good definition, or that's not what you were doing?"

He gave in gracefully. "Both, but never mind. Do you have any idea why those MAMAs came after us in such numbers?"

"The baby, of course."

"You mean Sandy?" asked Collis.

"I think so, if that's what Chuck's named his baby."

"She's not his baby, is she?" asked Collis.

"Well, she sure as hell ain't mine."

"Oh, I see." He probably did, too. "Where did that other baby come from? Is it Judy's?"

I started to say yes, and decided to save myself some trouble. "In the same way that Sandy is Chuck's. Somebody dumped her on us. I think he thought she was Sandy."

"How could he, when Sandy was here and you were somewhere else?"

"Presumably he thought I'd brought Sandy with me." I looked at Jamin. "Have you guys done anything about trying to find out where Sandy came from?"

He shook his head. "You first. How did it happen that this guy, whoever he was, got confused as to whether you'd brought Sandy with you? And where did he get another baby to mistake for Sandy and give to you? And why didn't her parents object? I never would have guessed the Solar System was so full of loose babies that people might decide belonged to you."

"Neither would I." My voice sounded positively badgered. "But as it happens, I think I know why Baby's parents didn't object. They must have died in the explosion."

"What explosion?" Collis looked excited again. "Did you get exploded at?"

I tousled his hair: a gesture I knew perfectly well he disliked. "Yes, and it was no fun, Toad. War and terrorist activities are no fun, as you should damn well remember."

He looked briefly chastened. "Oh. I know. It's just . . ."

"I know. At a distance it sounds exciting. Well, wait till Chuck and Judy get back, and I'll tell you the whole story. Then I guess you can decide for yourself."

Chapter Twenty-six

WHEN I LEFT FOR THE OUTER ROCKS I WAS ALONE AGAIN. The theory was that Chuck needed Judy's help tending the babies. The fact was that when those two met, something happened that couldn't be argued with. Love at first sight, chemistry, magic, I don't know, but I wasn't going to muck with it. I couldn't have separated them if I'd tried: if I had taken Judy with me to the Outer Rocks, she would really still have been with Chuck back on my rock. It had been almost a spark of recognition, as if the two of them had known each other in some former life or time or universe, and had been waiting all through this one just to meet again.

Perhaps not surprisingly, I was in a foul mood when I left them. Not that I had anything against love: quite the contrary, I found the concept exceedingly attractive. That was the problem. I was jealous of their apparently easy discovery and acceptance of love. I was envious of their joy.

I was, to put it quite simply, still miffed with Ian. Never mind any realizations I might have had since he left, about myself and my ability to maintain the mood of permanence Ian and I had shared. Obviously I couldn't maintain such a mood. I hadn't maintained such a mood. I was a loner not just by choice, or because it fit some outlaw image I had of myself, or out of habit, but because it really did fit my deepest philosophical inclinations. Love was attractive, certainly, but I could not really imagine myself contracted for life to one person, not even to Ian.

Errant thought: what about to Jamin?

That wasn't an option. I told myself to shut up, and I concentrated on hurling *Defiance* at the Outer Rocks as though my mission there were a race against time or the gods or destiny. It was none of the above. It was probably a wild rock chase. But I lost myself in the sound and fury of my shuttle's engines and eventually, as always, it was enough.

While I was on my rock with the others, we had all discussed the possible origin of the various babies in our care at considerable length and without any sensible result, just as Judy and I had done on the way back out from Earth. Now, utterly alone in space with my shuttle for the first time in what seemed like an eternity, I went over it all again, from the beginning.

Ian and I had been alone on my rock for nearly a month. Most of that time we had spent just playing house, though he'd had some computer project he worked on in his spare time, and I'd been doing some maintenance work on my rock when he was occupied with the computers and the CommNet. Outside, the world had been collecting itself for another war, but we hadn't known about that. . . .

Or had we? *I* hadn't: I had paid no attention whatsoever to world news since before I brought Ian to my rock, but I didn't know that he had ignored it too. He'd said nothing about it, but that could be because he knew how little general interest I had in world news. The Floater Factor's discovery had apparently been announced well before his arrival on my rock. Even if he knew about it, he might not have mentioned it simply because I didn't mention it. He might have assumed that it, like the rest of the world news, was of no particular interest to me.

Okay, so maybe Ian knew about the Floater Factor while he was on my rock. So what? So next somebody did what I would have thought nobody but Ian could do: docked with my rock without disturbing a single alarm on the way in. That didn't necessarily mean anything either. Sure, Ian was a computer genius, but he wasn't the only one in the Solar System. If he could bypass, mislead, or deactivate my alarms, so could somebody else. He'd been with me on my rock when that happened, so he couldn't have also been outside doing it.

But he could have told someone else how to do it. Hell, he could even have guided somebody in: I hadn't been lying when I told Jamin we'd been sleeping when the baby arrived, but I might have been mistaken. I'd been sleeping. I didn't know for sure that Ian had been. We'd awakened earlier, made love, and—I thought—fallen asleep again afterward. Maybe Ian hadn't fallen asleep. Maybe he'd gone to the control chamber to guide somebody in, then hurried back to the bedchamber before they docked so he could feign awakening when the airlock alarm went off.

Nonsense. Why would he? Besides, I'd been with him when we found the baby. He'd been as surprised as I was. And he was the best con man I'd ever met, so that didn't mean a damn thing. I did not like this line of reasoning. I tried to turn away from it, to dismiss it, to think of something else . . . anything else.

Like how suddenly our happy little love nest fell apart once the baby was on board. Well, hell, maybe he just didn't like babies any more than I did. But the baby wouldn't be around forever. He knew that. If all he wanted was to get rid of it as quickly as possible, why did he argue against orphanages?

Just because he'd been in one, and he knew they were a bad plan. Simple question, simple answer. So, having stuck me with the job of finding out where the kid came from before getting rid of it, why didn't he stick around to help get the job done faster? Why did he ask me to marry him and then take the earliest opportunity to pick a fight with me and get the hell off my rock?

That was a simple question with a simple answer too: he wasn't any more the marrying kind than I was. He had startled himself by proposing and picked a fight as the best way out of it. Quick, simple, efficient, and brutal. But then, nonmarrying types tended to get brutal when threatened with marriage. I ought to know.

Okay, next step: with Chuck's help, I tracked the attacking shuttles to Mars. Ian didn't know I'd have

Chuck's help, so he couldn't know I'd track them that fast. But he had to know I'd track them. It wouldn't have taken a lot longer without Chuck's help. And what was Ian doing, meantime? Depositing *Defiance* at Home Base where he'd left *Lady Luck*, and filing a flight plan for *Lady Luck* that led more easily to Mars than to anywhere else.

Yes, but I didn't *know* he'd gone to Mars. And so what if he had? I hadn't seen him there. He'd done nothing to either assist or interfere with my mission. The MAMA Warriors for Decency had done that, probably by accident. And some Belter ENI employee had stuck me with a second baby.

A Belter ENI employee who thought I'd brought the original baby with me. Who would think that except the people who'd given me the baby in the first place? Ian? He knew I was calling for a baby-sitter . . . didn't he? I couldn't remember. It didn't matter. He was a Belter, but he wasn't an ENI employee. And he'd seen the original baby, so he would have known the second one wasn't the same.

I heard myself telling Judy that all babies looked alike. She had said they didn't, but those two looked alike to me. Dark hair, dark puppy eyes, round little faces, and they were both Fallers. Judy could tell them apart. Could Ian? The guy who stuck me with the second one made sure, first, that it was a Faller, and found out in the process that it had the Floater Factor. The first baby didn't have that, and Ian knew it.

That wasn't right either. I was assuming it didn't have the Floater Factor because Ian and Collis both said it was more comfortable in freefall. But even with the Floater Factor, a Faller baby might be *emotionally* more comfortable in the environment for which its genes predisposed it. For that matter, I didn't *know* that the baby was more comfortable in freefall. Ian had told me it was, and I had told Chuck, and from then on its behavior could have been influenced by our expectations.

Damn! Well, Ian couldn't have had anything to do with the story Haruki-san had told me of the 'monster' baby's birth. That would have been about two months ago. I didn't know where he'd been then, but I was pretty sure he hadn't been either with Milicent B. Primm and her cohorts, or with anybody from ENI, and those were the two organizations that kept cropping up in this affair.

Pretty sure isn't exactly evidence. He could have been anywhere. I didn't know where he'd been. I'd never heard him speak of either MAMA or ENI, but that didn't mean he wasn't deeply involved with one or both of them.

He certainly hadn't been in the shuttle owned by Adrienne Martin that had attacked us on the way to Earth. He hadn't been at the ENI offices in the island city, and he hadn't been among the assassins we'd dealt with on leaving those offices. He hadn't left the booby trap on *Defiance*; if he wanted to booby-trap her, he could do it so the internal search system he had devised would miss the booby trap he left.

That didn't prove anything. I already knew that even if he was involved in some way, it wasn't in the effort to kill the baby. He'd wanted me to protect the baby. He'd left it in my care, and even if he'd been the Belter ENI employee on Mars, that guy had paid Judy to help take care of the baby, not to get rid of it.

"This whole idea is ridiculous." I listened to the echo of my voice in the empty cockpit and resisted the impulse to hit something. Damn it, the idea *was* ridiculous. I was groping in the dark, trying to find some solution to an absurd mystery that had nothing to do with Ian, and because my thoughts were centered on Ian I had managed to involve him, at least potentially, in the mystery. Obviously he had nothing to do with it: why would he?

I punched up the CommNet and looked for traces of Ian in the records of both MAMA and ENI. There were none, of course. He could be president of both agencies and still leave no traces of his existence in their records. (The thought of him as president of both agencies—which might in effect make him *both* parents of at least one of the two babies, if Judy's theory about Primm and Bone was right, almost made me laugh. Almost, but not quite.)

It occurred to me that I could eliminate Ian with certainty from at least one possible role in the mystery, and I called my rock and asked for Judy. When she came on-line, I asked her to go to the bedchamber and look in a certain drawer at a certain hologram, then come back to the Comm Link.

While she was gone I tried to chat cheerily with Collis, but my heart wasn't in it. He told me they had found, by CommNet, a possible lead on the parents of the baby from Mars. They had been able to find record of a couple who had brought a baby to the restaurant that night and died in the bomb blast. Their baby had not been found. I expected we might reinstate that one with whatever family it had left without much trouble, and Collis told me they were working on it. They were trying to get in touch with possible surviving relatives, and were even now waiting for a call-back. I tried to look pleased, but I hardly heard what he was saying. I kept glancing beyond him in the screen, watching for Judy's return.

I knew the answer as soon as I saw her. She waited for Collis to finish saying something to me, and I don't know what he said, because I could see her face and I knew what she was going to say and I didn't want to hear it. Ian was involved, all right. My wild, paranoid idea wasn't so wild and paranoid after all. And if he was involved in one little aspect, how much more deeply was he involved elsewhere? *What was he doing to me?*

Judy didn't say anything when she stepped up to the screen again; she just looked at me. I said, reluctantly, "That was the ENI Belter you saw on Mars?"

She nodded, looking sympathetic and puzzled and maybe shocked. In the hologram, which Ian had never known I'd taken, we had been in each other's arms. Fully clothed, mind you, but clearly affectionate. I'd instructed the computer to take it when we entered the galley one night, and I'd stage-managed our entrance so it would get a good shot of both of us. Jolly little love-nest behavior. Playing house. The happy couple. *Damn!*

Just to punch in the final rivet, I said carefully, "The one who paid you to help care for Baby and me?"

She nodded again. "Who is he, Skyrider?"

If she'd been in reach, I would have hit her. I couldn't stand the look of pity in her eyes. Since I couldn't hit her, I borrowed one of Ian's own sweet, deadly smiles and said in a voice I scarcely recognized, "Ask Jamin. It ought to give him a laugh when you tell him where you saw the guy before."

"Skyrider—"

I cut the connection, and listened to the Gypsies sing to me of stars.

Chapter Twenty-seven

ADRIENNE MARTIN STOPPED ME BEFORE I REACHED THE mining company in the Outer Rocks that supposedly had bought the two shuttles from Brenda Barraconda. I recognized Martin's shuttle before she fired on me, and I dodged skittishly out of her way, but there was no real need: her shot was not meant to do worse than singe my nose. Apparently she wanted to talk. The Comm Link signaled shrilly for attention, voice only.

Wary of traps, I scanned the screens and could see only one other shuttle anywhere nearby. It was headed our way, but still well out of range, so I kept an eye on it and opened the Comm Link to hear what Martin had to say. Having heard her once before, I didn't expect much, but I was curious. This time at least I got more than foul language. She opened with a diatribe against Fallers, but it segued into a diatribe against Milicent B. Primm that took me wholly by surprise.

"I thought you were a friend of Primm's," I said.

She threw another laser beam at me, this one a little more wickedly aimed than the last. If I hadn't dodged, it might have done me serious harm. I had slowed when I met her, and we were riding inertia still more or less in the direction I had been headed, but dodging that shot put me off course and I didn't bother to correct. I wasn't in a hurry. "I'm no friend of that damn murderous pig," Martin shouted. "I'll kill her, I'll kill that sleazy bitch; just as soon as I'm through with you I'm going to find her and kill the hell out of her."

Our new course was bringing us more quickly near the other shuttle I'd been keeping an eye on, and I put the screens on full magnification, trying to identify it, but we were still too far away. "That's nice," I told Martin. "And would you mind telling me what exactly your business is with me?"

"I want to know where you're keeping Ian's baby."

Something cold and hard and heavy settled in the pit of my stomach and stayed there, generating an icy calm that held my voice steady as I repeated, "Ian's baby?"

Martin laughed. "Old Alex thinks it's his, but I know better. Milicent's baby, you stupid half-breed. Why did you suppose Ian went to so much trouble to protect the little monster? Did you think he was doing it for Alex, for old times' sake or something? You don't know Ian as well as you thought you did, if you thought that. Ian doesn't do *any*thing for old times' sake. At least, not anything kind."

"Milicent Primm's baby is also Ian Spencer's? He fathered it?" My voice sounded dangerous, even to my own ears.

"That's what I said, lackwit. And I want to know where you're keeping it. I want to know *now*." She tossed another shot across my shuttle's nose, and it was all I could do to dodge without returning fire.

"Sure, okay, it's nothing to me," I said. "But first, how about telling me a little more about what's going on, will you?"

"I want that baby," she said suspiciously.

"Sure, sure. And I'll trade it for just a little more information."

It must have occurred to her that information would do me little good once she'd killed me, and of course she had every intention of killing me as soon as I told her where the baby was. She laughed abruptly and said almost eagerly, "Okay, sure. What do you want to know?"

What *did* I want to know? She had already confirmed that Ian was about as deeply involved in this tangled affair as he could get. She had said "Alex"—which presumably meant Alexander Bone—thought *he* was the baby's father rather than Ian, and while that didn't explain the unlikely pairing of Primm and Bone, it might explain why there were ENI people as well as MAMAs after the baby. The MAMAs would be intimates of Primm who for one reason or another were willing to ignore her "impure breeding" and help her kill the infant in an effort to conceal her impurity and protect the sanctity of their organization. The ENIs would be people who had somehow learned of the baby's existence and hoped its destruction would also destroy the liaison between Bone and Primm. Not many ENIs would want ENI in any way connected with MAMA, and some of them might go to bizarre extremes to prevent it. The radical left might do worse than kill infants to prevent their leader from marrying a leader from the radical right.

We hadn't much time left alone: that other shuttle was approaching more quickly now, though Martin didn't seem to have noticed it yet. I still couldn't make out its markings, even at maximum magnification. "What's your place in all this?" I asked Martin. "I guess Bone, Primm, and Spencer are united by their illicit love affairs, and I don't much give a damn where those came from, but where do you come in? What's your interest in the baby?"

"I don't give a damn about the baby, except I want it dead. Ian never should have screwed that pig. We were getting enough money from them just for keeping quiet about their histories. But he always wants his little extras."

"You . . ." My voice faltered and I cleared my throat. "You and Ian were getting money from . . . whom? Bone and Primm?"

"Sure, did you think he was with me out of love? Let me tell you, Ian Spencer never in his life loved anybody but Ian Spencer." Her voice took on a new, oddly triumphant note. "Or didn't you know he was with me at all? Did you think he was your own special conquest? Honey, nobody's ever conquered Ian Spencer that way, and nobody ever will. Yours wasn't the first little love nest he bedded down in for profit."

"What profit? He didn't take anything from me." I thought bleakly that I should, after all, have looked inside Martin's San Francisco home. It might have given me more answers than I wanted to know.

She laughed. "Have you looked at your CommNet bill lately? Or checked your secret stores? Believe me, your *Defiance* wasn't empty when he left your rock in it, but I bet it was when he deserted it at Home Base. You owed him, after all; he won your credit account fair and square, and they closed it down before he could spend it."

"He didn't win it exactly fairly." My defense of that was automatic and absentminded. I wasn't thinking of credit accounts won or lost. "That bet was about as crooked as a bet can get. If you know Ian, you must know that."

"Sure, I know it. But you fell for it, and you lost. The account should have been his."

"You still haven't told me where you fit into all this. You said nobody could conquer Ian through . . . love. Does that include you?"

"Sure, honey. There's no love lost between Ian and me, believe me. It just happens that I own the son of a bitch."

"You . . . *own* him?"

"I bought him out of the orphanage, I taught him his trade, I led him to the suckers he could fleece. I *made* Ian Spencer. And he's mine, all mine."

I had been so caught up in what she was telling me that I hadn't even wondered, before, why she kept the communication to a voice-only circuit. Now I wondered. "What the hell do you look like, anyway, that you have to buy yourself a man? Or do you have some other reason for missing out on the more ordinary ways of acquiring one?"

"I look okay, honey," she said sweetly. "And that's all you need to know. Now where's that monster brat he brought you?"

It occurred to me that her voice was oddly familiar, but I couldn't place it. "I'll tell you in a minute. First I want to be sure I understand all this. You're telling me that Ian and Alexander Bone were both . . . sleeping with Milicent Primm, right?"

She laughed. It was not a pleasant sound. "You're pretty prim yourself, aren't you, honey? They weren't just sleeping with the bitch, they were *screwing* her."

"Okay. And they both think they're the father of her kid. What makes you so sure it's Ian?"

She lowered her voice, an oddly chummy gesture. "I just happen to know that prissy Primm bitch a little better than some people think, that's all. I know the dates. And I saw that monster she gave birth to. It had brown eyes."

"But Ian's are blue."

"And so are Primm's. And so are Alex's. What you don't know and they don't realize is that Ian's parents had brown eyes. Yes, that's right, I know who his parents were. Oh, don't think about it, they were nobodies. Not anything like as important as Alex's parents. His were blue-eyed, of course. He could only pass on blue-eyed genes. Don't bother questioning it. I know the genetic history of the whole damn bunch of them. Hell, I knew Primm was a half-breed, and that's more than *she* knew."

"You knew she was a Floater?"

"Is that what you call yourselves? Cute. Floaters. Like a disease of the eyes. Yeah, I knew Milly wasn't the perfectly pure genetic wonder she claimed to be."

"Why didn't you tell her?"

"Why should I? What's it to me?"

"Or maybe you *did* tell her. Maybe you used it, maybe that's why she was paying you money. You said she and Bone were both paying you and Ian money."

"Sure, but not for that. We know a lot more about

them and their organizations than that. Didn't you ever read my novel?"

"I'm afraid I missed that pleasure."

"You should have read it. You'd have learned a lot. Oh, I didn't use their real names, but you might have recognized them. *They* did. They got in touch with me right away after it was published. Both of them. They wanted to be sure I didn't start telling the world who they were. Of course I told them I wouldn't. For a price."

"Sweet of you." The other shuttle was in hailing range now, but had made no effort at contact. She was a sleek, sweet Hawke-14, like Ian's *Lady Luck*, and for a wild moment I wondered if it might be Ian coming to explain away this madwoman's nonsense, but how could he? She might be a madwoman, but I didn't doubt the story she was telling. It fit too well with what I already knew. Even if the approaching shuttle were *Lady Luck*, Ian could not explain away the truth.

"Now where's that filthy brat?"

"In a minute, in a minute." There was yet another shuttle coming into range behind the Hawke-14. This was becoming quite a little party. I still couldn't read the reg. marks on either of them. "First tell me why—and how—it ended up on my rock."

"What, the baby? Ian, both counts. He wanted it protected, and he fondly imagined you could do it. He knew Milly and I would be after it at least, and possibly half Milly's MAMAs as well. Not to mention a bunch of Alex's buddies who found out about it. He must think a lot of your abilities, bitch; you were the second place he tried to hide the brat, and he hasn't taken it from you yet."

"What was the first place?"

"Some shipbuilders' farm on Mars he thought nobody'd think of. But that bitch Barraconda remembered it from her days with ENI. She got Alex's buddies and they went after it, so Ian had the kid moved to your rock."

"Where did Barraconda come from?"

I could almost hear her shrug. "She used to sleep with Alex, that's all. Now she sleeps with the Primm bitch. See how accommodating I am? I'm using your prissy little euphemism for you. Now where the hell is that brat? Is it still on your rock?"

"How did Ian get it to my rock?"

"He hired somebody to carry it there. Come on, come on, where is it?"

"How did they get through my alarms?"

"Christ, woman, what have you got for brains? Ian was on your rock, wasn't he?"

"He led them through?"

"He didn't need to. He keyed all the alarms to one code and, believe me, if he hadn't rekeyed them afterward I wouldn't be here playing games with you; I'd go knock your rock the hell out of the Belt just for the fun of it. Is the brat still there?"

"Why do you want it?"

"I told you. I need to kill it."

"Need"? "Why do you want to kill it?"

"I told you that too. Because it's a monster."

"Fallers are monsters?"

"Even you ought to be able to figure that out. But then, you're a monster yourself, and I've heard your best bed-buddy besides Ian is a Faller, so I guess you're not real particular."

"Fallers and Floaters aren't human, right? Only Grounders are human, is that it?"

"Anybody with half a brain can figure that out."

"So Ian's baby is a monster because it's a Faller. You know how you get a Faller. Each parent contributes a determinant gene, and they *both* have to be for freefall to turn out a Faller. That means the parents have to be Fallers or Floaters. Not Grounders."

"Yeah, yeah, so?"

"So that baby's parents are both monsters too."

I expected a reaction, but not a total abandonment of sanity. She literally tried to ram *Defiance* with her quick little Starbird, and it took me so much by surprise that she damn near made it. It would have killed us both, but probably she hadn't thought it through to that. She didn't seem to be very good at thinking things through. Her verbal response was completely unprintable, that part of it which was intelligible at all.

I was so bemused I didn't even try to kill her. I just dodged and stared while she tried to kill herself on my shuttle's hull. The Hawke-14 slid up to us, and it was Ian's *Lady Luck*, and I stared at that too.

Ian's voice stopped Martin as abruptly as one can stop in space. She rode inertia at an angle away from me without verbal response to him, while he repeated her name with infinite gentleness and love. "Adrienne. Adrienne, stop that, you'll hurt yourself. Adrienne." She thought he didn't love her. She was wrong.

The other shuttle that had been coming in behind Ian was rushing in now, and I could read its reg. marks but I didn't recognize them or it. I turned *Defiance* a

251

little, so I had them all under my guns, and I waited. I felt cold and tired and silly and scared. The world was a barren place in which not even Gypsies sang.

Chapter Twenty-eight

THE SHUTTLE THAT HAD COME IN BEHIND IAN'S *LADY LUCK* was piloted by Alexander Bone. It was old home week. He opened the Comm Link to Martin and made no effort to conceal his transmission from Ian or me. His face on the newsfax screen had been arrogant and self-assured. On the Comm Link, now, it was drawn, almost frail, the dark skin sunken in bruised hollows around his incongruously pale blue eyes and pulled tight over his cheekbones.

I didn't hear what he said to Martin, but apparently Ian did. He, like Martin, had kept the visual off during his earlier broadcast: now, speaking to Bone, he flipped on the visual and my Comm Link screen split in two to show them both. "She's Adrienne now," he said. "She doesn't remember."

I heard the words, but they didn't make any sense. Bone slowed his shuttle to ride effortlessly in silence beside *Lady Luck*. I backed off cautiously, keeping them all three under my guns, half my attention on the exterior view and half on the Comm Link screen where a dark face and a pale one side by side seemed to stare at me, their eyes transmitting secrets I could not understand. Of course they were, in fact, staring at each other over their own Comm Links. Whatever they had to say to each other did not seem to require words. I saw an odd sympathy and understanding between them, but could not guess what it was about.

"I remember *every*thing," shouted Martin. Bone's presence seemed to excite her, though with what emotion I couldn't guess. "It's not that easy, don't you ever think it will be. I remember, all right. I remember the orphanage, Ian. I remember what it was like, I remember how I got out, and much more important, sweetheart, I remember how *you* got out. And you, Alex, I remember your parents. Do you remember them? Even if you don't, you know who they were. Don't you think I'll ever forget it, and don't think I'll let *you* forget it either."

"Adrienne," said Bone.

Her voice took on a peculiar singsong quality. "Emma and Arthur Bonetti, founders of the first and last nuclear and toxic waste recycling city in space—"

"Adrienne," said Bone.

"—and murderers of the entire population of—"

"Adrienne!" said Bone. But if what he meant to do was keep me from realizing what she was talking about, he was too late. I didn't need the name of the city-colony Emma and Arthur Bonetti had founded and then killed in the most spectacular example in history of ecological disaster combined with bureaucratic idiocy, greed, and suicidal obstinacy. Emma and Arthur had died with their city, with the fifty thousand inhabitants they had bought and lured from Earth with promises of easy living and quick wealth. What the colonists had got was death, and it was neither easy nor quick. The whole scheme had been slipshod, poorly planned, and foolishly administered, an entire colony built and based upon the principle that safety margins destroy profits.

"Why didn't you die with them, Bone?" Perhaps I shouldn't have asked: it was by no means kind. But I was curious, and I'd never been given the impression that Bone was a particularly kind man, himself.

His eyes flickered as his Comm Link screen split to accommodate my transmission. "I was a baby," he said. "I was ill. I'd been sent to Earth." There was almost a note of pleading in his voice, but no sign of it in his hard blue eyes like shiny marbles in the dark of his face.

Martin laughed suddenly. "That's right," she said, her voice pulled high and thin by unspeakable, unknowable tensions. "He was the first victim, and the only one sent to Earth for medical care."

Bone's face was expressionless, his eyes cold, his voice flat. "It was my illness that alerted Earth to the danger to the colony. They tried to tell my parents, to get them to warn the population, to evacuate, to save lives. But that would have meant a loss of profits." He looked suddenly, unutterably weary. "And now that you know, if I don't kill you, you'll extract your price, of course."

"That's all right, Alex, I'm going to kill her."

Martin said it cheerfully, in much the same tone as one might use to announce the time of day. "But first I have to find out where Ian's baby is."

Bone looked startled. "Ian's baby?" His eyes flickered again, from my image to Ian's on his screen. "Did you say Ian's baby?"

"Of course, sweetie. Didn't Milly tell you? But no, of course she wouldn't. She'd want to play the two of you against each other, let you both think it's yours."

Bone's face settled back into the lines of taut and weary concern it had worn when he arrived. "It doesn't matter. Adrienne . . ." He seemed to have trouble with her name. "Adrienne, come home with me. You don't need to kill the baby."

"I do, I do!" She laughed like a child invited to the circus. "I need to kill it. It's a monster. Ask Milly: she'd tell you. Oh, you should have seen her face when they told her what it was!"

Ian spoke suddenly, his voice dangerously gentle. "Did you see her face, Adrienne?"

"Don't start," said Bone.

"I don't remember," said Martin, her voice suddenly less assured. "I think I must have."

"It doesn't matter," Bone said softly. "It doesn't matter . . . Adrienne. Just come home with me. Come home."

"To hell with that noise. I have work to do. You want a woman, go find Milly." She flipped her shuttle and fired on me so suddenly I barely dodged in time. I returned fire automatically, but without intent to kill; I just wanted to get her to back off. She didn't, but she did hold her fire. "You never told me," she said. "Is that baby still on your rock?"

"I don't know; I haven't been there in a while."

"You know what you told them to do with it." Her voice, naggingly familiar, was hoarse with rage.

"You're right, I do. Listen, who the hell are you, anyway? Why don't you show your face?"

She laughed. It was a gay, tinkling, party sound, without a hint of anger in it. "It wouldn't do you any good," she said. "You're dead, and so's the brat." She fired again.

This time I was ready: I dodged easily, and returned fire with every intention of killing her. She was getting on my nerves.

She skittered sideways with another gay little laugh, but she wasn't quite quick enough: my shot burned her port shield badly. It flared and sputtered and sheeted ugly, dying green. One more shot in the same place would have killed her. I didn't get a chance to make it. Both Bone and Ian hurled their shuttles between hers and mine. On the Comm Link screen, both their faces looked worried and intent and very, very dangerous.

"Leave her alone," said Ian. I didn't know whether he meant me or Martin. Martin answered.

"Why, is she that good in bed?"

"No more killing, Adrienne. There's been enough."

"What, one of you has a conscience?" I shouldn't have said that, but the three of them had just about used up all the patience I had.

Maybe none of them heard me, anyway; it was Ian's remark Martin responded to, and the response stunned me. She said in a clear, cold, calm, and completely sane voice, "My name is not Adrienne." She flipped her shuttle again and spun away from the three of us in a sudden curving dive that turned into an elegant, dwindling arc back toward the center of the Solar System. I tried to follow, but both Bone and Ian blocked my way. I would have had to kill them to get past them, and I wasn't quite cross enough with either of them to do that . . . yet.

Instead, I called after Martin, "Where are you going?"

Her only answer was sweet, jolly laughter.

"She'll go after the baby," Bone said urgently. He was speaking to Ian, but I answered anyway.

"If you hadn't stopped me, she wouldn't have a chance."

"That's the point," said Ian. "You'd kill her."

"You'd rather she killed your baby?"

His face did something I'd never seen it do before: it expressed genuine, naked emotion. Those jeweled mirror eyes were haunted, the curve of his cheek oddly hollow under suddenly white cheekbones, and his lips twisted in a grimace not at all like a boyish smile. "Oh, God," he said. "Oh, God."

"I could still stop her."

Bone's shuttle jumped at me, his face a harsh region of planes and dark shadows. "No."

Ian echoed him, not as strongly but still with deadly certainty. "No, Skyrider. You can't kill her."

"I *could*."

"You won't."

"You mean, not unless I kill you first."

He nodded slowly. "Maybe you could do it. You're as good with a shuttle as I am with computers. But that's what you'll have to do to get to her: you'll have to kill both of us." His gaze flicked sideways on the screen, as if to confirm Bone's support.

Bone wasn't backing down. He looked as torn and as haunted as Ian, but one thing they seemed firmly agreed on was to protect Martin from me. "I can't let you kill her," he said slowly.

"So you'll let her kill the baby, and probably my friends as well."

"They . . . Oh, *space*!" Ian looked again at Bone's image on his screen. "They'll kill her," he said. "We've got to . . . somehow, we've got to stop her."

"Not by killing." Bone was glaring at me when he said that, and I could tell he was deciding whether to obviate the danger by killing me.

I tensed my hands on my controls and said very gently, "Try it, Earther."

"Maybe she'll have sense enough to call in her Warriors for Decency," said Ian. "In a large enough group, they could take that rock."

I stared. "You really would rather let her kill six people, including two babies, one of them your own, rather than risk any danger to her life? What the hell *is* she to you? She can't be *that* good in bed."

He shook his head slowly. "It's not that."

"We grew up together," said Bone. "We're . . . family."

"Some family." I realized suddenly what Ian had said. "Wait a minute. *Her* Warriors for Decency? I thought that organization belonged to Primm, not Martin."

Bone produced a frayed and weary smile. "Haven't you figured it out yet, Skyrider? Primm *is* Martin."

I stared, working it out. "She was . . . what? Pretending to be somebody else? She pretends to be Martin? Is that what you're saying?"

"What he's saying," Ian said slowly, "is that Milly is stark, raving mad."

Bone glanced at him: a killing look. "So might you be, if you'd—"

"I know, I know." Ian looked at me, his eyes gone flat and guarded again, and yet hoping for understanding. "It was hard for her, Melacha. She . . . she got out of the orphanage before we did. By—"

"By screwing the right men," Bone said harshly.

Ian shook his head. "Not so right, as it turned out. The one who bought her out of the orphanage wanted a willing slave. When he tired of her, he sold her to a Faller who . . . treated her badly. She was eight years old when she killed him." He drew a breath. "He hadn't made a will. She made it for him, and it stood up in court. He was rich. She used the money to buy us out, and . . . Some of what I told you before is true. I did grow up in a gutter; Milly wasn't wholly sane, ever. She couldn't keep track of things. We tried to help her, and she did her best for us, but there were times—"

"The point is," said Bone, "we grew up. I founded ENI, I suppose in reaction to . . . what my parents had done. Milly founded MAMA: that Faller had really hurt her. And Ian did what he does best."

"Using people," I said.

"Using computers," Bone corrected mildly. "He helped us all get started, and stay legal."

"Or at least not arrested."

"Exactly." Bone seemed pleased with my understanding. "And he helped us stay solvent."

"And you're all three siblings under the skin, so you'd sooner see the rest of the universe go down in flames than stop Milly from burning it down, if the only way to stop her is to kill her."

"Harshly put." Ian had his old composure back,

and with it one of his sweet, deadly grins. "But accurate enough. You may as well face it, Melacha. We're not going to let you stop Milly."

"Then stop her yourselves, damn you. That's *your baby* she's trying to kill, Ian. Don't you care about that?"

He shrugged, and there were shadows in his eyes but not a hint of regret in his voice. "We can always have another."

"Space and damnation." I looked at him, studying the face I had thought I knew so well. "You're as crazy as she is. You know that, don't you?"

He shrugged again. "Maybe. Does it matter?"

I still couldn't kill him. I could not. I tightened my hands on the controls, and I had them both under my guns, and I could not pull the firing button.

I did the next-best thing: I kicked in the thrusters and hurled *Defiance* in a crazy dive right under the two of them, taking the chance I could get enough of a lead to get away before they realized what had happened, flipped their shuttles, and fired on me. I had damn little chance of making it. Still, at the time, it seemed the logical thing to do. I suppose, to Ian, it seemed just as logical to kill me. He certainly tried.

Chapter Twenty-nine

HE GOT IN ONE GOOD SHOT, AND IT WAS DAMN NEAR ALL HE needed: he was hell of quick. He got a killing angle on my starboard shield and I couldn't shake him. He tracked with me, keeping fire on that shield while it sparked and spat and sheeted blinding yellow like sudden sun outside my hull till I thought it must burn out. Maybe if I'd turned and fought I could have killed him: it was the way I usually solved that sort of problem, and so far I had always made it. This time I didn't even try. I dodged and jockeyed and ran, straining *Defiance*'s engines in evasive tactics she was never designed to perform, and just as my starboard shield sheeted unholy green and died I finally spun out from under him in a twisting, rolling dive he could not match.

In that last instant his laser had punched a hole right through *Defiance*'s hull, but it wasn't a killing blow, and then I was free of both of them and running for my rock in open space with the two of them, Ian and Bone, trailing behind and losing ground, but still coming . . . and still, uselessly, firing their lasers after me.

When I was sure they were falling behind, I took time to grab a bottle of sealant, upend it, and spray the holed bulkhead before escaping atmosphere could rip the hole any bigger. The reek of sealant mixed with the stench of burnt electronics, and the air filter fans hummed busily in their effort to clear my reduced atmosphere. I couldn't tell how much damage Ian's shot had done to anything besides the shield and the bulkhead. The computer was investigating and printing out damage reports, but I was too busy watching the screens to pay it any heed. I knew *Lady Luck* couldn't catch me in a straight run, but I wasn't sure about Bone's shuttle: he was flying a modified Falcon that looked a lot like *Defiance*, even to her enlarged engine nacelles. It was possible he had the same malite conversion drive I had, and that could make it hell of hard to outrun him.

If I'd been anybody else, I'd have been dead already, the way I'd been behaving. *Defiance* shouldn't have been able to do what I'd made her do, and it wasn't quite clear why I'd bothered. It would have been easier to kill Bone and Ian than to dodge them. If they'd been anyone else, I would have. Instead, I was running, and not half sure I could outrun them, or why I had done it that way.

Maybe I did it because of what Ian had said earlier: that there had been enough killing already. If so, it wasn't much of a reason. I knew if I got away from them, I was heading for more killing. I had let too many people into my life: Chuck and Judy, Jamin and Collis, and two babies: six hostages to fortune, and I was going to have to kill somebody else's hostages to keep mine alive.

I might have to kill one of mine to keep the others alive: in a sense, Ian was one of my hostages to fortune too. That was why I hadn't killed him already. I had loved him, or thought I loved him. Love or not, I did care for him too damn much to kill him just because he turned out to be crazy, and tried to keep me from killing the even crazier woman he obviously loved. But if he caught up with me before I'd chased that madwoman away from my rock. . . .

He would kill me to keep me from killing her. I would kill him, if I had to, to keep her from killing my friends. He was right: there had been enough killing already. There had been too much killing already. And there would almost certainly be more. . . .

But not yet. Bone and Ian were falling behind, slowly but steadily. I would reach my rock before they did, and I wouldn't have to kill them to do it. I let go a breath I hadn't known I held and turned from the exterior screens to the computer readout to see what damage Ian had done to my shuttle.

I was lucky: he'd hit nothing of importance at all. The burnt insulation I smelled was mostly from the shield electronics. One recycling circuit was damaged, and I switched to backup on that, but that was the worst he'd done besides the holed bulkhead. That would have to be mended before I hit atmosphere again, but in space the sealant with which I'd patched the hole would last indefinitely.

From there on, it was a straight run for my rock at

the best speed I could bully out of *Defiance*. She was a swift little shuttle. With any luck at all, I might reach my rock before Primm-Martin did, and I would certainly make it ahead of Ian and Bone.

Even at top speed, *Defiance* could run herself, and there wasn't much for me to do but wait. Never one of my better tricks. I used up some time calling ahead to my rock to warn them that there might be a battle on the way. The notion didn't alarm them: they'd already fought off contingents of MAMAs, and were confident they could fight off more. Not unreasonable: they hadn't talked to Primm-Martin.

Maybe it was only primitive fear of madness and monsters, but I feared that woman. I knew how determined she was, and I could not shake the belief that she would find her way through their defensive fire to destroy my rock if I didn't destroy her first. In desperation, because I couldn't get them to take the threat seriously, I lied: I told Jamin the Gypsies were singing for him.

They had sung to me once for him, and in spite of their warning I hadn't protected him well enough. He had damn near died. He knew enough to take it seriously when they sang me a warning for someone. He also knew me well enough to guess when I was telling a lie.

He was polite about it. He studied my face on the Comm screen for a long moment and finally said gently, "You're really worried about this, aren't you?"

"The Gypsies don't sing for the fun of it."

His mouth twitched, but he didn't—quite—grin. "From what you've said, I gather they sometimes do." When I started to respond to that he gestured quickly,

265

stopping me. "No, I'm sorry, I know you're serious about this. But they aren't really singing at all, are they?"

"Damn it, Jamin—"

His expression turned sober. "Skyrider, if it's serious enough for you to try out a lie on me, it's serious. We'll take it seriously. But what is it about this woman that's got you so nervous?"

"I don't know. She's stark, staring mad, Jamin. If she can't kill you any other way, she'll ram her shuttle right through the control-chamber viewport."

"That would do it."

"I know it would. Damn it, be ready for her. She may get there before I do. Don't underestimate her: she'll kill you if she possibly can."

"Okay, we'll be ready."

When I was sure he had taken me seriously, I cut the connection and checked the aft screens to see how Bone and Ian were doing. They were still with me. If they could keep their speed, they'd be fairly close behind me when I got to my rock. Out of sight, probably, but not for long. And if Primm-Martin did have some of MAMAs Warriors for Decency waiting in the wings, ready to fly into battle with her on a moment's notice, this might turn into one hell of a fight.

I didn't want to think about it. I remembered the way Ian had looked when he spoke to Adrienne Martin, and I sighed. There had been in his eyes something I had thought he and I had shared. I had been wrong. Love like that was a terrible and precious thing, one that I had not known in far too long a time, certainly not with Ian. Whatever we'd had, it had not been love like that. It had been tender and silly and fun. . . .

And it had been a lie. Ian had never been in love with me. He loved Primm-Martin: and if things went right, I was going to kill her. Hostages to fortune. *Damn*! I turned away from the screens and began a careful check of my weapons. The Gypsies weren't singing, but I didn't need a Gypsies' song to tell me I was going to need all the firepower the *Defiance* could provide.

Chapter Thirty

PRIMM HAD GOT HER WARRIORS FOR DECENCY TO MY ROCK ahead of me, all right; and she was crazy, but she was not stupid. She sent her Warriors on in and stayed behind them, waiting to cut me off when I came in from the Outer Rocks. She kept one other shuttle with her, and they were both good pilots. I was in sight of my rock when they stopped me. I could see the other Warriors attacking my rock, but I couldn't get through to stop them.

That was probably the only major mistake Primm made: she should have stopped me farther from my rock, where I couldn't see the battle. The mood I was in, worrying about other people's hostages to fortune as well as my own, I might have hesitated to kill her if we hadn't been in sight of the battle at my rock. That would have given her a serious advantage. Even as it was, at first I concentrated my attack on Primm's companion rather than on Primm herself: the companion was doubtless *some*body's hostage to fortune, but it was somebody I didn't know. Not very sound logic, I realize, but I've seldom been accused of sound logic.

When I saw Primm and her companion stationed to stop me, I angled for the companion and came in firing, and the companion had to scramble to get out of my way. I could see the big guns on my rock tracking one of the other Warriors, but I could also see that there were too damn many of them for Chuck to have a hope, alone with the big guns, if they were really determined . . . which they certainly seemed to be.

The dock where *Challenger II* had been parked was empty. Jamin must have decided he could be of more use in his shuttle than working the little guns on my rock. I couldn't see *Challenger II* anywhere, but I wasn't given much time to look: when Primm's companion scrambled out of my way, Primm was quick to get me under her own guns.

Her first shot was aimed at my missing starboard shield. I saw it coming and rolled out from under, so the red glare of her lasers caught on another shield and sparked brilliant yellow for an instant before I dived clear. That gave the companion a chance to recover from her initial alarm at the ferocity of my attack, and suddenly I was dodging both of them, trying to keep my starboard side clear of their lasers. It made maneuvering for an angle to fire a good deal more difficult than it would otherwise have been. They both saw very quickly that my shield was out, and they were both aiming their attacks at that side of *Defiance*.

Beyond them, I saw *Challenger II* arc into sight

from behind my rock, diving toward a foolishly clustered group of Primm's Warriors. He got two of them before they knew he was there. After that, I didn't have time to watch him: Primm and her companion were closing in, and I'd caught a glimpse of Bone and Ian approaching in my distance screens. If I didn't get rid of Primm and companion right quickly, I'd have all four of them after me.

I hurled *Defiance* away from Primm, back out toward Bone and Ian, and as I'd hoped, she followed me. Her companion was a little slower, but that was as well: I couldn't concentrate on both of them at once. Primm swung her shuttle too wide to catch me, and for a moment I thought she would sensibly give it up and return to her companion's side to await my return. She had to know I would return: I wasn't going to run off and leave my rock undefended.

She wasn't thinking that clearly. I judged her flight path carefully, compared it with mine, and ignored the laser bolts she threw at me: they weren't going to do me any harm. She had lost her temper and was firing wild. When the angles were right I flipped the *Defiance* end-for-end and kicked in full power to kill inertia while I centered Primm's shuttle on my laser screens.

She didn't even try to dodge me. Maybe she didn't have time. Maybe she didn't realize what I was doing. Maybe she was just too mad to care. In any event, she kept coming at me on exactly the same broadly curving flight path, and when it centered her perfectly in my screens, I fired.

The companion had seen what I was doing, and came after me with a scream of rage that made my Comm Link speakers rattle. Nobody had been saying much, before that, at least not on the channels I was monitoring, but when Primm's shuttle caught my lasers dead-center and died in a brief green haze of failing shields that disappeared almost instantly in a roiling explosion as the shields gave out, there was suddenly a lot of chatter over the Comm Link. I couldn't catch it all, but I caught enough to know that my brief hope that they would all give up and go home when Primm died was baseless. They intended to finish what she had begun.

And Ian: sweet Ian: beautiful, jewel-eyed, gentle Ian: he whose loving voice had whispered me to sleep at night . . . He was near enough to see Primm's shuttle go. He hurled curses like weapons, and while Primm's companion danced an expert block to keep me from my rock, he rushed in-system like an avenging angel. They would trap me between them, he and Bone and Primm's companion, and between them, they would kill me.

But not if I didn't stick around for the show. Right now there was only Primm's companion between me and the battle at my rock. I jockeyed as if to sneak past her starboard side and, when she bought the bait and jockeyed after me, I hurled *Defiance* past her port side and right on through to my rock. Ian's curses followed me all the way in.

There had been more than half a dozen Warriors for Decency after my rock when I'd first arrived. Between them, Chuck and Jamin had shot down all but three in the time it had taken me to kill Primm and dodge her companion. Now, with Bone and Ian and Primm's companion coming in after me, we were back up to half a dozen.

Well, Chuck and Jamin had fought off half a dozen

271

Warriors for Decency before. But those hadn't been enraged by Primm's death. It was as though, at her death, her madness had been passed on to all these others, undiminished by numbers; strengthened, rather than diluted, by diffusion. One of them tried to put her shuttle through the control-chamber viewport. She was too near for Chuck to hit, and Jamin was busy dealing with the two nearer him. I panicked. I wasn't near enough for a laser hit that would stop her. Without thinking, I set a photar to track and pulled the firing stud.

If I'd been off by the smallest margin, that photar would have blown my whole rock to hell and gone. They're distance weapons, and hell of powerful, never meant for infighting like that. If I'd been wholly sane, I probably wouldn't have tried it. But nothing else would stop that warrior's kamikaze dive in time. My aim wasn't off. The blast scarred the side of my rock, but the viewport held. There wasn't even any shrapnel left of the destroyed shuttle. All that was left of her was a dancing purple spot before my eyes where the light of the blast, inadequately shielded by my automatically dimmed screens, remained a ghostly visual image full seconds after the vacuum of space snuffed the real explosion.

There wasn't time to dwell on it. Bone and Ian came in so fast, they actually outran Primm's companion, who had been nearer my rock when Primm died. Chuck got one of the two shuttles that were after Jamin, and Jamin burned out a shield on the other before she spun out of his sights and jockeyed back again, looking for a weak spot in his defense.

I flipped *Defiance* to face the three shuttles coming in from the direction of the Outer Rocks, and I opened the visual on my Comm Link in the feeble hope of reasoning with them. When I saw Ian's face, I knew it would be a wasted effort, but I tried anyway. "Ian, there's nothing left here to fight for. There's no reason to kill the baby now."

"There's reason to kill you." His voice was as sweet and soft and gentle as always, and his grin as deadly as I had ever seen it, and his eyes were mad.

"Ian, please. There's been too much killing already. More won't bring her back. Let it go."

"You didn't let *her* go."

"I *couldn't*!" My voice sounded anguished, thin and high and strange; I barely recognized it. "She was trying to kill my friends."

"She was my family." His smile broadened, incongruously kind. "I'll finish her work for her. I won't even kill you: that would be too easy for you." Those jeweled eyes glittered like mirrors, and his smile was sweet. "You'll watch your friends die at your lover's hands. How will you live with that, my love?"

While Ian was talking, Bone slipped past us without a word. He just dived for my rock with all his weapons blazing, right past Ian and me without a second's hesitation: he knew I would be too busy with Ian to fire on him. Maybe he thought the last Warrior at my rock would keep Chuck and Jamin too busy to stop him. She didn't. She died.

In the instant my attention was diverted by that explosion, Ian threw a wild shot at me and skittered past in a swift, crazy jockeying maneuver I should have been able to stop. I didn't. I let him go, I don't know why. Maybe I still hoped he was sane enough to quit his idiot battle now that the reason for fighting it was gone. Maybe I just hoped I wouldn't have to kill him: maybe I even hoped that, if he must die, I could leave the killing to Chuck and Jamin and content myself with the destruction of strangers like Primm's companion. If that was it, I was out of luck.

Primm's companion saw Ian slide past me, and she saw where Bone was headed: toward the control-chamber viewport. Ian went in after him, right on his tail. I had let Ian pass, but Jamin wouldn't. Primm's companion couldn't do much about Chuck's big guns: they were too well set in the rock. She went for Jamin.

Chuck tracked Bone with the big guns and hit him just before he came in under them and out of range. The explosion sent shrapnel flying in every direction, some of it back out toward Ian, but that didn't slow him. I left Jamin to take care of Primm's companion. Flipping *Defiance* to face my rock again, I kicked in the thrusters for all they were worth and killed inertia in seconds, as only those powerful malite conversion-drive engines, strained to their limits, could do.

Even so, I couldn't catch Ian before he hit the viewport. I couldn't even get in range to use my lasers against him. As before, I had no choice but photars. With lasers, I might have stopped him without killing him: probably not, but I could have tried. Not with photars. With those I could only hit him or not. If I hit him, he would die.

I wanted to give him another chance: to beg him to quit the battle and leave my friends alone, now that his were gone: but I knew he wouldn't—couldn't—listen. If our positions were reversed, neither could I. I killed my engines and rode inertia silently toward my rock; I needed careful aim more than I needed forward momentum.

This time, at least, I had time to let the computer

augment my aim when I set the photars to track, so there was less danger to my rock. Pulling the firing stud wasn't even difficult. That much was automatic. The difficult part was sitting still and watching the results.

I think I called his name in the last instant before the photar hit. I know I saw the nose of his shuttle dip: but whether that was in a futile effort to dodge the photar, or just in preparation for colliding with my rock's viewport, I couldn't guess. If the photar hadn't stopped him, he would have collided with the viewport. It couldn't have withstood the collision, and neither could he. He would have been dead whether I fired or not.

It didn't help to know that. It didn't help to know that by killing him I saved my rock and my friends. The point was, I killed him. I centered him on the photar screens, set one tracking, pulled the firing stud, and watched him die.

The explosion stunned me. I must have imagined somehow, even after I fired, that he would escape. I remembered the curve of his cheek, the line of his jaw, the way his hair fell across his forehead in a disarming veil over one eye . . . His sleek, hard body, golden skin rippling smoothly over stringy muscles and elegant bones . . . His wide silver-blue eyes gemmed with amber . . . The sound of his voice, laughing, saying, "Will you marry me?"

I think I screamed. I may have cried. I know I did my damnedest to break every instrument, console, screen, and bulkhead in *Defiance*'s cockpit. I remember only blinding rage, bottomless grief, drowning despair; and a vast, starred darkness pulled close around the endless, aimless, enduring song of Gypsies and other ghosts gone down before him. Dead. And the knowledge, aching and deep, that I would never hear them again: that more than Ian had died under my photar; more than one life, more than innocence, more than love.

And then Jamin's voice, gentle, concerned, and oddly fierce and defiant in that dulling darkness, calling my name. . . .

Epilogue

WE NEVER FOUND LIVING RELATIVES FOR EITHER OF THE babies on my rock. It may be that one or both had Grounder relatives somewhere, but if so, they refused to acknowledge Faller babies. Chuck and Judy didn't mind: it gave them a ready-made family to start out with. I gave them the use of my rock as a wedding present. I wouldn't be needing it. Jamin and Collis and I were all moving to Mars Station, the center of the colonies' war effort and revolutionary government, such as it was.

With Primm's death, MAMA had lost momentum, but the Solar System was still gearing up for another of its seemingly interminable and inescapable wars. Most colonists kept hoping to find a way out of it, but perhaps it was a foolish hope: the Floater Factor, which should have made the race question unimportant since it would eventually make us all very much alike in our tolerances if not in our genes, instead made it a hotter issue than ever.

Attacks on colonists by racist Earthers were just as common in MAMA's absence as they had been during MAMA's reign of terror: and the Patrol, Earth-based and staffed with Earthers, did as little as ever to stop the attacks. The main topics on every newsfax channel were terrorist attacks and the Floater Factor. Broadcasts from Earth reported the terrorist attacks with muted excitement; broadcasts from Mars and the Belt reported them with rage; and every report on the Floater Factor, no matter where it originated, was tinged with wonder, concern, and confusion.

The human race had mutated, back when space colonization was just beginning, into three separate and distinct categories: now that mutation, taken one step further, was bringing us back together again whether we liked it or not, and people were spending a lot of time and effort letting it be known that they didn't like it. The gods didn't seem to be interested; the Floater Factor did not obligingly disappear.

There was at least one person in the Solar System who was glad it didn't disappear: Collis was eagerly awaiting adolescence, and consequent freedom from freefall sickness, as though it might occur at any moment. I had a feeling he was going to be checking out his tolerance to freefall about every five minutes for the next few years.

Meantime, Mars Station had gravity quarters in which he could comfortably live, and freefall work areas in which Jamin could comfortably spend his days. There was plenty of work to do. The station was as busy with shipbuilding and battle training as it had been before the Brief War: and this time there was no grandstand play with which I could save the world.

My cousin Michael tried to talk me into taking on a teaching job, trying to turn farm kids and misfits into warriors. "Even world-savers have to help with the dirty work once in a while." He said it with a wolfish grin.

If he hadn't said just that, in just those words, it's possible I would have done what he wanted. I'd done it before. But that remark sparked all my rebellious impulses. Rebelliousness has always been one of my better tricks. I may grow up someday, but meantime I figure a person ought to do whatever she does best. I returned Michael's grin with a fairly predatory one of my own and told him exactly what he could do with his classful of farm kids and misfits.

He glanced at Jamin, who was sitting beside me looking arrogant as he always did in gravity: we were in the gravity quarters necessitated by Collis's allergy, but I knew Michael wasn't sure whether I lived there with them. "You have something better to do?" he asked, looking at me meaningfully.

"I always have something better to do." I could feel Jamin grinning beside me, though I didn't look at him. He was used to my ways. I did live there.

"The war won't go away just because you ignore it." There were familiar shadows in Michael's eyes when he said that. I couldn't look at them.

"What war? I don't see any war."

"You will. Don't be obtuse."

"Watch your language," I said. Jamin shifted beside me, and I think he almost reached for my hand, but he knew better. Much as I needed his support in this, I might have hit him if he'd openly given me it. I wasn't much good at acknowledging needs like that.

"You can't get rid of this thing by pretending it doesn't exist." Michael sounded impatient.

"And you won't get rid of it by killing Earthers." I sounded fairly impatient myself.

"Melacha—"

"There's been enough killing already," I told him. "Too damn much killing. Aren't you tired of it yet?"

"Melacha—"

"Wars don't solve problems. They create problems. Fighting Earthers won't get rid of the Floater Factor, and killing Earthers won't make them accept it."

He tilted his head. "You have a better idea?" He sounded as though he really thought I might have one.

"Seems like I'm always trying to live up to my reputation."

"What does that mean?"

"You called me world-saver."

"Melacha, there's nothing you can do this time, except help teach people to fight. There's no way you can stop this war. Not this one."

"Would you like to make a bet on that?" I didn't really have anything in mind to stop it. But I did have a reputation to maintain.

He stared at me for a moment in silence. "Right. Sure. The Skyrider never does anything for free. You're trying to tell me you *could* stop this war if you were paid to?"

"I am a mercenary, don't forget."

"What do you know that I don't know? How could you possibly do it? You'd have to convince Earthers to leave us alone, to accept the Floater Factor, to accept the fact that they can't tell Fallers from anybody else anymore . . . In effect, you'd have to convince them that Fallers are people. That's something mankind hasn't achieved in all the years since the mutation developed, and you claim you could do it if you saw a direct profit in it for you?" He shook his head, glanced at Jamin, and looked back at me. "You're bluffing. You couldn't do that. You can't do a damn thing to stop this war. Nobody can."

Jamin grinned at Michael, sardonic and challenging. "The Skyrider can."

Michael made an impatient gesture. "Where have I heard that line before?"

Jamin transferred his grin to me. "When did it ever turn out to be a lie?"

Michael studied us both. "You really think you could do it." It wasn't quite a question.

"You offering me a profit?" I asked.

Jamin shook his head in affectionate despair. Michael gestured expansively. "Hell, whatever you want. Ask and it shall be granted. *If* you prevent this war."

"I'll draw up a list."

"I'll sign it." He tilted his head. "Then what will you do?"

Jamin was becoming very adept at judging my tolerances. This time he did take my hand. I didn't hit him. I clasped his hand, grinned at Michael, and said, "I'll save the world, of course."